BOUND TO SERVE

She had brought him plenty of rope and he used all of it, binding her breasts so that her nipples were squeezed into almost painful erection. Next, her elbows were tightly bound together behind the post, forcing her breasts further into prominence. He tied her ankles to a leg-spreader, leaving her totally helpless and very vulnerable.

'Where shall I beat you, hmm?' Liam's question was rhetorical, as he stood to one side of her, gently tapping at her thighs with the cane. The tapping increased in severity, until Caroline was gasping into her gag and desperately trying to twist away from the cruel implement.

'I think, before I go away, I'd like to leave you with a few marks – just so that you don't forget me.'

By the same author:

BOUND TO OBEY
BOUND TO SUBMIT

Other Nexus Classics:

A NEXUS CLASSIC

BOUND TO SERVE

Amanda Ware

This book is a work of fiction.
In real life, make sure you practise safe sex.

First published in 1996 by
Nexus
Thames Wharf Studios
Rainville Road
London W6 9HT

This Nexus Classic edition 1999

Typeset by TW Typesetting, Plymouth, Devon

Printed and bound by
Caledonian International Book Manufacturing Ltd,
Glasgow

ISBN 0 352 33457 6

One

Caroline opened her eyes and looked straight at her reflection. Still hazy with sleep, she stretched languorously, revelling in the way the slippery satin sheets felt against her skin. She had been a little unsure when Liam had told her of his intention to install a mirror on the canopy of their four-poster bed, but as she watched the whiteness of her body moving sensuously against the black satin, she had to admit that the effect was more than pleasing. She watched as her hand, almost of its own volition, moved to the empty space beside her. Everything was as it should be – except that Liam was not there. Remembering that she would not see him for at least a month, she felt tears stinging at the back of her eyes. She rolled over and smoothed the pillow next to her. It was an unnecessary movement. There was no indentation in the pillow. Liam had left the day before. Impatiently, she blinked away the unshed tears and looked at the bedside clock. Seven o'clock. He would be airborne by now. Despite her efforts, a tear slid down her cheek, making a tiny plopping sound as it dripped on to the satin pillow. Determinedly, she got out of bed. She was not going to spend the whole month pining away. There was plenty to do. The Master was away and the slave was in control.

Freshly showered and dressed in a white top and shorts that showed off her shapely figure to perfection, Caroline sat in front of the dressing-table mirror brushing her long, blonde hair, which shone with health. The sun streamed into the bedroom from the large, open windows. It was a perfect warm spring day, but Caroline had other things than the weather on her mind. She put the brush down and, cupping her chin in her hands, rested her elbows on the dressing-table, staring unseeingly at her reflection. Was it really only six months ago that it had all started? She felt that she and Liam had been together for much longer. She frowned as she remembered that, in fact, it was slightly less than six months. First there had been Francis – and Lynne. She shook her head as if that was all it took to take away the memory of the cruelly smiling dominatrix. Francis had been her first Master and Lynne, his wife, had been her Mistress. She thought back to that summer, six months ago, when she had been Caroline West, a girl without a job and without a home. Then, after her interview with Francis and Lynne, she had found both – at the expense of her freedom, but it had been worth it. She had loved her new position, despite the beatings and despite spending most of the time securely bound and gagged, or maybe because of it. She smiled at the irony of that thought. Francis and Lynne had brought out her naturally submissive feelings. They had taught her to enjoy the pain of the whippings and canings, because it always led, inexorably, to such intense pleasure. She enjoyed being tied and chained because it immeasurably increased the power of her orgasms.

She tried not to think of Liam, but she knew how much she would miss him. How strange to remember that Francis had sold her to Liam, like a piece of merchandise. Now she couldn't imagine life without him. Theirs was a Master/slave relationship with a difference. She was very much his slave. She smiled as she fingered the black leather collar that she had strapped around her neck after her shower this morning. Although he was away, he knew that she would continue to wear her collar. It was symbolic of her submission to him. She knew that he would think of her wearing it while he was away, and that the thought would give him immense pleasure. He trusted her and had appointed her to act as his deputy to look after his various businesses in his absence. Sexually, he treated her as his slave, but in business, he had acknowledged her intelligence by involving her more and more in these activities. To a large extent, she had taken over from Clive. Clive! She closed her eyes for a moment; even the name was capable of making her shudder. She quickly opened her eyes again, because beneath her closed lids she had seen his eyes. Those eyes had had such a mesmeric power over her. Clive had been Liam's close friend and business associate, but he was only interested in power and the utilisation of such power over people, particularly Caroline. She tried not to remember that day when Liam had found out about his so-called friend, that friend who had been discovered standing over a Caroline helplessly restrained in a rubber strait-jacket, ready to beat her and permanently mark her with the bull-whip he held raised in readiness. Caroline shivered. She could almost hear the whip whistling through the air as she tensed herself for the expected pain. But Liam had stopped him and had thrown him out. Neither of them knew where he had gone. Caroline hoped that he was far away and that she never had to look at him again. She had let Clive tie her into that strait-jacket and she had known what it was that he wanted to do to her. He had only to look at her with those dark eyes, speak in those persuasive tones, and she would have done anything for him.

Caroline got up from the dressing-table. That was all in the past. Now she had to breakfast and then begin looking after her Master's businesses. She loved Liam and she was determined to do a good job for him. The present was what mattered and Liam was her present and, she fervently hoped, her future, too.

* * *

3

Caroline was working in the study when she heard a knock on the door.

'Come in.'

Caroline looked up and smiled as Mrs Davies walked into the room. 'Do you want something, Carol?'

Mrs Davies didn't frighten Caroline now, not as she once had. When she had first arrived at Liam's house, she had been given into the none too tender care of the housekeeper, Carol Davies. As Liam's dutiful servant, Mrs Davies had considered it her duty to discipline the new slave and she had performed her task with great enthusiasm and obvious enjoyment. She had been retained as housekeeper on Caroline's petitioning Liam to allow her to stay, even after Liam's discovery of his housekeeper's sometimes cruel treatment of his slave. Mrs Davies had had nowhere else to go and, in all other respects, she had proved herself to be a loyal and trustworthy servant.

Mrs Davies seemed to be a little embarrassed as she stood before Caroline.

'I know it's not my usual day off and it's very short notice, but . . .'

'Carol, if you want some time off, you are more than entitled to it. Take the rest of the day off.'

Mrs Davies smiled, her relief obvious. Caroline bent her head over the file she was reading, but became aware that Mrs Davies was hesitating. She looked up. 'Is there anything else, Carol? I'm afraid I'm rather busy.'

'Yes – yes. I'm sorry to bother you, Mistress, but I was wondering about the Master.'

'Master Liam left yesterday. Surely you knew that?'

'Yes, I did, but . . . When is he expected to return?'

'Master Liam has some problems with one of his companies that need his personal attention. He's gone to America for a month – possibly a little longer. He's left me in charge so there's no need for you to worry. If there are any problems, come and see me.'

4

'Yes, Mistress. Thank you.'

After Mrs Davies had gone, Caroline threw down her pen in exasperation. Her train of thought had been completely broken. She poured herself a cup of the percolated coffee that was always kept in freshly-made readiness in the study and, sipping it slowly, walked thoughtfully towards the big picture-window on the back wall. Talking about Liam had upset her, reminded her of how long he was going to be away. She was also concerned about him. From what he had told her, the business in America was in serious trouble and that could affect all his other concerns. She had never seen him so worried before. She thought back to yesterday morning when they had lain in bed together. She had fought back her tears at the realisation that he was leaving her for a while.

'I'll miss you,' she had said, 'but I'll look after things for you, I promise.'

Liam had looked at her, his brown eyes feigning sternness. 'You'd better, my girl!'

'Or else?'

'Slaves should never question their Masters! I thought you had learned that. I see I was wrong. You obviously need further instruction. Get me the cane!'

'Yes, Master.'

Caroline hid her smile as she turned away. One of their games would make them both feel better. She cried out as Liam smacked her sharply on her bottom.

'Bring me some rope and something to keep you quiet as well! You are obviously going to be difficult!'

Rubbing her smarting backside, Caroline hurried to obey.

'Stand in front of the post!' Liam growled, as he gestured with the cane toward one of the bed's four posts.

'Now, my little slave. You will reap the rewards of your disobedience.'

Liam was standing very close to her, as Caroline

stood with her back to the post. Suddenly, he reached out and grabbed a handful of her long hair, twisting it around his fist and forcing her face closer to his. Her lips opened beneath the urgency of his kiss. Their tongues intermingled and she felt Liam's knowing fingers pushing back the hood of her clitoris. As he pushed against her, she felt the hardness of his penis. Abruptly, Liam released her hair. Then, without warning, he slapped her across the face, just hard enough to establish the ground rules.

'Slut! You're soaking! I hope you weren't thinking of coming without first asking permission! Eh?'

He slapped her again, before running the tip of the cane down her body. She found this sort of treatment exacerbated her sexual excitement. She wanted more and she knew how to get it.

'I was going to ask your permission, Master. Please don't hurt me. Please, I beg you.'

Feigning disgust, Liam stuffed a wadded-up cloth into her mouth. 'Shut up, slut! I hate whining women!'

Liam tied a piece of cord over the cloth, securing it in place. He wound the cord a couple of times around the post, so that she could not move her head. Grabbing her wrists, he tied them to the post behind her. Completing his work, he stood in front of her.

'I think we'll have your breasts bound.'

She had brought him plenty of rope and he used all of it, binding her breasts tightly, so that her nipples were squeezed into almost painful erection. Next, her elbows were tightly bound together behind the post, forcing her breasts further into prominence. He tied her ankles to a leg-spreader, leaving her totally helpless and very vulnerable.

'Where shall I beat you, hmmm?' Liam's question was rhetorical, as he stood to one side of her, gently tapping the front of her thighs with the cane. The tapping increased in severity, until Caroline was gasping into her gag and desperately trying to twist away from the cruel implement.

'I love to see you squirm, you little slut! I think, before I go away, I'd like to leave you with a few marks – just so that you don't forget me.'

The pain in her thighs as Liam laced them with a network of thin, red weals was intense. It was an intensity that made her clitoris pulse with pleasure. Liam dropped the cane and closed his fingers around her erect nipples, squeezing them and smiling with pleasure as he watched her helpless struggles. Without warning, he moved away and retrieved the cane. She felt the hard tip pushing into her slit and she moaned with pleasure.

'Not going to come are you, darling? I haven't said that you can, you know.'

Liam's fingers were at her clitoris again. He brought his fingers up to her nose. 'Smell yourself, my darling. You're ready for it, aren't you? Just remember that you have to wait until I say it's OK.'

He moved his fingers back to her clitoris, at the same time moving the cane inside her, and she knew that she was lost. She pulled furiously against her bindings and tried to scream against the saliva-sodden gag in her mouth as she came swiftly and strongly. Liam gave her no chance of recovery as he pulled the cane out of her and brought it down with some severity on the insides of her exposed and vulnerable thighs.

'You didn't wait for my permission, did you?'

The cane came down again and again. Liam was angry, not at Caroline, but at the whole situation. He didn't want to leave her for such a long time, but his business was in real trouble and someone had to remain here to look after things. There were tears in his eyes as Liam threw down the cane and pushed his hardness between her tender and abused thighs. He pounded into her, incapable of being gentle, incapable of stopping until he found some relief. He clung to her, gripping her

7

bound form tightly as he came, gasping into her hair. He moved one hand down and felt her wetness. He had known she would respond like this. It did not take long before she was shuddering within his grip, consumed by the paroxysms of her second orgasm.

'Oh, Caroline. I love you – I love you!' he whispered fiercely as he clung to her and, in answer, felt the wetness of her tears dripping on to his neck.

Mrs Davies stood outside the tall, Victorian terraced house and nervously checked her watch. She was a little early. Had she better wait or would it be in order to ring the bell? Perhaps she had better wait just a few minutes, she decided. He would not like her to be too early. She remembered how he had always admired punctuality above all things. She shifted the bulky manila folder to her other arm. Its contents had taken her many weeks to amass and she had kept it hidden in her room. She hoped he would be pleased. She wanted so much to please him. She remembered that morning, just a few weeks ago, when she had answered the telephone and heard his voice for the first time in several months. She had thought that she would never hear it again, that he had clearly shown his disinterest in her, but here he was speaking to her, telling her that he wanted – needed – to see her. She had gone to see him, still half-angry with him because he had left so suddenly, without any explanation or even a goodbye. Explanations had, of course, proved to be unnecessary. He had opened the door and taken her in his arms and it was just like he had never gone away.

She moved uncomfortably, trying to ignore the pulsing of her clitoris. That first time they had only kissed. Perhaps now – now that she had brought him what she knew he wanted – he would go further, fulfil all the promises he had ever made to her. She knew that she wasn't beautiful but, for her age, she was presentable.

She had scoured the shops, searching for just the right outfit. With nervous fingers, she smoothed the skirt of her tight-fitting black sheath dress. She didn't have a bad figure. Perhaps a little heavy on top, but black was so flattering, concealing unsightly bulges. She thought of the black corset that she wore. Yes, he would like that. He had always liked black on a woman. Sexy black he had called it the first time she had worn it. Surreptitiously, she smoothed the black stockings over her knees. Wouldn't do to have bagging around the knees. He'd never tolerate that. And it was only midday. They had the whole afternoon. Surely it would happen this time. He would be so grateful when he saw the contents of the file.

She looked at her watch again and then hurried up the worn stone steps, ringing the bell with a confidence she was far from feeling. She heard his footsteps, saw the blackness of his shape behind the frosted glass of the front door. She held her breath as the door swung open and she looked again into those black eyes.

'Carol . . . Right on time. Please come in, my dear.'

'Thank you, M – Master Clive.'

The house was typical of Clive. All the necessities were there, but there were none of the usual objects that were regarded as decorative in other homes. Everything was functional.

Mrs Davies stood in the middle of the room, clutching the folder. Clive stood in front of her, placing his hands on her shoulders.

'Carol, you look wonderful,' he said, as he reached forward to press his lips to her forehead.

She looked up at him, admiring his lean good looks. 'And you, Master Clive. You look even better than I remembered. I've wanted . . .'

'Ssh.' Clive put a finger to her lips, as his arms slid from her shoulders to her arms.

'No reminiscences, Carol. Not now. This is a new beginning for us.'

She thrilled to his words. He sounded as if she were to be included in his future plans.

'Do you have something for me?' Clive indicated the file.

'Oh, yes. I think you will find everything you need in there.'

Clive took the file and moved to the sofa. He indicated that Carol should sit and then sat beside her. He smiled as he quickly sifted through the papers. Then he turned to face Carol. Gently, he touched her face with his fingers. 'Carol, this is wonderful. With these documents, I can really help Liam. But remember, he must never know that we are in any kind of contact.'

'He won't, Clive. I didn't even tell Miss Caroline where I was going this afternoon.'

Clive's hand dropped to her shoulder, gripping it tightly. 'Caroline?'

'Master Clive! You're hurting me!'

Instantly, Clive's grip became nothing more than a caress.

'I'm sorry, Carol. Remember, you were to call me Clive.'

She blushed like a schoolgirl and looked up at him beneath lowered lids. 'Yes – Clive.'

'That's better. Now, how is Caroline?'

'She's well. Missing Master Liam, of course, but . . .'

'Missing him? Has he gone away?'

Mrs Davies looked at him, surprised at the intensity of his words. 'Why, yes. His company in America is in a lot of trouble and he's had to fly over to try and sort things out. Miss Caroline says that he'll be away for at least a month.'

Barely able to conceal his excitement, Clive got up and walked to the window. He had to be careful. He needed Mrs Davies. She was very loyal to Liam. She must not suspect – not yet. But this was amazing news. He had spent months, utilised some very disreputable people, in his endeavours to undermine Liam's business interests. Here was success beyond his wildest dreams. Liam had already gone away to try and sort out his ailing company and Caroline – poor little Caroline – was all on her own without her protector, so helpless and vulnerable: just as he liked her, so in need of help – his special kind of help. And Mrs Davies could assist, but first he had to make her totally his, make her desperate to do anything for him. There was only one way in which that could properly be achieved.

Smiling, Clive turned back from the window. 'Well, we'll have to make sure that Miss Caroline has everything that she needs, won't we, Carol? We must ensure that Master Liam has nothing to worry about in that department. You'll help me, won't you, Carol? You'll keep me informed of everything that Miss Caroline does and maybe even arrange a meeting between us . . . ?'

Carol rose to her feet. She wanted to help Clive, she really did, but she knew how Caroline felt about him.

'Clive, I don't know about a meeting. She – she still won't talk about you. I don't . . .'

'Carol, have I told you how much I've been looking forward to seeing you again? It's been so long, Carol and I've so longed for this.'

Clive enfolded an unresisting Mrs Davies into his arms. He closed his eyes as he kissed her, hard and passionately, forcing his tongue into her mouth, grazing her with his teeth. Perhaps he could pretend that she was Caroline – if he kept his eyes very firmly closed.

The sound of the shower formed a background to Clive's thoughts, as he lay back against the satin-covered headboard of his king-size bed. Carol Davies had proved surprisingly adept at giving him sexual satisfaction. Clive drew on his gold-monogrammed

11

cigarette, the gesture an exemplar of economy of movement. He had been right in his belief that it would be more than enough for Carol if he allowed her to give him non-reciprocal pleasure. Clive needed this woman's help, but there were limits beyond which even he would not go. He had closed his eyes as she went down on him with a practised ease which he had not expected. He had lain back, his arms above his head, clutching the headboard, imagining someone else's lips closed around his cock. He pictured Caroline, her long, blonde hair spread across his body, as she sucked and licked at him. Her hands were tied behind her and she wore a black leather collar around her neck – the slave collar he had placed there. If she did not succeed in giving him pleasure, he would have to beat her. He could see the unmarked contours of her bottom. He would change all that. He would mark that white skin; mark it permanently as he had so nearly done before. It was only Liam who had stopped him then, but Liam would pay for that. Clive would take his business away from him, just as easily as he would take his slave. She belonged to him. He would control her again, as he had done once before. The thought of it excited his mind, as the mouth sliding up and down his shaft was exciting his body. Clive did not cry out as he came, he was too much in control of himself for that, but the juddering motions of his body, together with the warm spunk that was jettisoned into her mouth, told Carol Davies that she had achieved her object. She had given Clive the pleasure she had longed to give him. At this realisation, she felt waves of pleasure wash over her. She gratefully swallowed the come that had filled her mouth. She would serve Clive as she had always wanted to, and there would be more moments like this. Whatever he wanted from her, she would give. If he wanted her to bring Caroline to him, she would find a way. Perhaps it might even be as it was before. She felt her clitoris pulse with renewed excitement as she remembered Caroline, bound, gagged and totally helpless, at the mercy of whatever Carol Davies wanted to do to her, and there was so very much she still wanted to do.

Clive slid out of bed and donned his black satin robe. It was an expensive, not totally essential, item for him to own. As he tied the sash of the robe, he looked at his reflection in the full-length mirror on one wall of his bedroom. It was important to Clive that he looked good. It was especially important that the men and women who shared his bed should think so. It made them so much easier to control.

He walked to the bathroom door and gently pushed it open. He stood in the doorway, smiling slightly as he watched Carol Davies, her naked body visible through the frosted glass of the shower cubicle. She was leaning against the back wall, her arm moving frantically as she brought herself to orgasm. As she cried out, Clive smiled and quietly closed the door. She was entitled to her pleasure. He appreciated the effort she had made to please him. As she pleasured him, she had kept the black corset on, not allowing him to see her naked. Thoughtfully, Clive stubbed out his cigarette in a black onyx ashtray. Yes, he had rewarded her for services to date. If all went according to plan, there would have to be further such payments. It was worth it. He opened a drawer in the dressing-table and lovingly fingered the wide black leather collar which lay inside. He would have to get a padlock for the collar. Once he had strapped it around Caroline's neck, he did not intend that it should ever be removed.

Two

'Five thousand pounds!'

Clive dropped the leash connected to the slave's collar and turned slowly to glare at the woman who stood behind him. She was tall, being just a little under six feet in height, and she had the sort of figure which most women would kill for. Her perfectly proportioned body was sheathed in black rubber, which flowed over her curves like a second skin. She wore impossibly high-heeled black rubber boots and the whip attached to the broad black rubber corset-belt at her waist clearly denoted her as a Mistress. She watched Clive with carmine lips curved into a sardonic smile. Her dark hair was pinioned on top of her head, increasing the overall severity of her appearance. Her red-painted nails rested elegantly on her rubber-clad hips as she returned Clive's glare with a challenging one of her own.

Clive evaluated her quickly. What a beautiful adversary she made and what a beautiful accomplice she would make. He narrowed his eyes. Dark eyes looked into even darker eyes and acknowledged her worth. Clive turned and looked at the slave-girl kneeling on the floor. She had willingly offered herself as a slave at to-night's auction. It was, after all, held in aid of charity. With his thoughts full of Caroline, Clive had nearly given this party a miss. Acknowledging that it was being held by one of his favourite fetish clubs, however, he had decided that he needed an evening of relaxation. Discovering that a slave auction was to be held had only

14

enhanced the evening's prospects for him. He had been willing to offer a substantial sum for the use of the blonde slave, who so reminded him of Caroline. He had offered one thousand pounds, which he was confident would be accepted. Now this woman had more than topped that offer. Clive's mind was working quickly. What better way to spend the night than with such an accomplished-looking Mistress and such a delicious-looking slave?

'I have a suggestion.' He spoke loudly to the gathering which had been silenced by the enormity of the sum offered. 'We both have an interest in this slave.' He looked at the imposing figure standing with her feet planted slightly apart and her hands on her curving hips. She inclined her head in acknowledgement. 'As I'm sure that we both want the charity to benefit as much as possible, I am prepared to match the offer by increasing my own to five thousand, making our joint donation one of ten thousand pounds, on the understanding that we both enjoy the slave equally.'

There was absolute silence, while eyes ranged from one to the other of the combatants. Even for this sophisticated gathering, this was serious money. The Mistress moved at last, striding elegantly towards the prostrate figure of the slave. She bent and picked up the leash which Clive had dropped and ran the tip gently across the girl's face. She flicked it sharply across the pale cheeks, smiling slightly at the startled cry of pain. She turned and looked at Clive. 'I accept the offer.'

Clive watched approvingly as his partner tied the slave's hands behind her back. He had never shared a slave with anyone before, but this woman had an economy about her movements which more than equalled his own. They had not talked much, but he knew that she was to be addressed as Mistress Lynne. As he watched her, he knew that his original feeling had been right. She would make the disciplining of Caroline he was planning an even more enjoyable affair, but that was later. Now he would concentrate on the more immediate matter. Mistress Lynne was running her hands along the naked girl's thighs and smiling at her, almost tenderly. Without a change of expression, she slapped the girl hard across both thighs. The girl cried out in pain, but looked at her new mistress with eyes that belied her cry. Lynne chuckled softly. This girl was a prize, to be enjoyed at length. She pushed a wadded-up piece of cloth into the girl's mouth, securing it with rope, which she tied tightly behind her helpless captive's head. She looked at the girl, the smile now gone.

'Can you speak?'

The girl made a muffled sound and shook her head. Satisfied, Lynne tied a black scarf over her slave's eyes, before turning to Clive.

'I think the slave is ready, Master Clive.'

'Not quite,' Clive said as he moved forward and knelt beside the girl. He tied her ankles together, drawing the rope tight as he knotted it. He had taken the measure of this slave and knew the sort of treatment to which she would respond well.

'Now, Mistress Lynne. Ladies first is, I think, the correct expression. By your leave, I will watch as you administer the first correction.'

At Lynne's nod, Clive got to his feet and drew a chair forward. He seated himself comfortably and looked forward to what he was sure would be an unparalleled entertainment. They had been given the use of this small room by the auction organisers. It was a room well equipped with instruments of correction.

Almost clinically, Lynne watched the captive's struggles. Like Clive, she could see that those struggles were as much for the girl's own pleasure as for theirs. Judging that the time was right, she unhooked the whip from her waist and unfurled it. She let the long, black

16

leather of the whip slide through her fingers as she chose the spot for her first blow. She looked at the well-shaped breasts, but they were not yet bound and would make better targets when they were squeezed between ropes. She transferred her gaze to the slave's quivering buttocks. So delicious and so unmarked. The whip slashed through the air, perfectly marking the white skin as it found its mark. Lynne smiled at the muffled moans emanating from the gagged girl. She knew that her willing victim could take more – much more. Lynne used the penis-shaped handle of her whip to massage the struggling girl's clitoris. Instantly, the struggles became sensuous movements as Lynne slid the handle into the girl's vagina. She watched with an almost professional interest as the captive threw her head from side to side, making incoherent mumblings through her gag. Lynne used her other hand to viciously tweak the hardened nipples, making the girl buck with pain and pleasure.

'It's so difficult isn't it, my dear?' she crooned, her voice like a caress. 'It hurts, but you like it, don't you?'

The girl's ceaseless movements continued and Lynne pinched her nipples again. This time, she was rewarded with a muffled shriek.

'I'll take that as a yes, shall I, my darling?' Lynne asked the question rhetorically as she continued to slide the whip handle in and out of the soaking slit. 'You see, you will receive pleasure. I always think that that only intensifies the pain when it comes, as it will come, my darling. Be assured of that. Let your mind dwell on it as you revel in the throes of your orgasm. Think of what awaits you. Pain beyond your wildest dreams, while you struggle, totally helpless. There is no one to help you. You came here of your own free will and you gave your Master and Mistress total domination over you. And we'll use it, my darling. We want you to remember this night for a long time.'

Lynne watched, smiling with anticipatory pleasure as

her words and actions propelled the girl inexorably to her orgasm. Lynne placed her hand firmly over the slave's mouth, to silence the wild, muffled cries.

'That's it, my darling. Soon you will have something to really cry about!'

Clive watched in admiration as Lynne, having carefully paved the girl's mind with suggestions of what was in store for her, brought her arm down again and again, carefully placing the raised weals in a delicious pattern on the previously white skin. The girl's buttocks quickly became an angry red from the beating, a red that Clive knew would become purple bruising before too long. He watched and waited, biding his time as he always did, because that patience brought its own reward when he was able to allow his own perverted desires their freedom.

When Lynne paused during the beating, breathing deeply with her exertions, Clive got slowly to his feet. Collecting some more rope from a table, he walked towards the girl and knelt down beside her. Lynne stood aside. Neither she nor Clive seemed to need words, both sensing the other's desires, respecting each other's needs.

'I want you to listen to me very carefully,' he told the slave, as he untied the blindfold, revealing limpid blue eyes that were stained with tears, yet excited and alert for more. She looked at Clive, at those mesmeric eyes that Caroline knew so well and that Clive used to great effect. 'I'm going to hurt you, because that is what I like to do. I will give you pleasure, but I will give you pain first. Will you let me do that, even though I have told you that it will hurt?'

She stared at him, hypnotised by the personality of this man, and slowly nodded. She watched with that same fascination as Clive unzipped his leather trousers and took out his engorged penis. He grabbed a handful of her blonde hair, forcing her head down.

'Look at it!'

She saw that the head of the swollen penis was already gleaming slickly with his excitement. Clive rubbed his penis over her nose and her gagged mouth, making her twist away involuntarily. Clive's grip on her hair intensified, making her emit muffled sounds of pained protest.

'Smell it!' Clive growled at her. 'I want you to smell my come.' He rubbed his penis again over her face. This time she did not resist. 'I want you to drink my semen, you little slut!' As he said this, Clive released her hair, just long enough to roughly pull down the gag. He pushed his penis into her mouth, grabbing a large handful of her hair and forcing her head down, until she took almost the whole length of him into her mouth. 'Suck it. If you don't please me, I will beat you very, very hard!'

As she sucked him, she twisted her hands behind her, trying to loosen the ropes. Seeing the knots slackening, Lynne moved forward and grabbed the girl's wrists with one hand, tightening the ropes with the other.

'Oh, no you don't, my girl! You will serve your Master properly!'

With growing excitement, Clive heard her words and watched the pleasure with which she pulled the ropes tighter. As he came, spurting his hot semen into his captive's mouth, he knew that Lynne could help him. He needed her. She had just the right edge of cruelty that, together with his own undoubted techniques, would teach Caroline to serve them both.

Clive tied the ropes tightly. He sat back and surveyed his work with satisfaction. The twin globes of the girl's ample breasts were now bulbous, pushed into swollen prominence by their bindings. The nipples were almost painfully erect. Lynne joined him and showed him the clamps that she held. Clive looked at their slave. It was time for a demonstration of his own. Nodding at Lynne, he watched as she opened the jaws of one of the ferocious-looking clamps and, bending down, snapped them closed on the girl's left nipple. Her gag had not been replaced and she screamed. Clive reached down and clamped his hand over her mouth. Through tears of pain, she looked pleadingly at him.

'Now, my dear, it would please me immeasurably to hear you thank your Mistress for the pain which she has just inflicted upon you.'

He saw the resistance in her eyes, but held them with his own, forcing his will on to hers. Eventually, he felt her relax against his hand. As a large tear trickled down her left cheek, she nodded.

'Good girl,' Clive said as he released her mouth and listened to her halting tones as she thanked Lynne for the pain which had been inflicted on her. 'Now, can you be a good girl and beg your Mistress to put the other clamp on you?'

This was much more difficult and Clive added a sweetener. 'My darling, I know it's hard, but shall I tell you what will happen if you don't please me? I am going to beat you very severely. I hate screaming slaves and so I had planned to replace your gag before I beat you. However, if you don't do as I ask, I shall refrain from gagging you and I will just add another ten strokes for every cry that you make. It's up to you, my dear. If you feel you can do that, I will ask Mistress Lynne not to apply the other clamp and we'll just get straight on with the beating. I plan to give you twenty strokes. Do you think that you can endure that without crying out?'

Clive smiled pleasantly. He might have been asking the girl if she wanted a cup of tea. He knew that she was excited, but also afraid. He was counting on her desire to please him overriding that fear. His reward was not long in coming, as she turned her head slightly and looked at Lynne. Trying not to look at the fearsome clamp, she smiled tremulously.

'Mistress, I ask that you please clamp my other nipple.'

Clive had not finished with his impressive display. 'Not quite right, my darling. Beg your Mistress.'

She took a deep, quivering breath before acceding to his request. 'Mistress, I beg you to put the other clamp on me.'

'Certainly, my dear,' Lynne said, snapping open the vicious jaws of the other clamp. Clive again put his hand over the slave's mouth, feeling her scream against his fingers as the clamp's steel jaws bit into her flesh. After he had replaced her gag, Clive pushed her into a sitting position and tied her elbows together, forcing her bound breasts into further prominence. He selected an innocuous-looking transparent plastic ruler from a table situated along one wall. Testing the ruler for flexibility, Clive well knew that, in the right hands, this innocent item could be used to inflict carefully selected levels of pain. Clive rejoined his captive and crouched down in front of her. He held her with his mesmeric gaze as he spoke.

'I am going to beat your breasts, my dear. As I promised you, it will hurt, but I want you to stick your tits out for me to beat them, no matter how hard that may be for you to do. Do you understand?'

Now it was Lynne's turn to watch with admiration as the girl nodded her head, fascinated by Clive as if she were a snake and he her charmer. Lynne watched as the girl steeled herself for the first blow. As a woman, Lynne felt an empathy with the girl's fear. The breasts were a very tender area. Her husband, Francis, had beaten her on her breasts only once and she had begged him not to do it again, threatening him with a return to her exclusively dominant way if he did not refrain from this activity. However, Lynne was in her dominant role now and it was not for her to advise a Master on how he should conduct his training. Besides which, she had to

21

admit to a feeling of wetness between her legs, the tight rubber of her suit sticking even more closely to her skin, as she prepared to witness the slave girl's punishment.

Clive teased the girl's clamped nipples with the tip of the ruler, knowing that, by now, they would be mercifully numb. The real pain would come when the clamps were released. Lightly at first, he flicked the ruler against the girl's breasts. He glanced at Lynne, noting with pleasure the way she leant forward in anticipation. The first real blow made a satisfying smacking sound as the ruler connected with the girl's skin. Clive interspersed the blows with probings of the girl's slit, sliding the tip of the ruler in and out, nudging her clitoris. Both Clive and Lynne admired the way in which the girl kept her breasts in position for the punishment they were receiving, even though each of the subsequent blows on the reddened flesh smarted intensely. Lynne could see the dampness on the insides of the girl's thighs and knew that she wanted to plunder that moist channel. She was impressed with the demonstration of Clive's control over this girl and was unexpectedly enjoying the sharing of the discipline that they were meting out to their helpless captive. Her mind roved back to the time when she and Francis had had their own slave. She remembered how she had enjoyed punishing the girl – Caroline, that was her name. She had missed that, maybe more than she had realised.

Clive finished the beating and stood back, admiring the girl's breasts. They looked very red, but he knew that the stinging sensations would quickly disappear well before the light bruising became manifest. He smiled at the girl, showing her his pleasure, and then looked at Lynne. Clive was an expert at judging people. It was one of the things that made his manipulative skills possible. He moved to the slave and untied her, removing the clamps before he untied the gag. He held her gently in his arms until the pain in her abused nipples had abated.

22

'There, there, my brave darling. I am very pleased with you.'

He watched Lynne over the girl's head, admiring her rubber-clad curves. He would like to have fucked her himself, but it was currently in his best interests to be as placatory to her as possible. He waited until the girl's sobs had subsided before moving back a little.

'I think that you would like to pleasure your Mistress. Am I right?' The girl looked at him with widened eyes. Slowly, she nodded. 'Good girl. While you are doing that, perhaps I will pleasure you.' Clive turned. 'Mistress Lynne. I think that the slave would like to thank you personally for your kindness towards her.'

Lynne smiled and beckoned the girl over to her. 'You may pleasure me, slave.'

The girl fell to her knees in front of her Mistress and her feverish fingers probed for the zip at Lynne's crotch. She found it and Lynne moaned softly as she leaned back in her chair. The slave was an expert. As the zip parted, her fingers slid inside the tight rubber and found Lynne's wet slit. Lynne's hand pressed against the back of the slave's head, pushing her face into the hot, moist rubber which contained her bush. She felt the girl's eager tongue insert itself into her sex, swirling around her clitoris and sending shuddering waves of pleasure through her. Clive fell on to his knees behind the girl and pushed his fingers into her wetness. When his fingers were sufficiently lubricated, Clive spread some of the wetness over the tight little entry to her anus. Pushing his fingers inside, he felt her bear down to allow him access. The hard knob of his penis was slick with his pre-come juices as he removed his fingers to make room for its swollen length. Clive found it relatively easy to slide his cock into the slickness of the girl's anus, until it was buried within her almost up to the hilt. The girl herself was on the verge of an orgasm, as she sucked at Lynne's clitoris and felt the increased moisture that told

23

her she had been successful, even if the tightening of Lynne's grasp in her hair had not. Waves of pleasure washed over her as Clive's fingers massaged her clitoris. She moved her mouth away from Lynne's bush as she sucked in air enough to scream her pleasure. She felt Clive's urgent thrusts becoming more intense and then screamed again, this time in pain, as Clive clamped his hands around her sore and swollen breasts, squeezing them unmercifully as he groaned out the intensity of his own orgasm.

'I am interested in control, Lynne. It excites me. I like to experiment with it, see how far I can take a person.'

'Any person? Or one particular person?'

Clive smiled and took a sip of his drink. He had invited Lynne to join him for a dinner to celebrate their successful collaboration.

'I can see that I'm going to have to be totally honest with you, Lynne, if I'm to secure your assistance.'

'My assistance?'

'Lynne, the other night . . . We were good together. You felt it, too, didn't you?'

Lynne inclined her head in acknowledgement, but her words were cautious. 'Clive, that was a one-off. I'm happily married and . . .'

'I'm not suggesting anything sexual between the two of us, Lynne. I won't say that I don't find you attractive. Of course I do, but there's a very special project that I would like your help with.'

The waiter arrived to take their order. Clive watched Lynne as she ordered. She wore an electric-blue leather mini-dress. Her dark hair was loose, its shining waves caressing her shoulders. It would be impossible for any man not to find her attractive, Clive reflected, but he had other things on his mind. He thought of Caroline. Such a contrast to this excitingly dominant creature seated opposite him. He had tried to forget the way her blonde hair lay along her bare shoulders, the way the ropes looked against her skin, and the feeling of triumph when his will had triumphed over hers. He had spent almost two years trying to forget, before acknowledging that it was impossible. He wanted Caroline. He wanted her body and he wanted her mind. Most of all, he wanted her will. He looked at Lynne as the waiter departed with their order. This woman could help him. He knew she could.

Smiling at his dinner partner, Clive settled himself more comfortably in his seat.

'Lynne, I have a proposition that I want to put to you. A business proposition that I think you'll like.'

Clive smiled as he replaced the telephone receiver. So it was all coming together. Sensible businesswoman that she was, Lynne had agreed to help him. He had not told her everything of course. Only that his control over a certain person would net him a substantial amount of money, which, if they were successful, Lynne would of course share. In the process, she would have an extremely enjoyable time doing what she did best. The idea of training a recalcitrant slave had interested and excited her. She did not yet know the name of the unsuspecting trainee, but that was not important. She would meet her soon enough – provided that Mrs Davies came though. Thinking of the woman caused Clive to glance at his watch. He had better get a move on. He wanted to look his best and impress Mrs Davies. He might even have to pleasure her, but it was all in a good cause. He needed her on board. If things went well, she would be the instigator of the whole plan, the one who set things in motion. Yes, he had to be very nice to Carol Davies. She could bring Caroline to him. He would do anything in order to achieve that.

Three

Caroline looked up at Mrs Davies as she placed a tray containing a silver coffee pot, silver milk jug and sugar bowl, a delicately wrought china cup and a plate of biscuits on the table before her. Caroline frowned at the expression on Carol Davies' face. The woman looked worried.

'Is there something wrong . . . Carol?'

Caroline sometimes found herself hesitating before she used Mrs Davies' Christian name and was angry with herself for this awkwardness. As time had passed, she had found it easier to deal with her memories of the atrocities that had been inflicted upon her by this woman. Because she was so happy, she wanted everyone to feel the same way. It was this, coupled with her genuine concern for the woman, that had prompted her to beg Liam to allow her to stay with them. Now she closed the file on which she had been working and prepared to listen sympathetically to the housekeeper.

'I don't want to bother you when you're so busy, madam,' Mrs Davies began, uncharacteristically twisting her hands together as she spoke.

Seriously alarmed by the woman's nervous attitude, Caroline patted the sofa cushion beside her.

'Carol, you obviously need to talk about something and, if there's anything I can do, I'd like to help. Please.'

Mrs Davies hesitated before settling herself on the sofa. She still seemed unable to unburden herself, so Caroline lifted the silver pot and poured some coffee into the cup. Adding some sugar, she passed the cup to Mrs Davies, who looked strangely at her for a few minutes before accepting the cup.

'Strange for you to be serving me, madam,' Mrs Davies said, smiling slightly in a way that made Caroline shiver.

'Never mind that now, Carol. Is there something that I can help you with?'

'It's, well, I don't know how to ...' Mrs Davies' words trailed off. Caroline was intrigued. The woman was definitely uncomfortable.

'Please, Carol,' Caroline said, a hint of impatience edging her voice. 'I haven't time to play guessing games. What's on your mind?'

'Well, it's Master Liam ...'

'Liam! What about him?' Caroline asked, unable to keep the fear from her voice. He'd been away for nearly a week and she missed him so much. Perhaps Mrs Davies had heard some bad news. In her agitation, Caroline grabbed Mrs Davies' arms and shook her. Mrs Davies smiled again in that strange way that somehow frightened Caroline and, surprisingly swiftly, circled Caroline's wrists with her hands, hands that to Caroline felt like steel bands.

'Now, madam. There's no need to get excited. As far as I know the Master is all right.'

The strength of her grip on Caroline's wrists brought all the fear back. Caroline remembered how she had been tied and beaten so mercilessly by this woman. She wrenched free of Mrs Davies' grasp and just sat there staring at her. She had said that Liam was all right. Caroline took a deep breath to calm herself.

'I'm sorry, Carol. I thought for a moment that ... Well, never mind. What is it you want to tell me?'

Mrs Davies took a sip from her coffee before resuming.

'I have this friend ... You know that I've been going off and seeing someone, madam?'

Caroline nodded. Mrs Davies had increasingly found it necessary to request extra time off and Caroline was aware that she had left the house for substantial periods of time.

'I haven't wanted to say anything before, but this friend of mine knows about Master Liam. About his . . . problems.'

Mrs Davies looked at Caroline expectantly, but if she expected a response, she was disappointed.

'Well, this friend says that he can help.'

'He?'

'Yes, madam. He's a good friend.'

Caroline looked at Mrs Davies, trying to see her in a new light. Mrs Davies with a male friend? How much of a friend? Caroline shook her head. What did it matter? Mrs Davies had said that her friend could help.

'Help?' she asked. 'In what way?'

'He's involved in company investigations and he says he has evidence that Master Liam's companies are being deliberately sabotaged. He says he has proof.'

Caroline rose from the sofa and went to the window. She didn't want to feel too hopeful. It might all come to nothing, but if there was a chance, any chance at all, it had to be followed up. Why not? Mrs Davies had every reason to be grateful to Liam. Whatever affected him would also inevitably affect Mrs Davies and her tenure at this house. Of course she would want to help all she could. Caroline knew that she had to trust the woman, even though that was something she had never thought possible. She turned back to the housekeeper, trying unsuccessfully to keep the excitement from her voice. 'This friend. Can I meet him?'

'Of course, madam. He suggested that you should. He's got documents that back up what he says. Oh, madam. There's a real chance, isn't there, that we can help the Master?'

'Let's hope so, Carol. Can you make the arrangements for us to meet?'

'Of course I will, madam. You leave everything to me.'

Mrs Davies hurried out of the room and leaned back against the closed door. Clive was right. The bitch would do anything to help Liam. It would all work out just as Clive had said it would. Mrs Davies smiled as she ran her hands down the bodice of her dress, feeling the erectness of her nipples as she thought of Clive. He had given her such pleasure and she would help him in any way she could. He had said that she would be invaluable to him in getting Caroline back into his power. She hoped that he would also want her continued assistance once he had Caroline. She had liked the feeling when Caroline had served her just now and she wanted that to be repeated . . . in many other ways.

Caroline stood in front of the imposing town house, her mind full of questions. How had Mrs Davies met this friend and what did they mean to each other? Life had taught her never to be surprised, but she had not expected this. Telling herself that she was being unfair to Carol Davies, she turned and smiled at the housekeeper. Caroline had to admit that she looked quite good in her black dress. She had always felt that, for her age, Carol Davies had a more than acceptable figure and the dress showed off her curves to good effect. Caroline did not know about the tightly confining corset into which the housekeeper had manoeuvred herself, but she smiled at the idea of Carol Davies dressing so well for her 'friend'.

'Shall we go in, madam?' Mrs Davies asked.

'Don't we have to ring the doorbell or something?'

'My friend won't be here for another fifteen minutes. Don't worry, madam. I have the key.'

Mrs Davies preceded her up the flight of steps to the front door. As she fitted the key into the lock and then stood aside for Caroline to enter, Caroline wondered why she suddenly felt afraid. She hesitated on the steps, but then thought of Liam and what this could mean for him. She had to meet this man and find out if he really could help. Summoning a smile, she walked past Mrs Davies and stood in the hallway. She was reassured as she looked around. The house felt warm and welcoming. Surely nothing could be wrong. She just had an overactive imagination.

As she looked around, Caroline was temporarily unaware of Mrs Davies. The housekeeper had silently locked the door from the inside and had pocketed the key. Now she stood watching Caroline, trying to keep her elation in check. She had her here! The little bitch had walked into the house of her own volition! Now she would pay for Mrs Davies' many humiliations! Oh, yes, she had been grateful to be allowed to stay in the only home she knew, but she felt that Caroline had gloried in her superiority over Mrs Davies. Of course she was pleased to give Mrs Davies a home, providing that the housekeeper knew her place and served her properly. Now it was Mrs Davies' turn. She would repay the bitch for every humiliation she had had to endure. Mrs Davies did not consider that her humiliations might have been of her own making or that they were simply the products of her own imagination. Her resentment had simmered for nearly six months. Now it was her moment.

Smiling pleasantly at Caroline, Mrs Davies indicated the stairs. 'Please go up, madam. I'll make us a nice cup of tea while we wait.'

Caroline put her cup down on the table in front of her and lay back against the soft cushions of the couch. She hoped that Mrs Davies' friend would not be long. She looked around the room. She had to admit that it was furnished very tastefully, if a little spartan in scope. The couch was undoubtedly comfortable but, apart from that, there were only a couple of chairs and a table in what she took to be the lounge. Strangely, there was no television or hi-fi, not even a bookcase. Everything appeared to be functional, as if the owner did not want to waste time on unnecessary items. Now why did that seem familiar? Caroline's thoughts were interrupted by the opening of the door. She looked up expectantly, only to see Mrs Davies standing there, her expression unreadable. She was carrying a small bag, which she placed on the floor before turning and closing the door.

'Will your friend be long, Carol?' Caroline asked, trying to still the rising feeling of panic that was prompting her to get up and run out of the room.

Mrs Davies turned towards her and smiled. It was a smile that was not reflected in her eyes. For a few moments, she remained silent; an impassively ominous bar to the front door and freedom. Caroline fought down her growing fear and tried to smile.

'Carol?'

'It's Mrs Davies to you, slut, and you'd better not forget it!'

Caroline remained frozen in her seat. Mrs Davies' attitude had completely changed. Without taking her eyes off the housekeeper, Caroline groped for her bag. 'Mrs Davies, I don't know what's happened, but I think we had better discuss this at home,' she said, striving to keep her voice from trembling as she rose to her feet.

'Sit down!' Mrs Davies barked out the command.

'Mrs Davies . . .'

'I said sit down! Would you like to be made to sit down?' Mrs Davies kept her tone even, but there was no mistaking the implied threat. Caroline sat and stared at the housekeeper.

'That's a sensible girl,' Mrs Davies said in a horribly familiar way which made Caroline shiver. 'There's been a tremendous lack of discipline in your life, my girl, but we aim to correct that.'

'We?' Caroline asked, amazed that her voice would still obey her.

31

'No questions, slut! For too long you have been the mistress,' Mrs Davies said, her voice laden with icy contempt. 'I've had to kowtow to you for long enough. Yes, madam. No, madam. Does madam require anything further?' She laughed harshly as she picked up the bag and walked towards Caroline.

Caroline's eyes flicked towards the door, trying to assess how quickly she could reach it. Mrs Davies stood in front of her and threw the bag on to the couch.

'Don't even think about it! I am much stronger than you, my girl. Don't you remember how strong I am?' Mrs Davies' voice was coldly firm. 'If you make one move towards that door, I'll stop you! Of course, if you made such a bad mistake, you would have to be punished for it! Would you like that?'

Caroline stared helplessly at the housekeeper. She had been foolish to even think that she could get past the woman. Seeing this acknowledgement in her eyes, Mrs Davies nodded.

'Even if you had succeeded in getting past me, the front door is locked. You will not be allowed to leave unless and until my friend says that you may be allowed your freedom.'

'What – what do you want? Who is this friend of yours and what does he want?' Caroline asked, her mind frantically groping around trying to make some sort of sense of what was happening to her.

Mrs Davies drew her arm back and slapped Caroline viciously across her face. 'I said no questions!' the housekeeper yelled.

Caroline subsided completely, now thoroughly frightened. Why had she let herself be tricked into coming here? What was it that Mrs Davies and her friend wanted? Keeping her hand pressed against the heat of her stinging cheek, Caroline kept her thoughts to herself. Mrs Davies bent down and opened the bag, keeping fully alert for any escape attempt.

'Do you have any idea of how difficult it's been for me?' the housekeeper asked rhetorically. 'Do you know how many times I've had to bite my tongue when you've humiliated me?'

Caroline wanted to shout at the woman and tell her that she had never knowingly humiliated her; that she was sorry if she had and that she would try and make amends. She knew, though, that silence was her best course. She knew how Mrs Davies liked to talk. Perhaps she would reveal everything without further prompting.

'I knew that if I bided my time, I would get my revenge,' Mrs Davies said, as she stared at Caroline. 'I knew that one day I would be in control again.'

Caroline could not suppress a cry of alarm, as Mrs Davies pulled some rope out of the bag. 'No, Mrs Davies! Please don't! I'll be quiet. I won't try and run away. Please don't tie me! Please!'

The housekeeper laughed malevolently and clamped one hand over Caroline's mouth, stilling her protests. She pushed her captive's head hard into the backrest of the couch and pushed her own face close to that of Caroline.

'You've no idea how much pleasure it gives me to hear you beg,' Mrs Davies said, her voice low and tense. 'You used to beg me, do you remember? You used to call me Mistress and beg me not to beat you. That was as much a waste of time then as it is now. We have six months to make up for, don't we? Six months of you ordering me around! Well, my girl, the situation has now changed. Once again, I am your Mistress and once again you will obey me without question or you will be punished!' Mrs Davies was breathing hard with excitement. She used her other hand to tear open Caroline's blouse, letting the girl's small breasts spring free from the fabric. Caroline started to struggle violently and Mrs Davies caught her wrists and held them firmly.

'Now listen to me, you stupid girl! I am going to tie

33

you and gag you. If you make any further noise, I will whip you the way I used to. Do you remember?'

Caroline stopped struggling, the coldness of common sense filtering into her brain.

'I thought you'd remember,' Mrs Davies said, her voice almost a caress. She picked up the rope and forced Caroline's arms behind her back. Caroline gasped with pain as the rope was tied cruelly tight, inexorably pinning her wrists together. Almost clinically, Mrs Davies pushed her back against the couch and tied a handkerchief between her lips. When she had finished, she surveyed her work with satisfaction.

'You look so good like that, my girl. I advise you not to struggle. You will remember that I always tie ropes very well.'

Caroline felt the woman's fingers softly stroking her breasts. She shook her head; as much to tell herself that she refused to feel arousal as in negation of what Mrs Davies was doing. The housekeeper laughed and moved one hand down beneath Caroline's skirt. Her probing fingers slid inside the girl's panties and she smiled as she saw Caroline's nipples harden. 'Oh, my little girl. You can't fool me. I know that this is just what you want. You'll get plenty of it and pain, too, of course. I remember how well you like that!'

In a vague, disconnected kind of way, Caroline wondered what time it was. How long had she been in this house?

'Easy, my little girl,' a voice spoke softly in her ear. 'I told you ... Don't struggle, my darling. You'll only hurt yourself. You know how efficient Mrs Davies' restraints can be. My friend will be here very soon, my darling. He will explain everything to you. There's no need to be frightened. You're quite safe with me. Mrs Davies will look after you, just like she always did. You see, we didn't think you'd come here if you knew who

34

my friend was. Don't worry. He doesn't want to hurt you. He only wants to talk to you. He really does want to help Master Liam. You'll see.'

Against her will, Caroline felt her nipples responding to the gently massaging fingers which stroked her breasts. She didn't want that. She didn't want to feel aroused, but her clitoris told her otherwise as it pulsed its need. Mrs Davies had dragged her into the bedroom and had secured her to the bed. She had also replaced the handkerchief with a more effective gag and had then blindfolded her helpless prisoner. Now, Caroline twisted against her bonds as those knowing fingers travelled down her body. She heard a murmur of pleasure as the fingers encountered her wetness, slipping easily into her slit and on to her engorged clitoris. She wouldn't give in to this woman who was holding her prisoner! However, the more she struggled against her bondage, the more her arousal grew. She felt lips close around her left nipple as the fingers continued their treacherous work on her engorged bud. Teeth grazed her as Mrs Davies bit gently on her nipple. She had guessed, rightly, that this would only serve to arouse Caroline further. She felt a tongue swirling around her nipple and then leaving it to begin a wet trail down her body towards her pulsating centre. Tears slipped beneath Caroline's blindfold. She would resist with every fibre of her being! She would!

'There, there, my darling. You know you cannot resist me. You never could. We will have such pleasure, my darling, just like before. Do you remember? Of course, I will need to correct you from time to time, but you know how easily that pain can turn to pleasure, don't you, my little darling? Oh, I've missed this so much.'

Mrs Davies fastened her lips on Caroline's clitoris, while continuing to squeeze her nipples. Caroline knew that she was lost. Her orgasm overwhelmed her, making her buck against the fastenings that held her. She didn't dislodge Mrs Davies, who sucked and licked at the increased moisture. The sucking continued until the waves of Caroline's orgasm abated, leaving her spent.

'It's such a shame that you have to be tied up, my darling. I would really like it if you brought me off, but my friend has given me strict instructions to ensure that you remain securely tied until he arrives. Perhaps, after he's dealt with you, I will be allowed a little more fun with you. We'll have to see, won't we, my poppet?'

Mrs Davies moved to kiss her forehead and, as she did so, Caroline heard a door open.

'Ah, Carol. You've been looking after her for me, I see.'

Caroline froze. No! It couldn't be! But that voice – the Scottish lilt in the tone . . .

'Well, Caroline. It's nice to see you again. Of course, I appreciate that you can't actually see me at the moment, but I think you'll be able to guess who I am. We have some unfinished business, you and I, my darling. You should know by now that I never leave a task unfinished!'

Clive stood looking down at Caroline. Mrs Davies had done her job well. Caroline lay helpless, secured to the bed by means of tightly strapped, thick leather handcuffs. A black scarf was tightly bound across her eyes and a black rubber ball-gag distorted her mouth, effectively preventing any kind of speech. As he had instructed, she was naked. Clive wanted her to feel completely helpless and vulnerable. He wanted to strike a bargain with Caroline, into which she would willingly enter. To achieve that, he needed to take control right at the beginning. She was already feeling frightened and unsure. He would leave her like that for a little while. He wanted her mind to get to work on all the possibilities as to why she was a prisoner and what she might expect. Then, when he offered her the deal that he had in mind, she would be so relieved that it was not as bad as she had feared and would be more inclined to accept. Clive's dark eyes narrowed as his gaze travelled the length of his gorgeous captive. How he had longed for this moment. The reality was so much better than he could have anticipated. There was plenty of time before he planned to untie her. Until then, he intended to feast himself on her delicious body, but first – first she must be punished. Punished for all those months he had been kept away from her. Punished because her skin did not yet carry his mark – but it would, he told himself grimly. Even if she refused his offer, she would not leave this house unbranded.

Caroline felt a fear such as she had never known as she realised that her captor was indeed Clive. Yet in conflict with that fear – perhaps even enhanced by it – was that familiar fascination. She couldn't see his eyes – and yet she could see them. As clearly as if she were not blindfolded, she could see those mesmeric eyes boring into hers, eating away at her will. She jumped as she felt something tickling her breasts, then sliding lower, splaying across the flatness of her abdomen. She tightened her muscles as she felt strands sliding ever downwards, coming to rest on her pubic bone.

'Still shaven, I see. Liam must like that.'

She felt something hard pushing at her damp slit and twisted her head from side to side in an attempt to dislodge the blindfold. She felt hands lifting her head, tightening the knot of the scarf.

'Oh, no, my darling. Your Master will take your blindfold off when it suits him. Until then, we must make sure that it remains on, mustn't we?' Mrs Davies crooned to her, making her shiver with the remembrance of how quickly this woman's sweetly honeyed tones could change to shrieks of anger.

'Thank you, Carol. You see, my dear, there is no

37

escape this time. Liam will not stop me from doing to you whatever I want.'

Clive smiled as he watched the effect that his words were having on Caroline. She moaned through her gag, desperately pulling at her fastenings. He brought the cat o'nine tails down on her shaven mound, just missing the tender leaves that protected her clitoris. Caroline screamed into the gag, but was given no time to recover. Clive set about whipping the tender insides of her thighs in a way that was guaranteed to mark her, but also likely to fuel her sexual pleasure. Initially, Caroline screamed into her gag at each stroke, trying unsuccessfully to tense herself each time she heard the sound of the implement whistling through the air prior to finding its mark. She had been well tied and was unable to struggle usefully or avoid the onslaught. Mrs Davies watched from a corner of the room, her fingers squeezing her own erect nipples as she observed Caroline's torment. As she watched the helpless girl trying to kick her way out of the ankle cuffs, Mrs Davies' fingers slid beneath her knickers and into her own wet slit, bringing herself to orgasm as she witnessed Caroline's punishment.

Imperceptibly, Caroline felt herself riding the waves of pain, to the extent that she almost listened eagerly for the tell-tale whistling, announcing further abuse of her crimson-coloured thighs. Clive was expertly letting the strands of the whip inch ever closer to her slit, even though he had no intention of hitting her in that tender area. He used his expertise to very good psychological effect. It was indeed the fear of the expected pain if the slashing leather got too close, coupled with the undoubted excitement which usually resulted from her being in restraints, which pushed Caroline towards a second orgasm, one which, this time, she didn't try to resist.

Clive smiled, gratified at his success, as he saw the

unmistakable paroxysms of her orgasm, but Caroline had not paid the full price yet. As she was helpless in the throes of her orgasm, Clive brought the whip down again, cracking it so smartly across her already abused thighs that her body jumped with the shock. Clive threw down the cat o'nine tails and hungrily stripped off his clothes. Climbing on to the bed, his lips fastened on Caroline's right nipple, while his fingers clamped around her left nipple in a vice-like squeeze. He knew that this new torment would take her mind off the stinging pain from the whipping. He could tell by the sounds coming from her throat that he had succeeded. She tried to twist away from him, but he merely laughed and clamped his hand across her gagged mouth, holding her head still.

'Oh, no, my darling. I'm in control now. And you like it, don't you, little slut? We have a lot of catching up to do, Caroline. It will be much easier for you if you simply go along for the ride.'

His words seemed to calm her, whether through fear or acknowledgement of her helpless predicament, he couldn't tell. His cock was pushing against her vagina. She made muffled sounds as he entered her and then was quiet. He rode her gently, moving his hands to her nipples and sensuously squeezing them. He could feel her bound body moving in rhythm with his movements and smiled as he felt her tense as she came to orgasm. As he let his own pleasure wash over him, he also felt the even greater pleasure of his triumph. She was his by force. Soon she would be his by choice.

'Don't give us any trouble, Caroline,' Clive murmured to her, as he bent to unstrap the cuffs from her wrists. She could feel other hands similarly busy at her ankles. 'I want to talk to you, but I'm afraid you will have to be tied until I'm finished.'

Caroline was helped to sit up and then urged to swing her legs over the side of the bed and stand up. Her captors were taking no chances with her and she felt two pairs of hands holding her firmly by the arms. She was guided to a chair and pushed into it, none too gently. Her arms were drawn behind her and she felt the bite of rope on her wrists as they were tightly secured to the chair. More rope bound her elbows together, making escape impossible. She felt hands behind her head as the blindfold was untied. As it fell away, she blinked in the unaccustomed light, her eyes gradually focusing on the familiarly sinister figure of Clive. He crouched down beside her and stroked her cheek.

'You are so lovely. I've thought about you often.'

Clive looked at her for a moment, his eyes scanning her from the shining waves of her hair to the tips of her bare feet. He watched approvingly as Mrs Davies forced her legs apart and bound her slim ankles to the legs of the chair. Clive's gaze returned to Caroline's face as Mrs Davies finished her task and moved behind the chair.

'Now, my darling, Carol is going to remove your gag. I need you to answer a question that I am going to put to you. She will remain behind you so that, upon any attempt that you may make to scream, she can immediately replace the gag. If you do decide to cause trouble, I will be compelled to whip you severely. Now, do you understand?'

Caroline stared at the black-clad figure crouching before her. His eyes held hers, as they had always done. She knew that she would obey him, not just because of the threatened whipping, but because this man demanded obedience. Slowly, she nodded. Clive's features relaxed into a smile and he nodded to Mrs Davies as he got to his feet. Caroline felt the straps behind her head being unbuckled and took a welcome deep breath of air as the abusive ball-gag was removed from her mouth. Clive went to a bar in the corner of the room. He poured a glass of sparkling spring water before returning to Caroline and holding the glass to her lips. She drank gratefully, the coolness of the water like a balm to her dry throat. When she pulled back, indicating that she had finished, Clive pulled another chair forward and sat in front of her. He smiled as he saw Caroline experimentally pull at the ropes that bound her. 'No, my dear, there is no escape. You will listen to what I have to say and then, depending on your answer to the question I will put to you, I will untie you and you can leave this house. Of course, I am rather hoping that you will decide to stay.'

'Never!' Caroline almost spat the word. 'As soon as you untie me, I want my clothes and I want to leave! You cannot hold me against my will!'

Clive smiled and, in a languid manner, crossed his legs. 'My darling, no one knows that you are here. I can keep you prisoner in this house for as long as I choose. Carol has agreed to be your keeper. She will live here and ensure that you don't leave.'

His words froze Caroline. When she next spoke, her strident tone had been replaced by a supplicatory whisper. 'But you said I could go. You said you'd untie me and let me leave.'

'And I'll keep my word – after you've heard and considered what I have to say.'

Clive rose and returned to the bar. He was enjoying himself and took his time in adding ice and whisky to a glass. Again seating himself before his helpless captive, he made his tone almost nonchalant as he asked, 'By the way, how is Liam?'

Caroline's eyes widened. 'He's fine. I'm expecting him home any day from his business trip, and . . .'

'Oh, Caroline, Caroline,' Clive said, shaking his head. 'Carol has told me everything, including how long you expect Liam to be away. He won't be back for over three weeks. Really, my darling, you are going to have to be honest with me. I know all about his business problems. In fact, that is why you are here.'

41

Clive reached beside him to a small table, retrieving the monogrammed cigarette case. Caroline watched the maddening way in which he took his time in selecting a cigarette before lighting it. He smiled at her as he exhaled a cloud of smoke. 'Filthy habit. One of my vices, I'm afraid.'

Caroline wriggled in her chair, her impatience becoming unbearable. The bite of the ropes against her limbs warned her to remain still.

'You are indeed very beautiful, my dear. I've always thought so. You look so good tied up like that.'

Caroline's patience broke. 'Please tell me what you want. These ropes are hurting me. I want to go home!'

Clive smiled at the pathetic child-like tone. 'I'm sorry, my darling. It's a pity about the ropes, but I do remember how very good you are at struggling.'

He stubbed his half-smoked cigarette into a silver ashtray and rose from his chair.

'Very well, my darling. I won't keep you in suspense any longer. I've been busy since you saw me last. I've been rather successful, working in a well-respected finance house. I have gained access to the records of many companies. I was naturally interested in keeping tabs on Liam's businesses. I like to follow the fortunes of old friends.' He paused and fixed Caroline with his hypnotic eyes. 'And we were friends, Caroline, Liam and I. We go back a long way, long before your arrival on the scene. Anyway, I quickly realised that outside influences were at work, seeking to undermine Liam's American company. That's why he's gone away, isn't it? He's trying to salvage what he can – but he won't succeed.'

Smiling pleasantly, Clive sat in front of Caroline. Putting his hands on his knees, he leant forward. 'I know who's behind all this, Caroline. I have proof which I can take to Companies House, proof which will destroy these manipulators and save Liam's ass.'

'What do you want?' Caroline tried to keep her voice steady, but she felt a growing excitement within her. Here was a real chance to help Liam, but she knew Clive. True, he had been a good friend to Liam before, but she wouldn't think about that now. Clive was a self-seeker. He would help Liam only if he could help himself at the same time.

'That's my Caroline! Always gets straight to the point.' Clive rose from his chair and walked around behind her. She felt his fingers brush her nipples, making them harden. His fingers trailed down her body, slipping into her dampening crease. He smiled at the evidence of arousal and slid his fingers in and out, just catching her clitoris with each movement. Mrs Davies stood back, watching with approval, fondling her own erect nipples as she surveyed the scene being enacted before her. Aroused in spite of herself, Caroline pulled against her tight bindings, causing fresh waves of excitement to shoot through her. Clive removed his fingers and brought them up to Caroline's nose, forcing her to sniff them. She twisted her head away, but Clive held her chin with his other hand.

'No, Caroline. I want you to suck them. Taste yourself.' He brushed his wet fingers across her lips, pushing until she opened her mouth and he was able to slide his fingers between her unwilling lips.

'That's it, my darling. It's not so hard to obey me, is it? Now, Caroline, this is what I want. I want you, my darling. I want you to come to me willingly. I want your obedience and, one day, I want your love.'

Caroline struggled against the ropes, biting the intruding fingers. Suddenly, Clive was in front of her, slapping her smartly across her face.

'That's the price of my help, Caroline. I will do everything I can to help Liam, but first I want you to spend three weeks in this house. I want to control you and I want you to enjoy that control. At the end of the three

43

weeks, if you don't willingly leave Liam and come to me, I will still keep my promise and help him. I want that three weeks, Caroline, to try to make you voluntarily mine. During that time, you will live here and obey me in all things, no matter what I may ask you to do. I want your promise to that effect. I have a contract already drawn up. It contains my promise to reveal what I know to the proper authorities, if you remain here with me for three weeks. It also says that, no matter what the outcome of that period may be, I will hold good to my promise. That document will be signed and notarised and kept under lock and key in the offices of an independent solicitor.'

Clive resumed his seat, turning the full force of his overpoweringly mesmeric eyes upon Caroline. 'Give me those three weeks, Caroline. What have you got to lose? If you're sure of your love for Liam . . .'

'I am! Very sure!'

'Then it is merely a short change of residence on your part, Caroline. When Liam returns you will have helped him immeasurably. If you return to him . . .'

'Which I will!'

Clive shrugged his shoulders. 'Then I will have gambled and lost. In that instance, I will get out of both of your lives for good and you will never see me again.' He studied the impassioned face before him. 'Think about it, Caroline. If I do nothing, Liam will lose his company – maybe all of his businesses. He'll be ruined. He'll lose everything.'

'He won't lose me!'

'But he can have it all, Caroline. He can have you and maintain his businesses. You could make him an extremely happy man.'

Caroline bowed her head. She was thinking furiously. She was absolutely certain that her love for Liam could withstand anything Clive might do to her. She thought of erasing the lines of worry that had furrowed Liam's

44

forehead for these past weeks. They could happily re-
sume their life together without these awful concerns
that had dogged them both. She raised her head and
looked at Clive. Yes, she could and would resist him.
She had dealt with Mrs Davies before and could do so
again. It was worth it for Liam. She would do it for him.
She looked intently at the man sitting before her. 'Untie
me, please. You've got yourself a deal!'

Caroline held the pen in a hand that trembled slightly.
The word 'obey' leapt out at her. If she signed this contract, she would be forced to obey Clive in everything.
He and Mrs Davies would be able to treat her as they
wished. With the memory of Liam's well-loved face in
her mind, she bent her head, signing her name in the
space provided.

'Excellent, my dear,' Clive said, scrutinising her signature before adding his own. 'You won't regret this.
Liam will be forever in your debt.'

'I don't want Liam to be in my debt, but neither do I
want to be in yours!'

Clive chuckled and walked over to stand behind
Caroline's chair as the solicitor added his signature, be-
fore folding the contract and placing it in his briefcase.
He leant over and shook the proffered hand.

'Many thanks, Miles. Perhaps you would care to join
us in a celebratory drink?'

The solicitor smiled lasciviously at Caroline. 'No time
at the present, but I look forward to furthering our
acquaintance when I collect my commission, Miss West.'

Nodding to them, he went out, closing the door behind him. Caroline turned in her chair and looked
accusingly at Clive. 'You said that it would be an independent solicitor!'

Clive laughed and reached down to squeeze both of
Caroline's breasts, now encased in the folds of a shiny
white satin robe.

'And so he is, my dear. He's not my solicitor nor, as far as I know, is he yours. I didn't say that I wouldn't be acquainted with the solicitor in question, now did I?'

'What did he mean about his commission?'

'My pet, I merely offered him an evening with my new slave – to repay him for his services.'

Caroline struggled wildly in his grip. 'I'm not your slave!'

'My pet, didn't anyone ever tell you always to read the small print before you sign anything?'

Mrs Davies came forward and placed a copy of the contract in front of them.

'Thank you, Carol. You see, my love,' Clive said, indicating one of the paragraphs with his finger, 'it says that you will be used by me and anyone else of my choosing. It also says that you will have no choice in the matter. And look here ...' Clive turned the page and indicated again. ' "For the agreed period, Caroline West will be known as Clive Craigen's slave and will be treated as such by everyone with whom she comes into contact." I think that just about covers it, don't you?'

'You lied to me! I didn't know anything about that!'

'But, my dear, you willingly signed this contract and agreed to abide by its terms, didn't you?'

Caroline stopped struggling and cursed herself for a fool. He was right. Of course he was right. She should have read the paper properly before signing it. She was bound by its terms. She looked up at Clive. For the next three weeks, she was this man's slave! Clive smiled and moved away slightly.

'And now, my dear, I think it's time that you were dressed as befits your new station. Carol, if you please.'

Mrs Davies moved forward and slipped the robe from Caroline's shoulders. Caroline made a feeble effort to grasp at the robe, but Mrs Davies tugged it away from her.

'We don't want any trouble, now do we?' She smiled

as she folded the robe. Clive had retrieved something from a table and Caroline sat sullenly in her chair as he approached. He held the collar that he had so lovingly kept for just this moment. He slipped it around her neck and smiled at her involuntary movement of resistance.

'Carol, I think we need the cuffs. The little slave needs to learn obedience before she can be trusted.' As he spoke, he reached down and gripped her wrists. Caroline looked at him, tears of frustration forming in her eyes, but she stopped struggling. He had every right to do what he wanted with her now. She had truly surrendered herself to him. Clive held her arms out for Mrs Davies to strap the heavy leather cuffs, with their short connecting chain, on to her slim wrists. When this task had been completed and Caroline's head was bowed in submission, Clive strapped the black leather slave collar around her neck, padlocking it firmly in place. He didn't know where the key that fitted the tiny gold padlock might be, but it didn't matter. As he had promised himself, now that the collar was at last locked around Caroline's neck, he had no intention of ever removing it.

As Clive stood behind her, stroking the luscious waves of her golden hair with a proprietary gesture, the doorbell sounded. As Caroline automatically opened her mouth to scream, Clive covered it with his hand.

'Carol, perhaps you'd be so good as to answer the door. I believe it will be the visitor that I'm expecting.'

Mrs Davies went out, closing the door behind her. Clive relaxed his grip on Caroline.

'Just remember, my dear, you are doing this for Liam and you are doing it of your own free will.'

Caroline reluctantly nodded and Clive moved away from her. The door opened and Caroline could not suppress a gasp of amazement as she instantly recognised the new arrival. It was Lynne who stood there. She looked just as Caroline remembered her: tall and imposing, her hair scraped back to accentuate the beautiful

47

angles of her face. She wore a black leather mistress dress, which ended just above her knees and completely concealed the tops of the black leather spike-heeled boots that she wore. She stared at Caroline with equal surprise and mounting anger.

'So! This is your new slave, Clive!' She walked slowly over to Caroline, bending to flick long red nails against the slave's nipples. 'So, little slut, we meet again!'

Surprised as he was that these two appeared to know each other, Clive still had the presence of mind to move swiftly over to Caroline and place his hands on her shoulders in a warningly firm grip.

'Yes, this is the slave that is in need of strict discipline, Lynne. More than suitable for your undoubted talents, I believe. She is aware that she needs training and has expressed a willingness to begin, haven't you, my sweet?'

Caroline did not need the increased pressure on her shoulders to encourage her to supply the answer that she knew was expected of her and that she had to give. 'Yes, Master. I am willing.'

Lynne selected a cane from an array contained in an upright stand, before crossing to stand in front of Caroline. 'I hear that Liam is away on business. So his little slut, whom he believes is waiting anxiously at home for him, has decided to have a little playtime of her own, yes?'

Caroline wanted to shout at Lynne that she didn't really want to be here and that things weren't how they appeared to be, but she was very conscious of the pressure on her shoulders and of what was at stake for Liam. She bowed her head, and said nothing.

'Well, you little slut, Liam may be away, but I am here! Nobody does the dirty on a good friend of mine and gets away with it!' She lifted Caroline's chin with the tip of the cane. 'Be assured, slut, that you are not going to get away with anything!' She moved the tip of the cane down, resting it on Caroline's thighs. 'Clive is

48

right. You do need discipline.' With that she brought the cane down sharply across the girl's thighs. Clive clamped his hand over her mouth, stilling her cry of pain. 'Oh, yes, slut. I'm going to see that you get everything that's coming to you! Everything!'

Four

Wearing nothing but her slave collar, Caroline stood with her back against one wall of the cheerless basement room. Things had happened much too quickly and she felt dazed. Mrs Davies? Why had she ever trusted that vengeful woman? Caroline shivered as she thought of how Mrs Davies must have watched and waited for her chance and of how much she seemed to hate her. Desperately, Caroline looked around the room. There was only one door, which she knew to be locked. There were no windows and Clive had assured her that the room had been very thoroughly sound-proofed. She felt tears sting her eyes as she thought of Liam. He had no idea where she was or what had happened to her. Thinking of Liam helped to strengthen her resolve. She would endure this for his sake. Clive had promised that he would help Liam and, strangely, she believed him. He was, after all, partly getting what he wanted. Caroline had signed the contract to which he knew she would keep. She would stay here in this house for the agreed period of time and then she would go back to Liam. Despite his confident assertions to the contrary, Clive could not impose his will on her to the extent that she would stay with him voluntarily beyond the agreed period. Fervently, she assured herself that she loved Liam and then wondered at her own fervency; was she really so confident? Unwittingly, she pictured the intensity of Clive's gaze. For a moment, his eyes seemed to fill her vision, blotting out everything else.

It was almost a relief when she heard a key grind in the lock and tensed herself as the door swung open. Lynne stood there, her eyes glittering. She carried a black leather cat o'nine tails in one hand. As if attracted by a magnet, Caroline fixed her eyes on the implement. Lynne gave a short, harsh laugh and entered the room, closing and locking the door. Caroline shrank back against the wall as Lynne approached her.

'Well, my little slave, it's so nice to spend time with you again,' Lynne said, her voice soft and low. Reaching Caroline, she stopped and reached out to cruelly pinch one of the girl's nipples. Caroline gasped with pain and Lynne laughed, idly flicking the cat o'nine tails across her prisoner's breasts. Measuring Caroline with an almost puzzled gaze, Lynne studied her for a moment. 'You know, I really thought that you and Liam had something special. I'd never seen him so happy and he seemed confident that you felt the same way about him.' Lynne paused, unwillingly conceding admiration as her eyes explored Caroline's shapely body. 'Liam is a good friend. I can see the attraction that Clive has. He's a very fascinating man – but then, so is Liam.' Lynne suddenly moved closer to Caroline, catching her chin and forcing her head up. 'What was the problem, little slave? One not good enough for you? Felt lonely with Liam away?'

Caroline wrenched her chin away from Lynne's grasp. 'It wasn't like that! I know how it looks, but ...' Caroline's voice faded. She couldn't say any more. If she did, Clive would not help Liam. She had to keep silent and let Lynne think the worst.

'Yes?' Lynne demanded. 'How is it different from the way it looks? Well, slave, I'm waiting.'

Caroline lowered her head. Enraged, Lynne grabbed a handful of her hair and jerked her head up, bringing their faces close together. Hopelessly, Caroline gave a slight shake of her head, then gasped with pain as the grip on her hair tightened.

'Nothing to say in your defence? Then I must make my own assumptions, mustn't I? I must punish you for those assumptions. I must avenge Liam. Isn't that right, slave?'

Feeling almost crushed by her own helplessness, Caroline swallowed her tears. She had willingly signed that contract and now was the pay-off time.

'You must do as you think fit, Mistress,' she managed and submissively dropped her eyes.

Lynne pushed her back against the wall and paced the room, studying her. Something was not right. What had Caroline been about to say before she had thought better of it? Usually in complete control of situations, Lynne felt slightly at a loss and tried to revive her earlier feelings of anger. Being the pragmatist that she was, she mentally shrugged her shoulders. She could only deal with the situation as it currently appeared to be. If the slave were indeed being unfaithful to her Master, Lynne felt that a strong dose of humiliation and discipline would teach the slut a lesson or even elicit the truth. Having reached her decision, she straightened her back and glared at Caroline.

'Undress me, slave,' Lynne ordered, her voice cold as ice.

Caroline just stared at her.

'I said undress me!' Lynne growled, her voice allowing for no doubt as to quick reprisal for any disobedience.

Caroline hurried over to her. She made to go behind Lynne, but was stopped as a vice-like grip encircled her wrists.

'I didn't hear your answer, slave.' Lynne's voice had changed again and her tone was now one of menacing sensuality. Caroline looked at her.

'I'm sorry, Mistress. I will immediately attend to your order,' Caroline said, lowering her eyes.

'Yes, you will,' Lynne purred. 'However, I have no

intention of making things easy for you. First of all, you will fetch me the rope that you will find in the cupboard.'

'No, Mistress, please. I will do anything that you say. There is no need . . .'

Caroline broke off as her wrists were released and she was sharply slapped across her face. Before she could recover from the blow, Lynne had again gripped her wrists.

'I did not give you permission to speak!' Lynne said, in a voice that was tightly controlled. 'It's no wonder that you felt able to chase after another man as soon as your Master went away. You are in great need of some discipline, slut! Get me that rope immediately!'

Lynne did not make any further threats. She knew there was an implied one that Caroline would not ignore. She released the girl's wrists, observing with satisfaction the red marks on Caroline's white skin. As the girl hurried over to the cupboard, Lynne watched the way her buttocks moved as she walked and felt a growing wetness between her legs. She had always desired Caroline. The girl's body excited her and she was looking forward to punishing and using the slave. As Caroline returned to her, Lynne's eyes swept over that perfect, small-waisted figure. With pleasure, she remembered sucking those deliciously large nipples; the breasts were small, but that was how she liked them. Yes, the girl was perfect and Lynne was determined to enjoy subduing and humiliating her.

Caroline placed the coil of rope in Lynne's hands. Her eyes were still downcast and Lynne refrained from the impulse she had to stroke the shining blonde head so meekly lowered. The rising passion that Lynne was experiencing translated into rough action, as she forced Caroline's arms behind her and tightly tied her wrists. Satisfied, she used the penis-shaped handle of the cat o'nine tails to tilt Caroline's chin upwards.

'That's better. Now, slave, as I was saying, I want you to undress me.'

Caroline opened her mouth to protest, but just as quickly closed her lips. Protesting would only bring another slap or worse. Taking a deep breath, she walked behind Lynne. In spite of everything, she was aroused - and challenged. She looked at the long zipper at the back of Lynne's black leather mistress dress. She would have to use her mouth – but how to get Lynne to bend down so that she could reach the lip of the zipper? She struggled with the ropes at her wrists knowing, even as she did so, that there was no escape. Her clitoris pulsed to her a warning of its need. Her nipples were hard and sensitive. Deliberately, she brushed against the soft leather, luxuriating in the smell of the sensuous material. She smelt something else; the unmistakeable smell of a woman's sexual arousal. Caroline instinctively grasped at the solution to her problem.

'Mistress, may I speak?' Caroline asked.

Lynne, who had felt the girl brushing against her, smiled. 'Permission granted.'

'When I have undressed you, Mistress, I would like to make you feel good, if the Mistress will allow.'

'In what way would my slave like to make me feel good?' Lynne asked, playing along with this delightful game. After all, Caroline was securely tied. She was not in a position to inflict harm.

'I would like to taste my Mistress' juices on my tongue,' Caroline said, with a docility that was overlaid with sexual excitement. 'If my Mistress would lie down, I would like to use my lips and tongue to give her pleasure.'

Silently congratulating Caroline on her successful ploy, Lynne, gracefully obliging, knelt on the floor and then lay down. She presented her back to Caroline and smiled as she felt the tug on her zipper as the slave set about undressing her. Lynne was impressed with the agility of the girl's mouth, as the zipper was pulled down and she felt the dress being gradually eased from her body. Caroline was enjoying herself, using her mouth to pull and tug at the dress. Appreciatively, Lynne breathed in the air of the room. It was redolent with the combined smells of the two women's arousal. Staying behind her, Caroline used her tongue to trail sensuously down Lynne's back. She didn't hesitate when she came to the cleft between Lynne's buttocks, but slipped the tip of her tongue inside the rosy opening to the dominatrix's anus. Lynne moaned with pleasure and opened her legs, allowing Caroline's tongue to move towards her slit and the swollen bud that had pushed out from beneath its hood. She jerked her knees towards her breasts with the strength of the feelings she was experiencing as Caroline's tongue swirled around her bud. She reached behind her and caught one of Caroline's small breasts in her hand, her usual instinct to twist such soft flesh and cause pain completely sublimated in the waves of desire and pleasure that washed over her. Instead, she kneaded and massaged the softness and felt an answering surge of passion in the tongue that caressed her clitoris. Lynne's spike-heeled boots drummed against the floor as she came in wave after wave of orgasmic pleasure that left her spent and sated. She lay still for some time. What a treasure this girl was. How had she and Francis let her get away? Eventually, she turned her head and looked at Caroline who, exhausted by her efforts, was lying a short distance from her. Lynne smiled as she looked at the eyelashes resting on the flushed cheeks. She really was a beautiful girl. Lynne frowned as she thought of the reason for her presence in this house. Was this girl really capable of such duplicity as she had at first thought? Maybe she shouldn't be concerned about getting vengeance for Liam. Maybe she should be thinking of how she could get this slave back to Beech House where she really belonged. If she had in fact done something wrong while Liam was away, then of course she must be punished for it. Lynne smiled as she thought of the pleasure she would derive from that.

Recovering herself, Lynne moved to Caroline, who opened her eyes and smiled at her.

'Is my little girl nicely rested?' Lynne asked, smiling pleasantly. 'Yes, thank you, Mistress,' Caroline responded.

'You have indeed made me feel good, little slave. Now, I think, it is my turn.'

Caroline looked up at Lynne, her eyes questioning. Was she going to be allowed some relief? Lynne smiled at her and got to her feet. Caroline watched admiringly as Lynne walked over to the cupboard. She was statuesque and beautifully proportioned. The spike-heeled boots clicked on the floor as she walked and Caroline shivered with excitement. Lynne got something from the cupboard and returned to the prone figure on the floor. Kneeling beside her, Lynne strapped a pair of ankle cuffs on to the girl, linking them with a long length of chain. Lynne looked at her again, her smile now strangely threatening. Caroline watched as Lynne gradually pulled on a pair of short black latex gloves, sensuously smoothing the soft rubber on to her hands. Flexing those hands before Caroline's eyes, she ran a finger over the girl's mouth, slipping it between the curved lips so that Caroline could taste the rubber.

'What does my little slave think I should do to her, eh?' Lynne purred the rhetorical question as she removed the finger from between Caroline's lips and pressed her hand over the girl's mouth.

'I wonder, should I gag you? Do you make much noise when you scream, little slave? I can't really remember whether or not you do. Perhaps I will gag you. It will stop you from screaming when you know what I intend, won't it?' Lynne's voice was low and soft. Caroline felt the fear that she was intended to feel, but also a sexual excitement that she could barely contain.

Keeping one hand firmly over the girl's mouth, Lynne stroked her other hand over those delicious breasts, revelling in the tautness of the large nipples. Her hand travelled further down, slipping over the smooth skin on the abdomen and downwards to the shaven mound. As Lynne's gloved hand reached Caroline's sex, she moaned beneath the hand that gagged her. The unrelenting questing fingers found the yearning bud and stroked around it. Caroline struggled helplessly. She wanted some relief. Lynne's fingers probing her slit and the smell of the latex that covered her mouth were driving her mad. As she slipped two fingers into Caroline's wetness, Lynne chuckled softly.

'Oh, my little slave. You are very wet. Anyone would think that you were enjoying yourself and we can't have that, can we?'

Suddenly, Lynne removed her fingers and brought them up to her nose. Sniffing appreciatively, she looked at Caroline with mock concern.

'Oh, I'm sorry, little slave. Would you like to taste yourself?'

Her eyes forbidding a response, Lynne removed her hand from Caroline's mouth and unpeeled both of the gloves. Pinching Caroline's nostrils, she forced the girl to open her mouth and thrust one of the rubber gloves between the slave's lips. Caroline tasted her own juices on the glove as Lynne secured the gag in position with a length of rope. Lynne sat back and looked at her, feeling the renewal of her arousal as she looked at the helpless girl.

'Oh, Caroline, how did we ever let you go? Francis cared about you, you know. A little too much, I think. You do need disciplining, my love. I think that perhaps Francis and I should take you back and continue where we left off. You need some good whippings and some good old-fashioned spankings . . .'

Excited, Lynne broke off and bent her head. She felt

Caroline buck beneath her as she swirled her tongue around the girl's clitoris. Teasing her, Lynne stopped and lifted her head.

'Clive wants me to discipline you, though. Perhaps I will do that to his satisfaction and then I'll talk to Francis about having you back.' Lynne bent her head again and stroked her tongue around Caroline's clitoris. The girl struggled in her arousal. Lynne raised her head. 'What shall I do, little slave?' she asked mischievously. 'Shall I bring you off or shall I whip you? Perhaps I'll do both. What do you think? Perhaps I'll just leave you tied up like this without doing anything. Oh, dear, it's so difficult.'

Lynne lay on top of Caroline, thrusting her pelvic bone against that of the girl. She stroked the girl's hard nipples, then bent her head and sucked each one in turn. She was pleasantly aware of their mingled juices, sealing their bodies together with their stickiness. She knew that one touch with her tongue or a finger would give Caroline the release that she craved. Still undecided, Lynne turned her head and saw the cat o'nine tails lying beside them on the floor. Smiling, she picked it up and let the soft leather strands slip through her fingers.

'I think I will beat you, little slave, for what you did to Liam.' Lynne let the soft leather trail across Caroline's breasts. 'Yes, I think I'd like to mark you and then let you try and work out some way to pleasure yourself. Difficult I know, with your hands tied behind you. However, you've shown yourself to be fairly adept at difficult situations. Perhaps I'll ask Mrs Davies to come down here . . .'

Lynne smiled at the immediate fear that her words sparked in Caroline. 'Would you like that, little slave? You are here for our pleasure, you know. You are to be used as we see fit. That's what being a slave means, little Caroline, and you know all about that, don't you?'

Deciding that she had had enough of this particular

play-acting, Lynne got into a kneeling position and pressed her mouth to Caroline's slit. It was only the work of a few seconds before she had Caroline bucking with the strength of her orgasm. Smiling almost clinically, Lynne got to her feet and tapped the penis-shaped head of the cat o'nine tails against the tops of her boots. She waited until Caroline's paroxysms had subsided and then knelt beside the girl, her eyes boring into those of the prisoner.

'Was that nice, my little slave? Yes? Good. You know what comes next, don't you? You've had the pleasure – now you must pay the price. I have to whip you, little Caroline, because you've been behaving very badly, and you know I can't allow that.' Lynne's smile almost begged forgiveness as she raised the punishment implement. 'This is for Liam and for what you've done to him, you little slut!'

Five

Clive lay back in bed and reached for his cigarettes. As he lit one, he reflected on the deep satisfaction that he felt. Caroline was here, in this house. He recalled the anger and fear that he had seen in her face, and then the resignation as she accepted the inevitable; he had gambled on her concern for Liam overcoming any repulsion that she might have felt for himself. He had no doubt that there was repulsion, just as he had no doubt that he could change all that. He felt invigorated by the challenge and did not for one moment think that he would not succeed. He was, however, surprised by the strength of feeling he had experienced on first seeing her again. He reached beneath the quilt and stroked his penis, already hard at the thought of Caroline and of what she must be experiencing at Lynne's hands. Perhaps he should go down to the basement? No, better to remove himself from the discipline that Lynne had promised to employ. If he was gentle with her, Caroline would respond to him favourably. He would give her pleasure after the pain and then, perhaps, he would give her to Carol. Between Lynne and Carol, exerting strict discipline, there would be his own gentle and considerate ministrations. Clive smiled as he imagined Caroline turning to him in gratitude; learning to rely on him as a protector from the termagants. Clive looked at his watch and stubbed out his cigarette. He would take great care over his appearance. His penis throbbed in anticipation as he got out of bed. Perhaps there would be time for a wank in the shower, but maybe not. Clive's eyes darkened as he thought about Caroline. He intended to spend a long time with her today, so it might be a good idea to conserve his energy. Regretfully, he looked down at his erect member and laughed. 'It'll be worth the wait,' he promised himself. He was still smiling as he walked into the bathroom.

Quietly opening the door, Clive stood for a moment on the threshold. Caroline was lying on the floor. Her hands were still tied and he could see the fresh weals on her bottom, the red stripes startling against the whiteness of her flesh. She was lying very still and it wasn't until he walked around to the other side of her that he could see that she was asleep. He wasn't prepared for the way he felt as he looked at the woman he wanted to control and dominate. She looked so vulnerable that he just wanted to reach out and gently touch her face. It was enough to wake her and her eyes flooded with fear.

'It's all right, my darling,' Clive said softly. 'I won't let anyone hurt you. I'm just going to take you upstairs.'

Caroline just stared at him. After the beating, Lynne had removed the gag before she had left the room, but it was her own confusion that now kept her silent. Clive bent down and gathered her into his arms. He lifted her so gently that, absurdly, she felt tears stinging at her eyes. She hadn't expected this. She had thought there would be more discipline – more pain – but Clive was treating her as tenderly as if she were a baby. He carried her upstairs and into the bedroom, laying her on the bed to which she had previously been tied. He closed the door and then, returning to her, sat on the bed. She felt his fingers gently stroking her hair. As if mesmerised, she watched him, her eyes searching his face for clues as to his state of mind and as to what she might expect. They remained like that for several moments. Clive now knew that he cared deeply for this woman, more deeply

61

than he would confess to her or to anyone. He knew that he would fight to win her and he also knew that he could not let her go. He wanted her to turn to him and look at him with even half the love that he felt. Clive tried to grasp at the reasons that had prompted him to get Caroline in his clutches. Revenge for what had previously happened, a desire to complete unfinished business: he knew that those things were no longer important. The challenge was still there and he still relished the prospect; but now for a different reason. Now he was really determined to make Caroline his woman and he would use whatever was necessary to achieve that goal.

Caroline felt the old sense of helplessness that she had felt whenever Clive had fixed her with those darkly compelling eyes. She felt as if she were being drawn into him and she was strongly aware of the futility of any resistance. Desperately, she tried to picture Liam's face, tried to recall the sound of his voice: all she could see was Clive's dark eyes and all she could hear was the sound of his breathing. His eyes filled her vision, blotting out everything else as he bent his head to kiss her. She felt his lips on hers, his tongue forcing her lips apart as it demanded entrance, and she knew that she could refuse him nothing. She closed her eyes, but still saw those eyes; eyes that compelled and commanded. She was aware of nothing else; not the rope around her wrists nor the soreness of her bottom. Still keeping his lips on hers, Clive's fingers stroked her breasts, lingering on the sensitive nipples. Their tongues entwined and she felt her sexual excitement growing and matching his. She didn't stop to think of what she was doing. She only knew that – now – this seemed right. Clive raised his head and looked at her. 'You are my slave, Caroline. I own you and I want to possess your body and your mind.'

He could see the confusion in her eyes as she shook

her head. 'No. I belong to Liam. You know that,' Caroline almost whispered.

Clive smiled and kissed her again. He sensed the eagerness of her response and felt a twinge of triumph, before he reminded himself that the battle was not yet won. She would have to go through many trials before she would admit the truth. She was his and one day she would own to that. When he again raised his head, he was smiling.

'Oh yes, you are mine, my love, but, until you admit to that, I will have to treat you as the slave that you are.'

'It doesn't matter what you do or what you say, I will always love Liam,' Caroline protested, more to convince herself than Clive.

Clive's smile broadened as he got off the bed. 'Then, my little slave, whether you like it or not, I had better ensure that you remain with me for the agreed period.'

Caroline watched as he retrieved some lengths of chain from a drawer in the bedside table. 'I have agreed to stay with you for a limited period of time, after which you have promised me that I will gain my freedom,' she pleaded.

'I will keep my promise – if that is what you really want,' Clive assured her, as he wound the chains around each of her ankles and fastened them to either side of the bed.

'You know it's what I really want ...' Caroline's voice was stilled as Clive kissed her again. She tried to fight her own body, tried to stop the arousal that flooded her, but it was a battle she could not win. As Clive's tongue invaded her mouth, gagging her protests, she was lost in the sensations that seemed to make her body deny what her mind really wanted. As the kiss deepened, Clive's fingers explored her body; it was as if he was patiently showing her what it was that she actually wanted. Her nipples strained towards his touch and her clitoris was so sensitive that the merest contact would have triggered a powerful orgasm.

'Oh, Caroline,' Clive murmured against her lips. 'I wonder if you know what it is that you really want? Your body is telling me something quite different to your words. Don't fight it. Give in to me, my darling. You know that you will eventually. Why go through all that pain?'

'It's you who wants to give me the pain,' Caroline said, desperately trying to latch on to some semblance of sanity.

Clive smiled and shook his head. He ran a finger over her lips. 'No, my dear. I don't want you to have to endure any pain. All that you have to do is come to me of your own accord. If you tell me that you want to stay with me, I will call off Lynne and Mrs Davies . . .'

'Mrs Davies!' Caroline shouted and struggled with her bonds. 'Why are you doing this to me?'

Clive kissed her again. When she had calmed a little, he looked at her. 'I see that Carol Davies frightens you, little one. That's a pity because I know that she is eager to become reacquainted with you . . .'

'No! Please! Please don't let her near me! You don't know what she's like!'

Clive put his hand over her mouth.

'Oh, but I do, my darling. She is going to persuade you to stay with me. If you are not in agreement, she will tie you and beat you and do whatever she likes. You can stop this immediately. You only have to agree to stay with me of your own free will and I will call her off. So you see, my darling, any pain that she might inflict is really of your own making. It's a shame, really. I understand that she feels you are responsible for what she considers to be her humiliating experiences in Liam's house. She has told me that she wants you to experience some of that humiliation . . .' Clive broke off as he saw the desperate pleading look in Caroline's eyes. 'Caroline, you are adorable when you look at me like that. Relax and enjoy, my darling. Carol will hurt you and I will pleasure you.'

64

Caroline shook her head, desperately trying to dislodge the hand that gagged her.

'Yes, my darling. You can stop this now. All you have to do is promise to stay with me and love me – love me of your own free will. Otherwise . . .' Clive regretfully shook his head. 'Let's not think about that now. Carol will want to see you later on today and I promised you some pleasure before the pain.'

Removing his hand, Clive kissed her again. Her frantic struggles, occasioned by his words, gradually stilled as her body again responded to him. Thoughts of Lynne and Mrs Davies slipped from her mind as she gave herself up to Clive's expert ministrations. She felt him easing out of his trousers and, had her hands been free, she would have helped him. Instead, her tongue plunged deeper, wanting to explore every crevice of his mouth. She felt his hardness pressing against her and strained her body towards him. If only she could just tell him what he wanted to hear. It would be so easy. Did Liam make her feel like this? Perhaps Lynne was right about her. Perhaps she was deceitful. Clive's cock penetrating her wetness stilled all the voices in her head. Vaguely, she heard the chink of chain against chain as her body moved with Clive. She strained against her bonds, fuelling her excitement. Clive's fingers were pinching her nipples; the pain, her helplessness and the welcome intruder within her vagina combined to push her into an orgasm so intense that she tore her mouth away from Clive's to enable her to gasp in great gulps of air. Her mind screamed that this was wrong but her body told her that it was very, very right.

For a long time, Clive lay still, allowing his breathing to return to normal. What was it about this girl? He had just experienced an orgasm so tremendous in its power that it had left him sated and momentarily powerless – and that frightened him. Power and the possession of it was what drove Clive. Exercising that power, by its use rendering others helpless, was the fuel that powered him. Now he was at the mercy of this slip of a girl. He could do nothing other than wait for her to turn to him and he wanted that more than anything else. She was necessary to him and he would not – could not – let her go. He turned his head to look at her. She lay quietly, but her eyes were open. He rolled over and looked at her, willing her to return his gaze. At first, she resisted. He could see the struggle that was being waged within her. Eventually, she turned her head and gazed at him. He was a little disconcerted to see that there were tears in her eyes. He reached out and gently stroked her hair.

'Caroline, we are good together. You know that. Why are you resisting me?'

Caroline shook her head and turned away. 'You know that I love Liam,' she managed before her voice broke.

Clive sat up and released the chains from her ankles. Pulling her to him, he was conscious of the renewed hardness of his penis. He could feel her body shaking with her sobs and pressed her to him. Eventually, she stopped crying and Clive tilted her chin toward him.

'Clive, please let me go. I won't tell Liam about any of this,' she begged him.

'My love, you signed a contract. You agreed . . .'

'No! I can't do it! You're asking too much!' Caroline looked at him, tears that threatened to overspill trembling on her lashes.

'I'm not asking too much, my love,' Clive said, brushing the wetness from her lids. 'All you have to do is to tell me that you will stay with me voluntarily. Are you so sure that that isn't what you want?'

'If I did say that, would you untie me and unlock the door? Would you trust me?' she challenged him.

'Not yet, my love. You wouldn't really expect me to, now would you? You have agreed to be my slave. After the expiration of the contract . . . Well, we'll see.'

Caroline searched his face with her eyes. 'If, at that time, I want to go back to Liam, do you really still intend to let me go?'

Clive felt a surge of hope. She had said 'if' she wanted to go back to Liam. Then she really was having doubts.

'Caroline, I have very strong feelings for you. Maybe you're really the one in the driving seat, I don't know. I don't know how I'll feel in a few weeks' time. If you want to go back to Liam, maybe I'll let you go, and . . .'

'Maybe you won't,' Caroline finished for him. There was a short silence before she turned her head back to him. 'Will you still keep your promise to help Liam . . . no matter what happens?'

Clive sighed and stroked her breasts. 'Yes, my love. No matter what happens, I will keep that part of my promise.'

'So I am to be your prisoner?' Caroline asked, her voice softly resigned.

'My love, I think you've always been that, haven't you?' Clive asked, as he bent his head and imprisoned her mouth with his own.

Caroline responded. She couldn't deny the urgings of her body. Right now, she wanted Clive – more perhaps than she had ever wanted Liam. Her thoughts were confused and were being swiftly overwhelmed by a return of the passion that Clive stirred in her. He pulled away from her and looked at her, the intensity of his gaze fuelling her arousal, even as it frightened her.

'You're mine, Caroline! Admit it!'

Dazedly, she shook her head. She wouldn't give in. She had to remember Liam. She had to fight for what they had had together.

'You're stubborn, young woman, do you know that?' Clive asked. 'I will have my way, Caroline. Resist me if you like. That only excites me.' He bent his head to taste her mouth again, before pulling back and grabbing some of the chains that he had used to bind her ankles. Leaning over her, he smiled, a sensuously menacing

67

smile that only excited her. 'You like it, too, don't you Caroline?'

She could only look at him, the truth of his words reflected in her eyes. With a grunt of satisfaction, Clive pushed her over on to her stomach. He tied one length of the chain around her mouth and head, stifling any protests she might have wanted to make. He linked the ends of the chain through the ring in her collar, padlocking them in place.

Satisfied, he lay on top of her. She could feel his cock, pressing gently at the entrance to her anus. She felt his fingers slip inside her wetness, which he used to lubricate the head of his cock. With one hand, he caught her bound wrists and held them still. The other hand guided his cock into her anus. As he gently slipped inside her, she felt his fingers move to her slit and stroke the straining bud of her clitoris. She screamed against the chains in her mouth, feeling an excitement that was almost more than she thought she could bear. She felt Clive's warm breath on her bare shoulder.

'You're mine, Caroline. You won't admit it yet, but soon you will. You are my slave and I will use you in whatever way that I choose. Tell me that this isn't what you want. Shake your head if, right now, you're not exactly where you want to be. Do that and I'll stop. Well, my love?'

Caroline moaned against her gag. She didn't shake her head because she didn't want him to stop. Clive was riding her with increasing ferocity and that was exactly what she wanted. Her climax was fast approaching and she tried to hold off as long as she could. She wanted them both to come together. As Clive shouted his pleasure at the same time as the waves of ecstasy washed over her, she could not repress the feeling of triumph that rose within her. She did not know that Clive was cresting his own wave of triumph – triumph in the sure knowledge that Caroline would soon belong to him completely.

Six

Caroline was reluctant to leave the warm darkness, but there was movement in the vicinity of her hiding place and perhaps it would be sensible just to look. Someone had removed the chains from her mouth and that same person was now busy at her wrists. As she welcomed the return of the freedom to move her arms, she groped for contact with other human flesh.

'Clive,' she murmured sleepily, making renewed efforts to open her eyes.

'How dare you call the Master by that name?' came an angry voice.

Mrs Davies! Caroline struggled to sit up but strong hands pushed her back down. Before she could properly collect her thoughts, a wide strip of adhesive tape sealed her mouth. She was pushed on to her stomach and felt cold steel at her wrists. Mrs Davies secured the handcuffs and turned Caroline on to her back. The housekeeper's face filled her vision.

'Yes, it's me, you little slut! The Master feels that you are in need of discipline and he has handed you over to me for the day. First things first. You smell disgusting! Let's get you into the shower!'

Mrs Davies clipped a length of chain into the ring of Caroline's collar and pulled her off the bed. She was pushed into the bathroom and chained to the shower control unit. She fearfully watched as Mrs Davies removed her own clothes and stood with her in the shower cubicle.

'I have to make sure that you're properly clean,' the housekeeper said, reaching above Caroline's head to turn on the water. Under normal circumstances, Caroline would have revelled in the feel of the warm water cascading over her skin. Now, however, she was too afraid of what might happen to be able to relax. The housekeeper studied Caroline critically. She felt a stirring in her clitoris as she looked at her helpless prisoner. How good it was to regain the control that she had lost. How good to again have the slut at her mercy. A lot had happened since Master Liam had threatened to throw her out. Oh, yes, Mrs Davies had Caroline to thank for her reinstatement, but how the bitch had made her pay. The housekeeper thought of all the humiliations she had had to endure. Well, things were different now. *She* was again in control. Miss Caroline would have to pay for the many slights that the older woman had had to endure. Mrs Davies ran her hands down her body and touched her swollen clitoris. There was plenty of time, though. She intended to derive as much pleasure as she possibly could from the new situation. She leant back against the wall of the cubicle, massaging herself. She fondled her nipples with her other hand, watching Caroline. The slut had always looked good when in restraints.

'We are going to have a very satisfying day, my pet,' Mrs Davies crooned. 'You are going to learn what it is like to be humiliated. You are going to fetch and carry for *me*. You are going to beg me to be kind and lenient. You are going to beg me to stop hurting you. You are going to beg my forgiveness for every single slight that you inflicted upon me. I am going to treat you like the slut that you are and then you will pleasure me and thank me for the privilege.'

Mrs Davies' breath was coming in gasps as she approached her climax. The sight of Caroline, struggling with the handcuffs and making piteous pleading noises behind the tape that gagged her, pushed Mrs Davies into an orgasm, the strength of which made her knees buckle beneath her. The housekeeper slid to the floor and lay gasping out her pleasure.

Some moments later, she pulled herself back up and stood before Caroline. She took the soap and lathered it in her hands before beginning to wash Caroline. She smoothed her hands over the girl's breasts, laughing delightedly as the nipples sprang to immediate erection.

'So, Mrs Davies has not lost her touch,' the housekeeper said, slipping her hands further down until she encountered Caroline's slit. She pushed two fingers inside and looked at her prisoner. 'Do you like that?' Mrs Davies queried rhetorically.

Caroline's eyes were closed. How was this woman able to make her feel so excited? She tried reminding herself of what, in all likelihood, was to come, but her body would not let her do anything but respond to the questing fingers within her. Regardless of the water, Mrs Davies bent her head and sucked at each of Caroline's nipples. The housekeeper was again becoming aroused. She would give the slut some pleasure; there would be precious little of it for her during the remainder of the day. Mrs Davies slid to the floor and sucked at the engorged bud of Caroline's clitoris. Caroline twisted her cuffed hands, moaning beneath her gag, as wave after wave of sexual pleasure consumed her. Had it not been for the chain at her collar, she would have fallen to the floor; instead, she could only lean against the wall of the cubicle, unable to resist and furious with herself at that very helplessness.

As Mrs Davies dragged Caroline down to the basement, they encountered Clive.

'Ah, Carol. Going about your duties, I see.'

'Yes, Master Clive,' Mrs Davies almost simpered at him.

Clive leant towards Caroline and stroked her face

71

with a gentle finger. 'Be good, my darling. Carol will report to me fully. I don't want to hear any disturbing reports of your disobedience.' Just for a moment, his eyes became softer. 'Oh, Caroline, if you'd only listen to reason.' As if a shutter dropped over any feelings of tenderness, Clive's eyes regained their usual coldness as he moved away from her and started to climb the stairs. Caroline turned her head towards him; she wanted to beg him to come back, but only muffled sounds could be heard and Clive continued on his way.

Now dressed in her normal black outfit, Mrs Davies thrust her prisoner into the basement room. With a triumphant smile, she closed and locked the door. Caroline stood before her, shivering with cold and fright. She yearned for Clive. If only he would come into the room now and remove the tape from her mouth. She would go on her knees to him and agree to stay with him. She would agree to anything if by doing so she could evade the clutches of this woman who had always caused her to feel such fear. Why hadn't she let Liam get rid of her? Too late now for recriminations. Mrs Davies slipped the key of the door into the pocket of her dress and walked towards Caroline.

'Cold are we, my dear? I know just the thing to warm you,' Mrs Davies said and turned towards the cupboard. Extracting a thin whippy cane, she turned and looked at Caroline. 'I think this should warm you up nicely,' she said and returned to stand before Caroline. 'You have to be punished for many things, slut! The humiliation that I have had to endure at your hands and the temerity that you displayed this morning in calling the Master by his first name.' She tapped Caroline's thighs with the cane and walked consideringly around her. 'Inspection first, I think, and then perhaps some exercise to really warm you up. Bend over, slut!'

Finding it difficult to keep her balance, Caroline bent

from the waist. She felt Mrs Davies' hands on her buttocks, patting and smoothing the white skin.

'Only a few marks on you as yet, but we'll soon change all that!' Mrs Davies said, tapping her sharply across the backs of her thighs.

Caroline fought to regain her balance, her cuffed hands making the task extremely difficult.

'Hmm. The little slut is very wet,' Mrs Davies commented after experimentally slipping her fingers into Caroline's slit. 'Are you finding this to your taste, my darling? Let me give you something else to suck on!'

Mrs Davies came round to the front of Caroline and ripped the tape from her mouth. Caroline gasped in pained surprise and Mrs Davies took that opportunity and pushed her fingers, fragrant with Caroline's juices, into the girl's mouth.

'Suck them, slut!' Mrs Davies ordered. 'I know that you are not unused to this sort of activity!'

Caroline had no choice but to comply. She felt the stirrings of sexual arousal and again wondered at herself. She was caught in an unenviable position, but as well as the undoubted fear that she felt, there was also an undeniable sexual excitement. Mrs Davies exacerbated that excitement by stroking the cleft between the girl's buttocks, making Caroline struggle to stay upright.

'Oh, dear. Is my little girl having trouble?' Mrs Davies asked, her voice heavily laced with sarcasm.

Suddenly, the housekeeper disappeared from Caroline's line of vision and in the next instant the world exploded with pain. Mrs Davies had pushed the fingers which were well lubricated with Caroline's juices into the girl's anus but, as she did so, kept up a continuous sharp tapping of the cane across the back of her thighs. Just as suddenly as she had started, Mrs Davies stopped and again stood before Caroline.

'Time for some exercise, I think. I want you to march

on the spot until I tell you to stop. You will keep your knees high as you march and point your toes before your feet connect with the ground. March!'

Mrs Davies stood slightly to one side as Caroline began to march. As she couldn't use her arms, retaining balance was extremely difficult. Caroline did her best, but she kept losing momentum.

'Please, Mistress. Please will you release my hands. I'm finding it so difficult to keep my balance.'

There was a silence, punctuated only by Caroline's gasping breaths. Mrs Davies appeared to be considering the request.

'Beg me!'

'Mistress?'

'Beg me to take off your handcuffs, little slut! Beg me nice and properly! I want to hear lots of humility in your voice!'

Caroline took a deep breath. 'Please, Mistress. I beg you to remove my handcuffs so that I can march for you properly. Please, Mistress, I beg you to do this.'

Another silence. Caroline's breathing became laboured as she waited for a response. Her steps were slowing as the pains grew in her aching muscles.

'Get on your knees and grovel to me, slut!' yelled Mrs Davies.

At first, Caroline was just relieved to be able to stop marching. The difficulty came when she tried to get to her knees without having the use of her hands.

'Mistress, please. I can't . . .'

'Didn't your mother ever tell you that there's no such word as can't, little girl?' Mrs Davies asked, her voice betraying just how much she was enjoying herself as she watched Caroline's discomfiture.

'Please, Mistress . . .'

Mrs Davies slapped Caroline so hard that she almost toppled over.

'On your knees, slut! Or perhaps you would like a little assistance from the cane . . ?'

Helplessly, Caroline fell forward on to her knees, falling sideways as she hit the ground.

'Get up! Get up on your knees!' Mrs Davies yelled, lashing the girl's buttocks with the cane.

Crying out with shock, Caroline managed to get up on to her knees and knelt, shivering, before her tormentor. Mrs Davies walked around Caroline and then stood before her, unable to conceal the satisfaction in her smile.

'Well, well. Miss high and mighty Caroline! The mistress of the house on her knees to her housekeeper.' Mrs Davies' eyes gleamed with her victory. 'It's almost worth it. All those months of kowtowing to you, slut, just to see you like this! Grovelling to Mrs Davies!'

Surprisingly, she bent down and bit gently on one of Caroline's nipples, swirling her tongue around the areola. Caroline struggled to resist, but her treacherous nipples betrayed her. Mrs Davies chuckled as she repeated the process on the other nipple, massaging the girl's breasts with tender fingers. She looked up at Caroline and smiled. 'My little girl can't resist Mrs Davies, can she? I can do anything I like to you, can't I? I wonder what should I do? Shall I beat you or shall I pleasure you? Maybe a little of both, hmm? First, though, I think you still have a lesson in humility to learn.'

She stood back and Caroline felt frustration as her clitoris pulsed anger at its denial.

'Shall I take off your handcuffs? Perhaps not yet. Before I do, there is something that I want you to do for me.'

With a resurgence of fear, Caroline looked up at Mrs Davies.

'Don't look so worried, my little girl. Mrs Davies wouldn't ask you to do anything that you couldn't easily do.' She paused, as though considering the problem. Smiling, she looked at Caroline. 'I have it. I want you to clean my shoes.'

Caroline felt a puzzled relief. She would gladly clean the woman's shoes and, for that, she would surely have to have her hands released. Expectantly, she looked at the housekeeper.

'Well, get on with it, girl!'

'Please, Mistress. My handcuffs . . .'

As if that thought had only just occurred to her, Mrs Davies walked around the girl. Resuming her previous position, she smiled pleasantly at Caroline. 'Yes, my darling. Your handcuffs are still locked on you very, very securely.'

'But, mistress, I can't clean your shoes . . .'

'Why ever not?'

'Mistress, I can't use my hands!'

'Yes?'

Nearly crying with frustration, Caroline looked pleadingly at her implacable tormentor. 'Mistress, I will gladly clean your shoes . . .'

'Yes, you will. You will clean my shoes immediately. You do not need to use your hands!'

Completely puzzled, Caroline looked at Mrs Davies. As if explaining to a small child, Mrs Davies bent toward her. 'Your handcuffs remain on. Use your tongue, my dear.'

Horrified, Caroline could only stare at Mrs Davies. Surely the woman couldn't mean that? As if reading her thoughts, Mrs Davies smiled and moved her feet to within Caroline's range.

'I know that you can do a good job, my darling. I have every confidence in you,' Mrs Davies said, tapping the cane meaningfully against her leg. 'If you tire, I can encourage your efforts with my little friend.'

To underline her point, she brought the cane sharply down across Caroline's knees.

'Now, I suggest you get to it, my dear. Every smear and every little bit that you miss will earn you twenty strokes for each error. You have ten minutes. Time penalties will also incur further strokes.'

For a long moment, Caroline stared into Mrs Davies' eyes. She read several things in those cold depths: hate mingled with lust; a desire to hurt and humiliate and an implacable determination that would not be gainsaid. Submissively, Caroline bowed her head and took a deep breath. She bent her head and began her task. The leather felt cold and rough on her tongue. Fortunately, she didn't have time to become aware of any taste. She was too aware of the clock speeding through the allotted time, too aware of the cane that Mrs Davies smoothed over her hair and down her back. She had to stop frequently in order to gather enough spittle in her mouth to continue with her task. She licked and cleaned for all she was worth, as Mrs Davies began to count down the minutes and then the seconds remaining. When the ten minutes was up, she tapped the girl sharply across her shoulders, indicating that she should stop. Desperately trying to swallow and lubricate the dryness of her throat, Caroline looked up as Mrs Davies pulled a chair forward and sat down. Clinically, she inspected her shoes. Caroline could only sit and wait for the result of that inspection. Absurdly, she remembered how she had felt when at school, awaiting the results of a test. This was just as important to her – maybe even more so.

'You've done a good job, my dear,' Mrs Davies eventually pronounced.

Caroline felt weak with relief, a relief which lasted only for as long as it took Mrs Davies to rise and cross the room to stand before her prisoner. Using the tip of the cane, she raised the girl's chin. 'Congratulations, my dear. There are only two smears.'

Frozen with shock at the implication within those words, Caroline stared at Mrs Davies. 'Please, madam . . . I beg you . . .'

'That's right, my dear. Beg your Mistress. Beg her not to be cruel to you. Beg her to let you off. Beg her forgiveness. You know that that won't help you, don't you?'

If Caroline's wrists had not been locked into the handcuffs, she would have thrown her arms about Mrs Davies' knees. As it was, all she could do was use her mouth and eyes to beg for mercy. 'Please, Mistress, I do beg you . . .'

Mrs Davies shook her head and tapped the cane against the girl's lips. 'You know that that's no use, my little girl. You beg so very prettily, but I have to do my duty and you have to be punished.'

Still shaking her head, Mrs Davies extracted a roll of adhesive tape from the pocket of her dress.

'No! Please, Mistress!'

Mrs Davies knelt in front of Caroline and placed a finger over the girl's lips. 'Hush, my darling. It's only forty strokes. That's not so very many. You can be a brave little girl, can't you?'

Smiling in a regretfully sensuous way, Mrs Davies tore off a strip of the tape and pressed it firmly across Caroline's mouth.

'There we are, my love. We can't have you screaming, can we? I'm looking forward to this, my darling, and, when it's over, you can pleasure me. I feel very, very excited and I remember how well you used to bring me off. It'll be quite like old times, won't it?'

Frantically, Caroline shook her head.

'You will do as I say, my little girl. You have no choice. Now, I need to have you bent over this chair, so up you get, my darling.'

Resistance was futile as Mrs Davies grabbed her under both arms and dragged her to her feet.

'We'll just go to the cupboard first, my darling. I need to get some rope to tie you to the chair.'

Although she knew it was useless, Caroline continued to struggle and make pitiful noises behind the tape that covered her mouth. Mrs Davies retrieved the rope and dragged Caroline to the chair. Forcing her to bend over the chair, Mrs Davies tied her in position, mercilessly tightening the knots before she was satisfied. Standing behind Caroline, she probed the girl's wetness.

'My little girl is very excited. That's good. It makes the punishment so much more bearable, doesn't it?'

Caroline couldn't believe it, but she *was* excited. She pushed back against Mrs Davies' fingers, wanting to feel them go even further inside; she wanted to feel her captor's fingers on her clitoris, massaging the swollen bud. Mrs Davies chuckled softly. 'Later, my dear. First you must be punished for being such a bad girl.'

Mrs Davies spent a long time running the cane across the girl's back and legs, delighting in the way that she squirmed. How delicious it was to have Caroline in her power. How she had missed using the girl. It had been almost worth those humiliating months to reach this point.

'It's good to be back with you, my dear. Perhaps you deliberately humiliated me just so that I would punish you. You've missed it, too, haven't you?'

Caroline was still furiously shaking her head in negation when the first blow fell. She thought she had prepared herself and that she could handle the pain; Mrs Davies, however, gave her no chance to adapt as blow after blow fell on her buttocks and no amount of struggling or muffled pleas for mercy on her part had any affect on her tormentor. She lost count of the number of blows, lost in a swirling mist of pain. She continued to twist and pull at the ropes that held her so tightly, until gradually she became dimly aware that, almost effortlessly, she was riding the pain and her struggles became more a source of pleasure than a genuine desire to escape. She knew she was wet between her legs and she could feel her clitoris pulsating its need for attention. Amazingly, Mrs Davies supplied that need. Never pausing in her caning of her cowed and submissive prisoner, she reached down and stroked the swollen bud. The stroking became insistent and matched in rhythm the stinging strokes of the cane. Pleasure and pain became irrevocably linked and Caroline's orgasm flooded through her with such strength that, had not Mrs Davies held on to her with a firm and steadying hand, she and the chair would have crashed to the floor.

'There, there, my little girl. You have taken your punishment very well indeed,' said Mrs Davies as she dropped the cane and stroked the reddened flesh of Caroline's buttocks with tender hands.

Exhausted and sated, Caroline closed her eyes and felt the ropes being removed. Incredibly, she felt a greater sexual satisfaction than she had previously known. What was it about this woman? She could be so cruel and yet so understanding of Caroline's needs. Mrs Davies helped her to sit down on the chair. Caroline winced at the soreness in her bottom as she came into contact with the hard wooden seat, but the pain had dulled significantly into a bearable throbbing warmth. Mrs Davies stood beside her and gently stroked her breasts.

'You are so beautiful, my little girl. Why do you have to be so disobedient?' As she spoke, Mrs Davies ripped the strip of tape from Caroline's mouth. The girl licked her dry and momentarily stinging lips and looked at Mrs Davies. She looked quite kind, really, Caroline thought, and she was right: by her standards, Caroline had been disobedient. Hoping that Mrs Davies would remove the handcuffs, Caroline smiled at her.

'That's better, my love. Master Clive was right. You just needed some discipline. We will have such fun, the three of us. Master Clive says that I can live here with you, just to keep an eye on you, of course. That means that we can have some fun together, my love. I don't like being angry with you. You won't make me angry, will you?'

Caroline's puzzlement showed in her eyes. 'What . . . what do you mean? Live here with you? I can't. You know that, in a few weeks, I'm going back to Liam. This is only temporary. Surely you knew that?'

Mrs Davies' eyes glittered. The slut hadn't learned a thing! She still needed further humiliation. Clive was counting on her to get the slut to agree to stay with them and she would not let him down. Mrs Davies felt a swiftly growing sexual arousal as she contemplated Caroline's next lesson.

'You still haven't learned, have you?' Mrs Davies asked, keeping her tone light and pleasant. 'I'm sorry about that, because it means that our business for the day has not yet concluded. All you have to do is to agree to stay here voluntarily with myself and Master Clive . . .'

She let her voice trail off, leaving an opening for Caroline to voice her acceptance, but hoping that the slut wouldn't be tempted. She received her reward when Caroline shook her head and looked pleadingly at Mrs Davies.

'You know that I can't do that. I love Liam and . . . I want to go home.' The last part of that sentence became an almost childish wail.

Mrs Davies grabbed Caroline's arms and forced her to stand. 'Well, I'm afraid that you can't. Master Clive and Mistress Lynne and I are going to persuade you to stay – whatever that may take!'

Dragging Caroline across the room, she showed the frightened girl the recent addition which the prisoner had not before noticed. A long, smooth wooden beam had been anchored at right angles to the wall. The beam was just wide enough to accommodate one person and had leather straps attached to it. Caroline froze as she looked at the leather hood-like attachment at the top of the beam. Turning, she struggled frantically in Mrs Davies' vice-like grip.

'Changed our mind, have we?' Mrs Davies asked. 'I hope not, because I have really been looking forward to this!'

She forced the struggling girl backwards, until she tripped over the beam.

'No, please, Mrs Davies! Don't do this!' Caroline begged. 'You can come back with Liam and me! I won't tell him about this! Please let me go! Please!'

Mrs Davies laughed harshly as she forced Caroline to lie on the beam. 'Come back with you! For what? More humiliation? That's what you want, isn't it? That's what you've always wanted! Well, it's your turn now, Miss Caroline. You're going to find out what it's like to be really humiliated!'

Ignoring the girl's pleas and cries for mercy, Mrs Davies tightly fastened the broad black leather straps over Caroline's waist, knees and ankles. She paused and looked without pity at the still struggling girl.

'Mrs Davies, I'll do anything you want! I'll pleasure you! You like it when I do that, don't you! We can spend the day having fun, just like we used to! You remember, don't you?'

Mrs Davies' eyes bore into Caroline's. 'You'll stay here with us? You'll do whatever we say?'

'I ... I ...'

The hesitation was all the answer that Mrs Davies needed. She bent down and pulled out the flap of the black leather hood.

'Just remember, slut. This was your choice!' Mrs Davies said, barely controlling the excitement in her voice as she pulled the hood over Caroline's face and closed it by feeding the straps through the buckles which were attached to the other side of the beam. Caroline could not move her head. There were eyeholes in the mask and an aperture by her nose which enabled her to breathe when Mrs Davies had closed the zip on that part of the leather that covered her mouth. Caroline's screams were effectively muffled and she could only use her eyes to plead piteously for mercy. The implacable Mrs Davies stood back and admired her handiwork.

'Yes, my girl. Humiliation is what you need to teach you not to be so high and mighty.'

Mrs Davies moved to stand with one leg planted on either side of the beam. She stood very close to Caroline's head.

'Can you guess what I am going to do, my love? It's all for your own good, you know. Remember that you could have avoided this if you hadn't been so disobedient.'

Caroline's eyes widened with horror and she struggled desperately but ineffectually within her bonds. She could feel the metal of the handcuffs rubbing against the skin of her wrists as her weight inexorably pressed against them; but even that pain was as nothing compared to her sense of incredulous horror as she watched Mrs Davies reach beneath her dress and pull her knickers slowly down her legs, all the while keeping her eyes on Caroline.

'Yes, my darling. I'm going to relieve myself now and, as I piss over your face, remember that you asked for this!'

Mrs Davies reached down and opened the zip on the mouth piece of the hood.

'Mrs Davies . . . Carol . . . please don't do this! Please let me go!'

Mrs Davies merely laughed. As soon as the girl's mouth opened, Mrs Davies released the first trickle of urine.

'I told Master Clive what I wanted to do and he was most obliging in constructing this little device for me,' Mrs Davies said conversationally, as she continued to let the stream of liquid fill the girl's mouth. 'Swallow it, little girl,' she urged. 'We don't want you choking now, do we?'

Unable to move her head within the constricting confines of the leather hood, Caroline had no choice. Mrs Davies kept her hand over her nostrils and she had to keep her mouth open to breathe. She was crying as she opened her mouth to swallow and could only hope that her ordeal would soon be over. As she gulped down the strong-smelling liquid, she keenly felt the humiliation that Mrs Davies had intended. She knew that she would agree to anything that Mrs Davies and Clive wanted – anything to avoid such a repetition.

At last, the stream slowed and stopped. Mrs Davies removed her hand from Caroline's nostrils, bent her knees and knelt down, pushing her wet bush close to Caroline's face.

'That's a good girl. It wasn't so bad, was it? Now you can wash me with that lovely little tongue of yours.'

Hesitantly, Caroline extended her tongue. She knew that there was no point in refusing. Clive and Mrs Davies were stronger than she and she bowed to the inevitable. Slowly, she moved her tongue across Mrs Davies' slit. After the degradation she had endured, she could not have said why it was that her tongue slipped inside Mrs Davies' labia, or why her nipples were hardening. She could not explain it and decided not to even try. Mrs Davies was stroking her breasts and she began to feel a little better, especially when the house-keeper leant back and slipped her hand on to Caroline's shaven mound. She was aware of a growing arousal that seemed to clear everything else from her mind. She felt knowing fingers on her clitoris and responded by pro-bing her tongue deeper into Mrs Davies' luxuriant bush, pulling back to swirl her tongue around the hard little nubbin. It wouldn't be so bad. She didn't exactly love Clive; but there was something indefinable between them. Mrs Davies could be tolerated, too, especially when she made her feel this way. Caroline revelled in her feelings of utter helplessness as she struggled against the straps that held her so firmly to the beam. As she came strongly and surely, feeling in her mouth the in-crease in juices which told of her own success, she knew it would indeed not be so bad. Coming down from her orgasm, she felt a momentary sadness as she thought of Liam. She would miss him, but at least she would have saved his businesses from ruin. That wasn't such a bad farewell gift.

Seven

Lynne looked at the blonde head lying on the pillow beside her and smiled. Careful not to wake him, she slipped out of bed and went to stand by the window. As always, the drapes were open. She and Francis loved to lie awake and watch the stars and the changing face of the moon. She noted that it was full tonight. Staring at its beauty, Lynne thought back over the events of the day. She had had another session with Caroline. Despite the enjoyment that this occasioned both of them, Lynne couldn't shake the growing certainty that there was something wrong. Caroline hadn't said anything to arouse her suspicions, so perhaps it was just an instinct. Lynne shook her head as she acknowledged that she had more than a passing interest in the girl. She had felt a resurgence of her original attraction to Caroline. She loved dominating her and now accepted that the earlier reason for this had long since disappeared. She remembered how, that afternoon, the girl had submissively knelt before her; her hands bound behind her and her bottom bearing the evidence of Lynne's recent beating. There had been other marks, too. When questioned about these, Caroline had merely shaken her head. She had seemed more subdued than usual and even accepted a whipping at Lynne's hands rather than reveal anything about the reason behind the fierce redness of the stripes.

'Lynne?'

Disturbed in her reverie, Lynne turned in surprise,

relaxing into a smile as she saw Francis' exciting lean-ness walking towards her. She held her arms open to him, holding him passionately as his warmth enfolded her.

'I missed you,' he said.

'I'm sorry, darling. I couldn't sleep and didn't want to wake you.'

Francis pulled back a little and looked in her face. 'What's wrong?'

She laughed uncertainly. 'Nothing's wrong, Francis. I'm just . . .'

'Lying,' Francis said, catching her chin in his hand and forcing her to look at him. 'Lynne, I thought that we had been through all of this. I thought that we were at last being honest with each other. I don't know about you but, to me, honesty means that we don't have secrets from each other.'

For a long time, she looked at him, before pulling him back into her arms and pressing her head against his shoulder.

'Francis, I don't want to lose you . . .'

His arms tightened around her. 'You're not going to lose me. Tell me what the problem is.'

This time, she was the one to pull back. He was right; there shouldn't be any secrets between them.

'Make me a drink, please my darling,' Lynne said. 'I have something to tell you.'

'Caroline. I don't believe it!' Francis exclaimed, setting his drink down on the coffee table.

'It's true. At first, I couldn't believe it, either. I mean, Liam had told us both how happy he was. He seemed so sure of her. I was so angry with her when I thought that she must have taken advantage of Liam's absence to go with someone else that I jumped at the chance to discipline her. I thought I would repay her for what she had done.'

87

'And now?' Francis asked.

'Francis, I don't know what to think. From the first I had the feeling that she was hiding something from me and then when I saw her this afternoon she seemed different . . .'

'Different?' Francis said, leaning forward and taking his wife's hands between his own. 'In what way?'

'Well, for one thing, she'd been thoroughly beaten by someone else. When I asked her about it, she just clammed up and wouldn't say a word. She seems quieter somehow. Resigned, even.'

'Do you think it's this Clive who's responsible for the beating?'

Lynne shook her head. 'Not directly, I think he really cares about her. Perhaps this Mrs Davies has something to do with it. I can't work out the reason behind her presence in that house.'

'Never mind Mrs Davies, how do you think Caroline feels about Clive?' Francis asked.

'She calls him Master and will obviously do anything that he says. Francis, I'm just not sure. I only know that there's something wrong and I just wish that Liam was here . . .'

Francis jumped up and began pacing.

'Francis, I'm sorry. I should have told you earlier, but I was afraid,' Lynne said.

Instantly, he came back to her and put his arms around her.

'Afraid? My Lynne afraid?' he asked humorously, but then his face became serious. 'What were you afraid of, Lynne?'

She took a deep steadying breath. 'The more I've seen of Caroline, the more I've felt how good it would be to have her back with us, here in this house. I thought, if I told you, you'd want that, too.'

There was a short silence.

'Would that be so bad?' Francis asked quietly.

She turned to him, her fear reflecting in her eyes.

'Don't you remember how it was when she came here? Don't you remember how upset you were when Liam took her? You cared about her, Francis, and you can't deny it.'

Francis leant back against the cushions of the couch and closed his eyes. He remembered so clearly how it had been when Caroline had left him. She had looked adorable in that plastic cape he had draped over her shoulders. She had been so trusting, standing there looking at him, her hands tied behind her and a gag silencing her pleas to be allowed to remain with him. She had thought that she was only going to be away from him for one night, but instead Liam had refused to let her come back to him. As he remembered this, Francis' eyes opened. Liam had been the catalyst for all of this. By taking Caroline away, he had betrayed the trust of a good friend. Sighing, Francis turned to Lynne and took her in his arms.

'Lynne, my darling. You are forgetting one thing. Caroline brought us together. If she hadn't come into our lives, we might have carried on as we were – drifting inexorably further apart. If it hadn't been for her, we might by now be living quite separately. If she came back into our lives, it wouldn't make any difference between us. I nearly lost you once and I don't intend to do that again.'

Francis bent his head and kissed away any disquiet she might have felt. Lynne responded to his embrace and then rested her head on his shoulder.

'Francis, what shall we do – about Caroline?'

'Do you think she's being held against her will?'

Lynne thought for a moment and then shook her head. 'I don't think so. She's had plenty of opportunity to ask me for help. I just get the impression that Clive has some sort of hold over her.'

'Do you think he's blackmailing her?'

89

He felt Lynne shrug her shoulders.

'I don't know, Francis. I wish I'd spoken to you about this before.'

Francis bent and kissed the top of her head. 'It doesn't matter, my sweet. You've told me now. I think that we had both better go and see Clive and Mrs Davies. In the meantime . . .'

She smiled as she looked up at him. 'In the meantime?'

Francis looked meaningfully at his wife. All the sexual arousal that had been stirred in him by his reminiscences of Caroline was now focused on Lynne.

'Get the ropes, slave. Tonight I feel like dominating my beautiful wife.'

'Clive, I'd like you to meet my husband,' Lynne said, smiling innocuously.

'I'd be delighted, but may I ask why you want us to meet?' Clive responded, as always admiring his guest who had dressed in her usual provocative fashion.

Lynne moved her legs a little, allowing the hem of her black PVC dress to slip another enticing inch towards her crotch.

'Francis is very interested in your little project. We have kept slaves in the past and he is thinking of returning to that very exciting pastime. I hope you don't mind, but I've told him all about Caroline and he would welcome the opportunity of watching us work with her.'

Lynne reflected on the truth of her words. Francis had certainly welcomed with alacrity the thought of Caroline returning to their house. She watched Clive as he considered what she had said. Lynne had to admit that there was something special about Clive. Perhaps she could understand why Caroline seemed to have chosen being with him in preference to living with Liam. As she became aware of her own moistness, Lynne shifted slightly in her seat. With eyes that seemed to miss nothing, Clive followed the small movement. There was no doubting the admiration in his eyes as he looked at his co-conspirator.

'What would it be worth?' Clive asked, moving to sit next to her on the couch.

'Worth?' Lynne asked, feigning puzzlement. 'I'm sorry . . .'

'Come now, my dear, we are adults. You want something from me and I –' Clive paused, letting his eyes roam over Lynne's PVC-covered slenderness. '– I would be most happy to oblige.'

With a suddenness of movement that completely disoriented her, Clive pushed her back against the couch and closed his mouth over hers. She felt his tongue intruding between her lips and the fingers of one hand massaging her breasts. His other hand was behind her neck, searching amongst her dark tresses for the zip of her dress. As he pulled the zip down, she moved against him. Why not? she thought. It's all in a good cause. She could not repress a momentary resistance as his hand slipped beneath her skirt, but he slapped her hand away.

'No, my dear,' Clive said, raising his head to look at her. 'I'm in control now. Relax and enjoy it.'

Lynne looked into those dark eyes and felt all tendencies to resist slip away. She knew that she wanted this man and she also knew that, in any event, resistance would be futile. He was very used to getting his own way and took anything he wanted as if it was his by right. She felt her dress slide from her shoulders and found herself hoping that he wouldn't tie her. That was something that she let Francis do to her, but no one else.

'Clive . . .'

'Hush, my dear. Relax and enjoy it. We are two very dominant people. I fully appreciate that and I wouldn't do anything that would cause you problems. From the first moment I saw you, Lynne, I wanted you. Together we are brilliant – you know that. I want to make you feel as good as I do whenever I look at you. Your Francis will never know. I would never do anything to hurt you, Lynne. Let's just enjoy the moment.'

Lynne listened to Clive's hypnotic voice with a pleasurable feeling of helplessness. Yet it was more a bowing to the inevitable than an affirmation of her own inability to resist this man. They were two powerful people, taking from each other and giving back with a passion unequalled for either of them. Clive gently pushed her back and this time she opened herself to him willingly. Clive fastened his mouth on her left nipple as he entered her. His movements were gentle and unhurried, yet she was conscious of the power within him that seemed to ignite and fuel her own passion. They moved together, for those few moments in perfect harmony. Clive's breath came faster as his climax neared. For once, he did not need to dominate; he could just enjoy. As his orgasm shuddered through him, he was vaguely aware of a question forming in his mind. Was this the real Clive Craigen? As he reached down to part the willing lips beneath his own, he knew that he would never arrive at an answer. He had been playing a part for too long and now didn't know who he really was any more.

Far from sating her, the excellence of Lynne's orgasm had left her greedy for more. She was still determined to get to the bottom of the mystery surrounding Caroline's presence in this house, but she was now aware of a grudging respect for Clive. She had enjoyed some great sex, without damaging her relationship with Francis. She might even tell her husband of what had transpired. She was confident enough of the strength of their relationship to consider doing that. Now, as she went downstairs, Lynne realised that she was looking forward to another encounter with Caroline. She was not, therefore, prepared for the sight that greeted her entry to the basement room. Caroline was sitting on the floor, her head buried in her knees. Her arms were wrapped tightly around herself as she rocked to and fro, shaking with sobs. For a moment, Lynne paused on the threshold. She was not without kindness and she was concerned to see Caroline in this state. Quietly closing the door, she walked over to the sobbing girl and knelt beside her. Hesitantly at first, she put her arm around the younger girl's shoulders.

'Caroline, tell me what's wrong.'

Caroline looked up at her and wiped her face with her arms. 'Nothing's wrong, Mistress. I'm ...' Caroline managed, before tears again overwhelmed her.

'Caroline, you must talk to me. What's going on here? What's keeping you here?'

Choking back sobs, Caroline again looked up at Lynne. For a long moment, the two of them looked at one another. Lynne could see that Caroline was weighing up how much she could and should reveal. Reaching out a gentle hand, Lynne smoothed back the girl's hair.

'Caroline, I know there's something not right here. I know how happy you and Liam were together. Please tell me what happened to change that. If I can help you, I will.'

Seeing a ray of hope, Caroline grasped Lynne's arm. 'Promise me you won't tell Clive. If you do, he won't help Liam,' she begged in a tone that would have exacted pity from a statue.

'All right, I promise. Tell me what's been happening,' Lynne said, sitting beside the girl. She noted that Caroline wore wrist and ankle restraints, the chains of which clinke: softly as she moved.

Haltingly, Caroline began her narrative. She left nothing out and made no further appeals for help. All she could now do was to tell Lynne the truth and leave it to her to make a decision on whether or not such help would be forthcoming. When Caroline had finished speaking, Lynne silently digested all the information she had just received. That she believed Caroline was not in doubt; the girl's obvious distress and the clarity with which past events could now be viewed in the light of this new information made Lynne's acceptance of all she had heard an absolute certainty. She turned to the girl beside her and could not resist reaching out her hand to stroke the nipples which the girl's nudity so appealingly presented. In spite of herself, Caroline moaned softly with pleasure. She closed her eyes and felt Lynne's fingers probe a little lower until, gradually, they slipped inside the wetness of her slit. Caroline gasped with pleasure as Lynne's fingers moved within her. Lynne was watching her closely.

'Caroline, do you want to stay here? If Clive keeps to his word and helps Liam, what then?'

Caroline's questing hands moved towards Lynne. She opened her eyes in some surprise as Lynne gripped both of her wrists and held them tightly.

'Answer me, slave! What then?'

'I ... I don't know. Clive ...'

'Clive what? What does he do to you?' Lynne asked, roughly pulling Caroline on to her lap. 'Does he do this? Do you like it?'

As she spoke, Lynne punctuated her words with hard slaps to the girl's bottom. Caroline squirmed on her lap, but Lynne forcibly pushed her down.

'I can give you this and much more, you little slut! Francis and I want you to come back with us. You used to get this and much worse, didn't you? I know you liked it, little slave. You liked Francis, didn't you? Would you like to be with Francis again?'

Lynne's words were spurring her on as feelings that she had kept largely repressed since Caroline had left came to the surface. The slaps were coming with increasing frequency and severity.

'What do you say, little slut? Would you like to come back?'

Caroline was crying with the pain, but also with her growing need for Lynne to probe her clitoris, to massage the little bud that pulsated its desire. Sensing this, Lynne used one hand to stroke the engorged bud whilst, with the other hand, she continued to spank the girl. In spite of the fact that Lynne was no longer holding her down, Caroline did not attempt to escape. She was enjoying the sensations that were flooding through her too much for that. She was close to orgasm and suddenly the path that was opening up to her seemed increasingly attractive. She could go back with Lynne and Francis. Why not? There would be no more Mrs Davies, but there would also be no more Clive. And what about Liam? Caroline didn't know if she wanted that. She didn't know anything any more as she came, her screams of pleasure stifled beneath Lynne's hand.

Lynne was already slipping out of her dress, as Caroline's paroxysms of pleasure subsided. Lying back, Lynne grabbed a handful of Caroline's hair and pulled the girl with her.

'Pleasure me, slut! Do it now!' Lynne yelled at her and Caroline hastened to obey. The hand remained twisted in her hair while she used her tongue to massage Lynne's clitoris. She didn't have long to wait, as the increased pulling on her hair denoted that Lynne was enjoying her climax. It was a long and satisfying orgasm and only when the shudderings of her body had subsided did she relax the fingers that still tugged on Caroline's hair. For a long while, Mistress and slave lay sated in each other's arms. Lynne was the first to move, gently stroking the girl's shoulders.

'We can have a good time together, Caroline. You, me and Francis. Maybe we'll all go away somewhere, but it's you who has to make the first decision, Caroline. It's up to you, little slave. What's it to be?'

Eight

The handshake was firm; more of a challenge than a greeting.

'My wife has told me all about you,' Francis said, his smile not quite reaching his eyes.

'Nothing bad, I hope,' Clive responded.

'Intriguing, I'd say,' Francis returned equably. He looked at the couch and then raised a questioning eyebrow in Clive's direction.

'Please,' Clive said, gesturing towards the couch.

Lynne and Francis both sat down and Clive stood back to admire the very handsome pair they made. Francis wore a black turtle-neck sweater and a pair of supple black leather trousers. His blonde hair was brushed and gleaming and he made a perfect complement to Lynne, whose dark hair was loose and brushed her nipples, clearly visible through the tight rubber of her dress.

'I understand that you and my wife get on rather well together,' Francis began, his tone conversational.

Clive raised an eyebrow in Lynne's direction, but received no help from that quarter. 'We do indeed. I trust that you do not find this in any way offensive?'

'By no means, provided that the limits of courtesy are observed,' Francis said, his voice as smooth as polished glass.

'Would you both like a drink?' Clive asked to cover the silence which appeared awkward only to him. Lynne and Francis both declined the offer, expressing a desire to begin their sessions with Caroline.

'I'm grateful for the opportunity to observe my wife at work,' Francis explained. 'Will you be joining us?'

Clive shook his head regretfully. 'Any other time and I would be delighted.· Unfortunately, I have a pressing business engagement which cannot wait. However, Mrs Davies will see to anything which you might require.'

'Mrs Davies?' Francis enquired.

'Yes. She is my – assistant. She will be present at your meeting with Caroline,' Clive said, collecting his coat and briefcase as he spoke. 'If you'll excuse me, it's been a pleasure to meet you, Francis.'

Clive extended his hand and Francis took it.

'Will Mrs Davies be joining us for the whole morning?' Francis asked.

Clive paused in the doorway, smiling at his guests. 'Oh, yes. Mrs Davies will not leave you alone for one minute.'

As the door closed behind Clive, Francis turned to his wife. 'Not very trusting, your Clive?'

'He is not *my* anything, darling. Did you expect him to trust us?' Lynne asked.

'I suppose not. Anyway, it doesn't really matter. I want to meet the famous Mrs Davies and here she is being presented to me. It should indeed be an interesting morning.'

As Francis finished speaking, there was a knock on the door. Francis and Lynne turned as the door was opened. Arrayed in her usual black dress, Mrs Davies stood in the doorway looking at them. After a moment's hesitation, Francis crossed the floor and kissed Mrs Davies on both cheeks. The housekeeper reeled a little in surprise at this unexpected greeting.

'Mrs Davies at last! Lynne has told me so much about you that I almost feel as if I know you!'

Crimson with embarrassment, Mrs Davies hesitated in the doorway.

'You must be Mr Francis,' she said, recovering herself

a little. 'Master Clive has asked that I see that you and Miss Lynne have everything you need.'

'Everything, Mrs Davies? Well, we'll have to see about that, won't we?' Francis said, jocularly. 'Perhaps we could see Caroline now?'

Mrs Davies nodded and produced a bunch of keys from her pocket. Francis smiled.

'I see that Master Clive is taking no chances?'

Mrs Davies lowered her eyes and turned into the corridor. 'If you'll follow me, sir, madam, I'll take you to her.'

'Lead on, Mrs Davies. I'd follow you anywhere,' Francis said, gallantly indicating that his wife should precede him.

Suppressing a smile, Lynne walked past Francis, reaching out a hand to squeeze one of his pierced and ringed nipples as she did so.

Mrs Davies ushered them into a bedroom, slightly smaller than the one occupied by Clive. Smiling, Mrs Davies stood aside so that they could both see Caroline who, bound hand and foot, lay on the double bed. Her eyes were large and frightened above the scarf that gagged her, but those eyes lost their fear as they alighted on Francis.

'Well, my darling. It's been a long time,' Francis said as he sat beside the bound girl. He kept his voice low in order to lessen the chances of Mrs Davies eavesdropping on their conversation. His fingers slid gently into Caroline's luxuriant hair and gently massaged her scalp. His eyes devoured her. She was every bit as beautiful as he remembered and he felt his penis stir in empathy with his thoughts.

Lynne stood by the door and watched her husband. She felt an expected surge of jealousy, but also a feeling of sympathy. He needed time to be alone with Caroline and she would ensure that he could enjoy an uninterrupted reunion with the girl.

'Mrs Davies, is this where the slave is usually kept?' she asked, keeping her eyes on the two people who now most concerned her.

'No, madam. She has a cell in the basement,' Mrs Davies answered, also unable to look away from the two people on the bed. There was something strange here. As far as she knew, Francis had never before set eyes on Caroline, but the looks these two were exchanging were not the looks that strangers give to each other.

'I'd like to see it, please.' Lynne's voice came more insistently. She turned her gaze to the housekeeper. There was a slight pause, during which Mrs Davies continued to stare at Caroline and Francis.

'Now, please, Mrs Davies!'

This time, there was no denying the authority in Lynne's voice and, reluctantly, Mrs Davies looked at her. 'Madam, the Master said . . .'

'The Master told us that you have been ordered to give us every assistance.' Lynne's voice had become hard and unyielding.

'I'm not supposed to leave . . .'

'*Every* assistance, Mrs Davies!'

With one last look towards Francis and Caroline, and a rather mutinous expression, Mrs Davies turned and walked out of the door.

'Thank you, my darling,' Francis said to his wife, his eyes warmly appreciative of the sacrifice she was making.

Lynne smiled at him before abruptly turning and following Mrs Davies from the room.

'This is the cell where the slave is kept, madam,' Mrs Davies said, standing aside for Lynne to enter the small room.

When she did so, Lynne saw that it was sparsely but adequately furnished, functional only to the bare necessities of life for one person. There was a narrow single bed, a chair and a table, upon which rested a water pitcher and a small bowl. Lynne could imagine Caroline standing at this table, supervised of course, as she washed herself. She looked around and then turned to Mrs Davies. 'Where does the slave relieve herself?' she asked imperiously.

Suitably cowed, Mrs Davies folded her hands in front of her and nodded toward a cupboard in one corner of the room. 'There is a bucket kept for the purpose which the slave has to keep clean.'

Lynne wrinkled her nose in disgust as she pictured Caroline having to clean up after herself, but an idea was taking shape in her mind. She needed to give Francis and Caroline time together without Mrs Davies' intrusive presence. She walked over to the bed and fingered the leather cuffs that dangled from the headboard.

'How does the slave sleep? Is she always restrained?' Lynne asked, her attitude one of mild curiosity.

Mrs Davies responded with enthusiasm. They were on her territory now! She joined Lynne, her eyes sparkling with excitement. 'Yes indeed, madam. That is one of my duties. When Master Clive has finished with the slave for the day, I bring her down here and – settle her down for the night.'

Lynne ignored Mrs Davies' implied hint and sat down on the bed. Positioning herself in a sleeper's attitude, she looked up at the housekeeper, her eyes empty of everything except a naive questioning.

'How do you do that, Mrs Davies?' she asked innocuously. In spite of herself, she was aware of a growing sexual excitement. She needed some release and Mrs Davies might just provide it.

Mrs Davies hesitated. She looked at Lynne and felt her nipples harden as she studied the slim form encased in tight black latex. She could imagine herself pushing up the rubber and greedily inserting her tongue in Lynne's waiting slit.

'Can you show me, Mrs Davies? Please.' Lynne's voice had become soft and pleading.

Mrs Davies needed no further encouragement. Bending down, she grasped Lynne's unresisting wrists and pulled them over her head.

'Why, I just lock the slave's wrists into the handcuffs – just like this.' Mrs Davies could not repress a note of triumph, as she fastened the leather cuffs around Lynne's slim wrists and snapped the padlocks closed.

Obligingly, Lynne struggled to free her hands, while Mrs Davies watched. Lynne almost laughed out loud at the expression in the housekeeper's eyes. She knew only too well that, in many ways, far from being the passive partner, the submissive actually had a lot of power in a relationship and, if they so chose, could effortlessly dominate the proceedings. Mrs Davies, however, obviously did not appreciate this fact. She looked down at Lynne's apparently helpless form and saw only a woman who had become her prisoner and with whom she felt she could do anything that she chose.

'Oh, Mrs Davies. I think perhaps you had better release me.' Lynne's voice sounded false to her own ears, but she knew that Mrs Davies thought she had complete control of the situation.

'I think not, madam. I think that you are no longer in any condition to give orders.' The housekeeper sat on the bed, her eyes alight with sexual greed. 'I think instead that I am the one who is now giving the orders.'

Mrs Davies reached out and stroked Lynne's latex-covered breasts, making her shiver with excitement. Taking the shiver for a sign of fear, Mrs Davies became even more daring. She slipped one hand beneath the tight rubber of the dress' skirt and inched her way up until she found the wetness of Lynne's sex.

'Oh, Mrs Davies! What do you think you are doing?' Lynne demanded, playing the outraged guest to perfection.

'What I'm doing is no more than you deserve, Miss!' Mrs Davies responded, slipping here fingers further inside and massaging the exposed bud.

Lynne, all pretence abandoned, groaned with pleasure. She gratefully acknowledged Mrs Davies' skill, but she wanted more.

'Mrs Davies, use your mouth. Please, use your mouth,' Lynne pleaded.

Too excited herself to consider the abrupt change in roles, Mrs Davies slid down the bed and pushed the latex dress further up. Expertly, her agile tongue flicked around Lynne's clit, causing her 'prisoner' to writhe and twist on the bed.

'That's it, my little love,' Mrs Davies crooned. 'Mrs Davies knows what's best.' She again bent her head and applied her tongue.

'Oh, yes!' Lynne cried. 'She does indeed!'

Lynne's orgasm overwhelmed her. With a small part of her mind, she wondered how Francis was faring with Caroline – but it was only a very small part.

Francis had removed the scarf that gagged Caroline and they had both remained looking wordlessly at each other for some moments. Caroline stared at Francis almost as if he were a ghost. He returned her look with an incredulity that seemed to relegate the months since they had last seen each other to another time. She hadn't changed, Francis decided. Perhaps she had become even more desirable. All the questions which he had wanted to put to her faded from his mind. What was important was that she was here with him. At last, he spoke. 'I've missed you, Caroline.'

Her answer lay in her eyes as she looked at him. She had also missed him – but so much had happened. Caroline felt confused; she was glad to see Francis again, but she was also worried. Francis and Liam were very good friends. If he told Liam about where she was, she might never be able to get Clive to keep his word and save Liam from ruin. Her lips formed the words and Francis bent to catch the almost inaudible whisper.

'Don't tell him. Please don't tell him.'

Francis felt alarmed. There was something very wrong here.

'Tell Liam? Why, Caroline. What's going on?' Francis asked, although he really wanted to touch her; to stroke that beautiful body and see the response that he knew so well.

'Liam's in trouble, Francis. Clive can help him, *will* help him if . . .'

'If?'

'If I stay with him voluntarily,' Caroline finished, her eyes searching his face for a sign of understanding.

'Do you want to? Stay with him, I mean?' Francis asked, gently stroking her hair.

'Yes, Francis. I do. There's something about him . . .'

'What about Liam?' Francis asked. 'I suppose that I shouldn't be surprised, though, should I, Caroline? You went from me to Liam willingly enough . . .'

'That's a lie!' Caroline exclaimed. 'You sold me to him . . .'

'For one evening!'

'Was it my fault that he wouldn't let me go back to you? It took me a long time to accept that, Francis.'

Francis lowered his eyes and looked at her pert, inviting nipples. She was so easily aroused.

'You're excited, aren't you, Caroline? You seem to be happy to serve the strongest Master.'

She opened her mouth to refute his accusation, but Francis bent his head and covered her mouth with his. Feeling her immediate response, he chuckled mentally. Caroline was the perfect sex slave, he thought. She was a loyal little thing, but her loyalties seemed to be bought easily enough. His tongue probed the willing mouth beneath his own and he gave in to the overriding sexual need that blotted out everything else. He was smiling as he raised his head.

'You are a little slut, Caroline. Can't complain,

though, can I? I think I must bear some of the blame for making you as you are. You like bondage now, don't you? I remember a time when you professed not to. Perhaps that was only because you wanted it so much, eh?'

Caroline shook her head, but Francis covered her mouth with his hand, smothering the half-formed denial.

'It doesn't matter, my pet. I like you just the way that you are. I'm sure that you are telling me the truth about Clive. He seems the sort of bastard that would do anyone a favour for the sake of a good fuck! It's a shame, little Caroline. Lynne and I have been talking about you. We had almost decided that you should come back with us. Yes, my little pet, I will tell Liam. I will bring him back and get him to try and make you see some sense. If he does, perhaps we can all come to a mutually convenient arrangement. Would you like that, little girl? Liam can have you during the week and Lynne and I will have you at the weekends. How does that sound?'

Caroline desperately shook her head; at what, she couldn't have said. She wondered if Francis was right about her and what Liam would say when he came back. Clive would never let her see him. She wasn't sure any more what it was that she wanted.

'Oh, I'm sorry. You can't answer me, can you?' Francis asked, bringing his face close to that of Caroline. 'Well, I tell you what, my dear. I'll just replace my hand with the scarf. I intend to beat you, my darling, and I don't like screaming.'

Francis retied the scarf on Caroline's mouth, smiling at her as he tied the knot. 'There, that's much better, my darling. You have always looked good when tied up, my love. Shall I beat you hard, Caroline? Do you think that you deserve it?'

Caroline looked at him, trying to discern in his eyes what it was that he was truly feeling. Did he believe her, or did he think she was just making excuses for her defection from Liam? She felt ashamed, yet also excited at the prospect of a beating at the hands of Francis. He was standing now, taking off the broad leather belt from his waist. She tensed in excited expectation of the leather slapping against her bottom. Suddenly, Francis pushed her over on to her stomach. She felt his hands stroking her bottom, felt him slip two fingers into her slit. He chuckled at the wetness that he found there and immediately transferred his lubricated fingers to her anus. She found herself opening for him as he himself had taught her to do. She wondered if he remembered. His next words answered her unspoken question.

'Do you recall how it was when I used to do this? Do you remember the feel of my cock in your rectum? I hope so, darling, because you are going to feel it again. Pleasure after the pain, yes?'

Caroline struggled ineffectually with the ropes that bound her. They were the soft white cords that Clive used on her, telling her that he did not want to hurt her. It didn't matter how much she struggled, the cords held but did not hurt. The struggling excited both herself and Francis. She heard movement behind her and realised that Francis had removed his clothes when she felt his warmth and hardness pressing into her buttocks.

'I don't care what you are, Caroline. How I've missed this,' Francis whispered softly. 'I am going to beat you, my darling, because you are in great need of such discipline, but afterwards ...' He let his voice trail off suggestively. Caroline wriggled with anticipation as he stood up. She didn't know that he was still so close to her until the belt stroked silently across her buttocks.

'You already have some marks, I see, you little slut. I'll try to improve on those.' Francis kept his tone light, but it was becoming increasingly difficult to keep himself in check. He raised the belt and revelled in the slapping sound as leather struck flesh. He didn't need to feel between Caroline's legs to know that she was wet. What an inestimable treasure she was! As the beating continued, he alternated the thwacking of the belt with some urgent probings of his fingers into her slit. Eventually, the growing urgency of his own needs made him throw down the belt and kneel over her on the bed. His cock was lubricated with dribbles of the clear fluid that denoted his excitement. Her anus was easy to enter, his cock sliding in almost up to the hilt. Careless of the weals which he had inflicted, Francis kneaded the tender flesh of her buttocks, knowing that this fresh soreness would only add to Caroline's pleasure. He could feel his orgasm building, demanding release, and felt a similar response in Caroline. As his semen spurted into her rectum, Francis felt Caroline shuddering beneath him in an enforced silent orgasm. As his hands reached around her to cup her small breasts, Francis smiled.

It was almost like coming home.

Nine

Clive entered the bedroom, opening and closing the door as silently as he could. It was dark in the room but, by a bar of light filtering through a gap in the drawn curtains, he was able to make out Caroline's inert body lying on the bed. She seemed to be asleep and he watched her for a moment, watching the way her breasts rose and fell as she breathed. Clive had returned from his business meeting only a short while before. He had not even seen Mrs Davies and so had no idea how the meeting between Lynne, Francis and Caroline had progressed. She had been in his house for nearly a fortnight, he reflected. During that time, she had become very important to him. It was true that she had agreed to stay with him permanently, but he knew her agreement had been extracted more through her wish to help Liam and a fear of Mrs Davies than through her own genuine desire. That wasn't what Clive wanted. He had her body but, as yet, she still retained free use of her mind. Clive wanted to control her – all of her. Silently, he moved to the bed and looked down at Caroline. She was lying on her side and, now that he was closer, he could see the fresh red stripes across her backside. He wondered who it was that had inflicted the punishment, then dismissed the thought from his mind. Right now, that wasn't important. What was of more immediate concern to him was his control over Caroline. He eased himself down on to the bed and gently ran his fingers over the cords that still bound her. She stirred in her sleep and moaned softly. He smiled and wondered what dreams she was having and whether or not they were troubled. He was aware of his own arousal as, gently, he pulled the scarf from her mouth and kissed her. Sensuously, she moved beneath him, waking to the reality of Clive's stroking fingers and her own excitement.

'Have you missed me, baby?' Clive asked, kissing her neck and then her breasts.

'Clive . . ,' she murmured, still not fully awake. 'I need you.'

Clive pulled back and looked at her. 'Caroline, what did you say?' he asked with an unintentional sharpness.

Caroline's eyes opened wider. 'I'm sorry. I . . .' she said, as she struggled to remember what it was that she had said. She was still smarting, more from Francis' comments to her than his beating. Was he right? Would she go with anyone, provided that they were strong enough to dominate her? Although being unaware of the cause, Clive sensed her difficulty and pulled her into his arms.

'It doesn't matter, my love. I have something that I want to say to you, Caroline, but first . . .'

Clive untied the ropes that bound Caroline and gently rubbed at the marks they had left on her wrists. Caroline watched him. She didn't understand what Clive was thinking. He seemed somehow different. He bent his head and gently kissed her on the lips. His very gentleness sent a shiver of arousal through her. Gradually, her arms went around his neck. She wasn't used to this. Since coming to this house, she had been subjected to every kind of sexual deviance and punishment, but there had not been too much gentleness or kindness. Now she was confused. Clive looked at her.

'Caroline, I want you to be truthful with me. Can you do that?'

She looked as innocent as a child as she nodded.

'You know I care about you, Caroline. I know that I

tricked you into coming to this house, but I only wanted to be with you. Since I first saw you, I knew that we could be good together. Over the past days, I've come to feel that even more strongly. I want to know how you feel about me. Tell me honestly, Caroline. I have no whip in my hand and I promise you that your total truthfulness will not be rewarded with any kind of punishment.'

'Mrs Davies . . .'

'Forget Mrs Davies! I used her to bring you here. You have nothing to fear from her and I don't want her image to distort what you may feel you have to say to me. I just want the truth, Caroline. Do we have a future together, or do you want to leave me and go back to Liam? If that's what you really want, I won't try and stop you, Caroline.'

'You promised . . .'

'I promised to help Liam and I will. Whatever you say to me will have no bearing on that. I wanted you here in this house so that we could have a chance. Now I need to know where I stand with you.'

As he spoke, Clive gently stroked her hair. She looked at him, trying to pierce his control in order to see what lay beneath. It also gave her time to think. The irony of the situation was not lost on her. Once, just over six months before, Liam had asked her much the same question. He had offered her her freedom and she had chosen to stay with him. Now Clive was offering her the same thing. She could have her freedom and she would be able to return to Liam. She looked into the dark eyes so close to her own and wondered what it was about Clive. He intrigued and fascinated her – but did she love him?

'Before I can answer you, Clive, I would like you to do something for me.'

Without hesitation, Clive smiled openly at her. This time, there was no other motive behind his smile. He looked at her with honesty. 'Whatever you want will be done, my love.'

'I want you to make love to me. No ropes or gags. Just you and me. Will you do that for me?'

In answer, Clive touched her lips with his own, parting her mouth with his tongue and feeling her immediate response. He had never before had her like this. She came into his arms willingly and, for the moment, Clive's true feelings for her dominated his usually cold personality. It was Caroline who caught his hand and urged him off the bed. He followed her into the bathroom, softly laughing at the impatience with which she divested him of his clothes. When he was naked, she pulled him into the shower cubicle and they both gasped as a jet of cold water hit his back. She laughed with him as they clung together beneath the rapidly warming water. It was quite a new thing for Clive to allow himself to be soaped all over and expertly massaged as the water cascaded over them both. He smiled when she presented him with the soap and he performed a similar service in return, his fingers lingering a little longer than absolutely necessary when he soaped her slit. After she had turned off the water, they dried each other using a fluffy white towel and, hand-in-hand, returned to the bedroom. He pressed her back on to the bed and lay on top of her. He took each one of her nipples into his mouth in turn, first sucking and then gently biting at the hard buds. He kissed her all the way down to her sex, where he tasted the sweetness of her juices. Gently, he pushed her on to her stomach and trailed lingeringly wet kisses down her spine until his tongue slipped between the cleft in her buttocks. Caroline gasped as his tongue twitched around the entry to her anus, before slipping inside and agitating the sensitive nerve endings. He reached around her and squeezed her nipples.

'Hurt me! Please hurt me!' she gasped.

'Caroline, are you sure?' Clive asked. He didn't want to make a mistake now – not now when he was so close.

'I'm sure, Clive! It's what I want!'

As his cock, moistened by his own excitement, slipped inside her anus, Clive increased the pressure on her nipples, pinching the aroused flesh. Caroline yelled with pained delight and Clive put one hand over her mouth.

'All right, you little slut! You've had your fun! Enjoyed being in control, did you? Well, I hope you made the most of it, because it won't happen again! I am the only one in control and you'd better learn to accept that, my girl!'

Caroline revelled in his words; the implied threat and the pain she felt, both in her nipples and in the renewed stinging from her buttocks as Clive pounded into her, joined to fuel the strength of her orgasm. Clive's hand was removed from her mouth. As he shouted out his own pleasure, he again squeezed her nipples, leaving her in no doubt as to how, if she stayed, she might expect the relationship to continue.

For a long time, neither of them moved. Clive was conscious of the fact that he did not feel the expected triumph. He had won and now she was his. Perhaps it was because, as yet, she hadn't verbally confirmed what her body had already told him. Perhaps it was because he cared for her more than even he had realised. For the moment, Clive was quietly content in his victory.

Caroline was unsure of how she felt: she was sure of her feelings for Clive, but it was how she felt about herself that was giving rise to the doubts. She had loved Liam – she still did – but the fascination she felt for this man who had come back into her life so unexpectedly was a real and tangible thing. She couldn't ignore it. Maybe it was something that had to be explored to the full before she could end it – if she ever wanted to.

'Clive?'

'Yes?' he answered.

'If I agree to stay with you, will I still be treated as a slave?'

There was a long silence, the only sound being their mutual breathing. At last, Clive moved to lie over her, propping himself up with his elbows on either side of her. His position was one of total dominance, a fact which they both silently acknowledged.

'Caroline, I am going to be as honest with you as I feel that you have been with me. I am a dominant person and I always have been. I can't change now and I hope that you wouldn't want me to.' Clive paused and tenderly stroked her hair, while his eyes caressed her. 'Darling, I love dominating you. I love controlling you. Sometimes I will want to use you as my sex slave. That means that I will expect you to do whatever I may want you to do. I love tying you and exerting control in that way, Caroline; it excites me to do that. Sometimes I will hurt you, because you deserve it and because I want to. I don't believe that you will have a problem in that respect.'

It was not really a question, but she shook her head anyway, denoting her agreement.

'What about when you have to go out?' she asked.

'It excites me to think of you tied up and helpless awaiting my return. Do you think you'll object to that?'

His tone was light, but she wasn't sure whether or not he would beat her if her answer was not the one he sought. She smiled and shook her head. Clive bent to kiss her.

'Clive, what about Mrs Davies?'

He thought for a moment. 'I think I will ask her to stay, my darling,' he answered, chuckling at the fear in her eyes. 'My love, I will need her help. You can hardly answer the door if you are tied up. Besides, I firmly believe that it is not a good idea to tie and gag your partner and then leave them alone while you go out. Your safety is paramount, my love. Mrs Davies can look after you when I'm not here –' Clive laughed, smothering her protests with one hand clamped firmly over her mouth. ' but she will be given a set of guidelines which I shall insist upon her following. The main one will be that she is not to do anything to you without my knowledge and consent.'

Clive removed his hand from her mouth and cocked his head to one side as he looked at her. 'Any other queries?' he asked.

'How do I know that you won't give your consent to Mrs Davies doing all manner of unspeakable things to me?' Caroline asked, her question only half serious.

'You will have to trust me, my love. You had also better behave yourself so that I don't feel the need to authorise extra discipline,' Clive answered, his smile belying the seriousness of his intent.

'Extra discipline?' Caroline asked, relaxing beneath him.

'Of course. You will receive regular punishment just to remind you of who is the boss around here,' Clive said.

'Then I think I'll stay,' Caroline said happily, as she reached up to kiss him.

'I'm very pleased to hear it, my darling, but I meant what I said.' Caroline looked at him questioningly. 'About the fact that I will expect you to do everything that I say,' he clarified, running his finger down her cheek and slipping it inside her mouth.

'Of course,' she answered. 'Whatever you say will be done, my Master.'

Clive's smile disappeared as he looked at her. 'Are you sure, Caroline? Is this what you really want?'

Surprised at his seriousness, Caroline nodded.

'You won't change your mind?' Clive asked, with an intensity that puzzled her.

Again she shook her head. Relieved, Clive gathered her in his arms and kissed her; it was a fierce kiss, almost as if he were marking his territory and setting down his stamp of ownership.

* * *

'Yesterday my love, I had a very important business meeting.'

With some surprise, Caroline looked at Clive. This was the first time he had discussed his business dealings with her. They were seated at the breakfast table. Mrs Davies had served them with a fairly bad grace. Clive had spent an arduous half an hour with her while he explained the new situation. He had been compelled to make some sexual overtures to the woman in order to pacify her, but he felt that it was worth it. She could indeed be very helpful to him and he smiled as he watched her tolerably respectful attitude to Caroline. Her eyes seemed to warn Caroline of what she could expect if she stepped out of line. He had given Mrs Davies to understand that she would, on occasion, be allowed to discipline her 'Mistress'. He looked approvingly at the way that Caroline's tight black lycra dress clung to her breasts as she moved.

'James Ogilby is very close to signing a contract with me,' Clive continued.

'Is there something preventing him signing?' Caroline asked innocuously.

Clive laid down the knife with which he had been buttering some toast and smiled at her. 'Not exactly preventing, my dear. It is merely on hold for the moment, pending . . .'

Unusually, Clive seemed to be in some difficulty.

'Pending?' Caroline prompted. Mrs Davies hovered near the door, anxious to follow the conversation.

'Thank you, Mrs Davies. We have all that we need,' Clive said, in a voice that brooked no argument.

'Certainly, Cl . . . Master Clive. You will call me if you need anything?' Mrs Davies allowed the hint of a suggestion to linger in her voice.

'Yes, Mrs Davies, be assured that we will,' Clive said, keeping his temper in check with an effort. How, he wondered, had Liam put up with the woman for so long?

They both watched the door close behind Mrs Davies. Caroline turned back to Clive. 'Pending what, Clive? Can I help?'

She watched as Clive dabbed a napkin to his lips, reciprocating his earlier admiration of her apparel. As usual, he looked darkly handsome in a black turtle-neck sweater and sharply creased black trousers.

'As a matter of fact, my dear, you can,' Clive said as he smiled at her warmly. 'I'm going to put you to the test.'

Caroline felt a faint stab of alarm. 'To the test? In what way?' she asked.

'You agreed that you would do anything that I might require of you, did you not, my dear?'

Caroline was swallowed up in the depths of the eyes that were boring into her own.

'Yes, of course, Clive. What is it that you want me to do?'

Clive reached across the table and caught both her hands in his. If she had tried, she would not have been able to pull away from his grasp. He kept his hypnotic eyes fixed on her with an irresistible intensity.

'Mr Ogilby is somewhat reticent about entering into new contracts with unknown partners. I feel that he needs a little encouragement and I have invited him here tonight.'

Caroline could only nod. He was gripping her so tightly that she was unable to tell where his hands ended and her own began.

'Tonight, my Caroline, you will provide that encouragement. I have done some research into Mr Ogilby's preferences in the sexual department. He likes his women to be tied up, my love, and sometimes he likes to beat them.'

Caroline tried to pull away, but Clive effortlessly held her still.

'He is an American and, when in this country, usually

has to use professional services to get what he wants. Tonight, however, I have promised him a delightful little surprise,' Clive said.

Caroline could only stare at him, the enormity of his words sinking gradually into her consciousness. Clive's smile could not have been more charming.

'You, my dear, are to be that delightful little surprise.'

Ten

Caroline stood before Clive. She felt nervous and unsure. So much seemed to be at stake. She wanted to help Clive but she was concerned about what would happen if she failed. If, following this night, James Ogilby did not enter into a contract with Clive, what then? Would she be blamed for that and what would it mean for her relationship with Clive. She was not concerned about the fact that Clive was using her in this way; in some ways it showed that he trusted her and needed her help. As she looked at him, she knew that she was very anxious to please him, but so much could go wrong.

'Suppose he doesn't like me?' she asked suddenly, surprising Clive who had been studying her naked form appraisingly.

'Don't be silly, my love. Of course he will like you,' Clive replied, almost absent-mindedly.

Walking to the mirrored wardrobe which occupied the whole length of one wall, he slid back one of the doors and selected something from the hanging rail. Turning back to her, he paused. Seeing her concern, he dropped the black garment which he had selected on to the bed and took her in his arms.

'My love, you're shivering. What's wrong? Would you prefer not to go through with this?'

As he asked the question, Clive mentally added another: 'And if that were so, would I care?'

'Oh, Clive, you know I want to help you. I'm just . . .'

Confused, Caroline broke off and buried her head in Clive's shoulder.

Surprisingly gentle, Clive stroked the long, blonde hair. 'Then what is the trouble, my pet?' he asked, pulling away a little and tilting her face up towards him.

'Suppose I'm not good enough for him? I don't know if I can give him what he wants and if I don't how you'll feel about me and . . .' Her words tumbled out, jumbling together, making Clive smile and put a finger across her lips.

'My love, your concerns are groundless. James Ogilby will love you and I will be very pleased with you.'

'But what if . . ?'

'If, my love, is one of the most futile words in the English language.'

Seeing that she was about to add further protests, Clive smiled. 'All right, let's suppose that, for whatever reason, this doesn't work and James Ogilby leaves without entering into the contract with me. What of it? It will make no difference to the way that I feel about you. Of course, I may have to punish you for your failure, but we'd both enjoy that, wouldn't we?'

Smiling tremulously, she nodded. She felt relieved and determined that James Ogilby would not be disappointed. Seeing that she was feeling better, Clive released her and turned to pick up the garment he had laid on the bed. 'Now, I think we'll dress you just a little – just enough to titillate!' Clive said, holding up the garment for her inspection. She recognised it as a skin-tight pair of black latex trousers, the zip of which went all the way around from the crotch to the waist-band at the back. She watched while Clive powdered the inside of the trousers so that they could be eased on without too much difficulty. She sat on the bed and extended her legs, smiling at Clive. Now that her fears had been allayed, she had begun to feel a little excitement. After all, this could be very interesting. She felt her nipples harden as Clive smoothed the sensuous rubber on to her legs, pausing in his work to slip a finger into her slit and approvingly note the wetness that he discovered. He removed and licked his finger. 'James Ogilby will not be able to resist you, my love. Perhaps I should feel a little jealous. You are obviously looking forward to this encounter.'

They laughed together but, watching his smile fade, Caroline wondered how much truth lay behind the lightness of his banter. She couldn't help feeling a twinge of pride as she thought that the total control of himself which Clive had previously always exhibited might be shaken by something as routinely normal as jealousy.

'Perhaps he'll want to keep me!' she said, looking archly at Clive.

Suddenly, the tops of her arms were gripped fiercely. Clive's face filled her vision as his eyes seemed to devour her. 'You'd better hope that he doesn't! I've waited a long time for you, Caroline, and now that you're mine, I don't intend to let you go! Get that inside your head!'

Instantly, she regretted her words. She had meant to make a joke of it and she had not expected this savage reaction. She felt a fear of this stranger who held her and then she remembered that it was Clive and that he must really care for her; this reaction of his proved how much. As his grip lightened and his features relaxed into a smile, she found herself returning that smile.

'I'm sorry, my love. I didn't mean to scare you. I'm just not too happy at the prospect of losing you,' Clive said.

She reached up and touched his face. 'You won't lose me, Clive.'

'Do you promise that I won't?' Clive asked, with a return to his eyes of that intensity which she could not resist.

'Yes, I promise. Clive, I . . .'

For some reason, Caroline could not finish the sentence. Did she really love Clive? Did she prefer him over

Liam, or was it just the fascination that she undoubtedly had for this usually totally controlled man? Clive caught her wrists, again gripping her so tightly that she felt a momentary, inexplicable fear.

'Finish it, Caroline! What were you going to say? Tell me!' Clive urged her in a voice that trembled with an obsessive passion.

'I won't leave you, Clive,' Caroline said, wanting more than anything to reassure him. 'I won't leave you because I love you.'

The grip on her wrists tightened.

'Say it again!' he demanded, his eyes burning into her.

'I said I love you, Clive,' Caroline repeated with utter sincerity.

Clive pulled her to him and kissed her with a savagery that told of his inner triumph. At last she was his! She had declared his victory in a way that could not be doubted. He felt her returning his kiss, her tongue entwining with his. Just as suddenly, he roughly pushed her away.

'Come on, little sex slave! We have to get you ready!' he said, his expression jovial but with an underlying seriousness that told her something of the effect her recent words had had. Clive went back to the wardrobe and pulled from a top shelf a long piece of thick white rope.

'I think that Mr Ogilby would like to find you pleasingly packaged for him. White rope, I think, will make an extremely good contrast to the black latex.'

Although his tone was now businesslike, Clive was enjoying himself. Assured of her love, he could afford to ignore the virgin feelings of what, for a moment, he had feared might be jealousy – at least for now. He tied the rope around Caroline's arms, the hard and unyielding texture of the binding pushing her breasts into prominence. As he tied her wrists together behind her, she wondered at the use of this rope as opposed to the soft, forgiving cords with which she was usually bound.

'I'm sorry about the rope, my sweet. I gather that

James Ogilby likes his women to be well tied and he isn't too concerned about their comfort. He will enjoy the knowledge that, although you may want to struggle, the severity of the ropes 'will discourage this,' Clive said, answering her unspoken question.

He urged her to lie down and then tied the rope around her ankles, knotting it just tightly enough to cause her some discomfort but not enough to cut off her circulation. When he had finished, he stroked a gentle finger across her swollen clitoris, which was visible through the open zip of the trousers. He smiled at this evidence of her need. Caroline found that he was right about the ropes. As she moved in response to his finger, the unyielding ropes warned her that the pressure on her limbs could quickly become soreness. In frustration, she lay still. Clive chuckled and smeared her own wetness across her lips.

'I should have thought of this sooner. I think this might be another form of discipline for you, sweetheart. Now, you will have to be a good girl, won't you?'

Mutinously, she looked at him as he folded a large white handkerchief and forced it between her lips, tying it tightly behind her head.

'Bear up, my sweet. After James has finished with you, I'll come and ease your frustrations!'

Smiling, Clive bent down and kissed her forehead, before lowering his head and taking her left nipple between his teeth. His fingers probed between the open zip on her trousers, causing her to moan with pleasure. Quickly, he raised his head and removed his fingers.

'Oh, no. That's not fair, is it, my sweet? I'm just increasing your frustrations.' Smiling, Clive got to his feet and looked down at the sexually exciting picture that she presented.

'I think I'd better go and prepare that contract for signature. I have the distinct feeling that James will want to sign it before he leaves!'

* * *

James Ogilby gave the taxi driver the address and then settled himself in the back seat. He felt tired, but pleased, after a very successful day in the City. He enjoyed his visits to London; the capital was always a delight with its successful melding of history and modern technology. James ran a hand through his luxuriant chestnut-brown hair as he contemplated the coming night's entertainment. Clive had been very mysterious, hinting at all sorts of delights, without being specific. James frowned. He liked Clive and was more than a little well-disposed toward doing business with him. He was not averse to a little bribe, providing that it was enjoyable and was unlikely to involve him in a scandal. He had had several narrow escapes on previous visits to England, when his sexual predilections had often left him open to the risk of blackmail. Clive had assured him that he would cater for his guest with the greatest of discretion. James eased his six-foot form into a more comfortable position and thought about his predisposition to unusual sexual practices. Now in his forties, James had at last achieved an acceptance of his sexuality. This acceptance had been a long time in coming; for many years, he had striven to have acceptably 'normal' sex in his many relationships with the opposite sex. After the usual experimental fling with homosexuality (which had proven to him that that was definitely not his particular bag), he had settled for unsatisfactory relationships with women who occasionally gave in to his sexual preferences. They let him tie them up and even endured anal intercourse – all without enthusiasm. He had been married and had really tried to make it work, but the subsequent divorce came as no real surprise. James sighed sufficiently to make the taxi driver curiously eye him in the driving mirror.

'You wouldn't last in New York, bud,' he said in a non-condemnatory manner and relapsed into the tangled web of his thoughts.

James acknowledged that he was lonely. Yet he was a very successful businessman on the boards of directors of several companies and with a finger in many pies. He had a duplex apartment in New York, a country estate in New England and a beach house in California; all staffed by understanding and discreet members of staff. He had a playroom in his New England estate, which was sadly underused. Once he had lived there with a woman who had enjoyed several exciting excursions with him to the playroom. He had had great hopes for that relationship, James reflected, before – what was her name? Oh, yes, Leila – before Leila had become too greedy in her financial demands and, reluctantly, he had had to ask her to leave. Since Leila, there had been many others; one-night stands, the occasional weekends, but nothing that even looked like lasting. It was ironic, James thought. At long last, he had been able to come to terms with his own sexuality; he accepted the fact that he needed to be the Master in any relationship and now, having accepted that, he found it almost impossible to find someone who could share his sexuality and his life. Well, James reflected, at least he could afford to buy some good times – or accept pleasant bribes like tonight.

'Six pounds, please,' repeated the cockney voice, now with a hint of impatience. James looked up and realised that the taxi had stopped outside a large town house.

'Oh, I'm sorry,' James apologised, feeling for his wallet.

Extracting a ten-pound note, James asked the driver to give him three pounds change and asked for a receipt. Why not? he thought. It was a legitimate business expense!

James caught his breath as he looked at the beautiful girl lying on the bed.

'James, I'd like you to meet Caroline,' Clive said. 'You will obviously excuse her inability to properly greet you. She is, as you see, rather tied up at the moment.'

James could not at that moment form a reply. His eyes had to be allowed time to feast on this vision of submissiveness – a real dream come true. The gag in her mouth could not conceal her beauty; that wonderful long, blonde hair and the shapely figure adorned in rope and black latex. Excitingly, he could see that the ropes were already marking her tender white skin, where they pressed unyieldingly. His eyes took in the open zip that left her anus free for his use. Wordlessly, he turned to Clive.

'She is yours for the night, James. I will leave you to it and perhaps you will join me for breakfast?'

Clive let the invitation and its implication linger in the air behind him as he left the room, softly closing the door.

'My dear, you are very beautiful,' James said, sitting on the bed beside Caroline.

Her eyes expressed the gratitude that her mouth could not. She was glad that she couldn't speak. She wouldn't have known what to say. James Ogilby was undoubtedly the handsomest man she had ever seen; handsome in the old-fashioned sense with very masculine features and an inherent sense of strength that exuded from him as he moved. It was a strength that did not frighten her – but did very much to excite her. She knew that her nipples were erect and that she was very wet. She knew that he must be able to smell her aroused excitement. She felt his finger gently trace her features, hovering fractionally on the gag in her mouth.

'No, I think I will keep you gagged for the moment, my dear. A gag on a woman as beautiful as you is really quite exciting.'

He bent lower and kissed her mouth and then raised his head again to look at her. 'It is really exciting, my dear, because it means that you are completely under my control, yet Clive tells me that you are consenting to my being here?'

She nodded in immediate response.

'You mean that? You are not just accepting the situation for – shall we say – business advancement? You are not at all under duress?'

She shook her head and James, delighting in her, determined that, at some stage in the evening, he would remove the gag because he wanted to hear her voice. He couldn't believe his luck. Clive had not told him much about her, other than the fact that she was his sex slave and lived in this house. James felt unbearably envious of Clive as he looked at Caroline; tied up and helpless she might be, but her eyes told him of her total willingness for him to use her as he chose. If only he had met her before this, he thought, running his hands across the restrictive ropes.

'How lucky Clive is,' James murmured. 'To have you as his slave is something for which he is truly to be envied.'

James slipped his fingers inside Caroline and felt her wetness. She was so willing; so ready for him. He felt her move beneath him as much as she was able to without hurting herself. He felt tremendous excitement. He would have tied her like this, in these unforgiving ropes. They forced her to impose her own self-discipline. She knew that it would only hurt if she struggled too much.

'Later, I may want to beat you, Caroline. Because of the way that you are tied, it will be hard to bear,' James said, then listened in amazement as he heard his own voice make her an offer. 'I can untie you and use something a little less harsh to restrain you. Would you like that?'

Caroline showed her gratitude in her eyes, but slowly shook her head. She knew that it was the way in which she was tied that was exciting James. She had to admit that that excitement was not one-sided. She was finding the very restrictive nature of the ropes tremendously arousing. Unable even to struggle, she felt very vulnerable and helpless; a fact which only fuelled her sexual arousal.

'Good girl,' James said, using his fingers to greater effect and making Caroline moan through her gag.

Caroline knew that it would not take much to trigger her orgasm and she tried to hold it back. She wanted to hold on to the sensations that this man was evoking within her for as long as she possibly could.

'Let it go, my little love,' James whispered to her. 'The night is young. This will be the first of many, I promise.'

She did as she was told, giving way to a flood of exquisite sensations as James considerately held her in his arms, not allowing her to struggle.

'Was that good for you, little one?' James asked. 'I will give you much pleasure during this night and, afterwards, I want to sleep with you tied up and helpless beside me. I'm afraid that there will also be pain, but I promise that I will make that pleasurable for you. For tonight, Caroline, I want you to think of me as your Master   I insist upon it!'

As he smiled at her, James' mind was already formulating a plan to ensure that this would not be his only night with Caroline.

Caroline moaned with frustration as yet again her desires were not met. James had proved himself to be an expert in exquisitely subtle sexual torture; constantly bringing her to a peak of excitement without allowing her to orgasm. There was silence and Caroline strained her ears to try and locate James. Where was he and what was he doing? After that first incredible release, he had blindfolded her and then proceeded to arouse her unbearably before stopping. Now, she lay helpless, unable to see or speak; the only movements she was able to make were little tremors of agitated frustration, eliciting delighted chuckles from James. Suddenly, she felt something stroking across her body. Her muscles tensed as she realised that it was a cane.

'Relax, my dear,' James urged soothingly. 'You don't know when or even if I am going to strike you with the cane. Just enjoy the feeling of it stroking along your body, while your mind wonders where it is that I may first choose to punish. One of the exciting things about being blindfold, my darling, is that you cannot see me and therefore you can only guess at my intentions. I find such an increase in the sexual tension to be highly desirable. I myself may not yet have decided what it is that I am going to do, so it is as much a pleasure for me as it is for you, my darling. I may indeed decide to hit you with the cane, but I may also decide that there are other uses for which it could be employed.'

The cane slithered down Caroline's body until it was pressed against her slit. Then, teasingly slowly, the cane was inserted into her vagina, sliding easily into an already well-oiled path. Caroline's muscles tightened around the cane. Surely this time he would let her come. She had begun the wonderfully inexorable climb towards a sexual pinnacle that would clamour for release.

'Shall I let you come, my darling? It would be so easy. I only have to leave the cane in place and perhaps stroke your little bud – just like this. Oh, yes. You like that, don't you? If I could only just make up my mind. I think perhaps the cane should be removed and put to its original purpose . . .' James' voice trailed off suggestively, letting her think that he was only considering this option. She moaned desperately into her gag and James chuckled, before resuming a tender massage of her clitoris. She sighed with relief and relaxed back into her pool of enjoyment, unaware that James was closely watching her reactions. Just as he sensed that she was on the very brink of her orgasm, he extracted the cane so swiftly that she gasped in pained surprise.

'No, my darling, not yet. I have other plans for you.' James' voice contained an underlying hint of menace; just enough to excite but not really scare her. There was a resumption of the sort of empty silence which meant that he had moved away from her. Mentally screaming with frustration, Caroline tried to wriggle herself into a different position to try and ease her pulsating clitoris. The silence continued and she wondered whether James had actually left the room. She strained to hear his breathing, but there was no sound. For a few minutes, she lay still. Surely he hadn't left her?

So suddenly that she had no time to collect her thoughts, the blindfold and gag were removed. She only caught a glimpse of James' face before something soft was pressed over her face. Momentarily, she panicked but then relaxed as she realised that she could still breathe in a perfectly normal fashion. She was aware of the smell of leather and of the tightening of the material as it was fastened behind her head. She realised that James had placed some kind of hood over her head. Now, in addition to being unable to see and speak, she could only hear very muffled sounds. Soon, even these stopped. She was left in an abyss of totally dark silence. The hood was quite a snug fit and she was not convinced that even her moans could be heard.

She didn't know that James was silently studying her, admiring the beautiful picture that she presented. He knelt on the bed and gently turned Caroline on to her side. He knew that her sense of feeling would now be intensified by her almost total sensory deprivation. He also knew that her nerve endings would be so much more receptive to his touch and that, accordingly, both of them would derive greater pleasure from the experience. When he had collected the hood, he had also divested himself of his clothes. Gently and sensuously, he lubricated the sensitive opening to Caroline's anus and also the head of his erect penis. His cock slipped easily inside Caroline and he sighed with pleasure as his nakedness came into contact with the rubber that covered the lower part of her body. He reached around her and gripped her bound breasts, revelling in the feel of the rope-covered flesh. He had intended to cane her, but his sexual needs had become too urgent to ignore. His thrusts became more urgent and the incoherent mumblings coming from Caroline told him that she was also approaching a climax. Just before his semen spurted inside Caroline's rectum, he moved one hand to massage her clitoris, ensuring that they both came together. He held her tightly as he screamed his pleasure and the intensity of it left him gasping. This was real pleasure. This was how it really felt to be a Master, and Master of such a beautiful submissive at that. This was the elusive thing he had been searching for; knowing it was out there, but constantly frustrated in his attempts to secure it. As his breathing slowed to something approaching normal, he retained his hold on Caroline. As he felt her moving exhaustedly in his arms, he knew that, whatever it took, he would not rest until he could make her his very own slave.

Caroline felt as if she were moving through a dream. This incredible man had walked into her life and in a matter of a few hours irrevocably changed its course. She had found it very exciting to have sex with him whilst she was almost anonymous beneath the confines of the enclosing hood. Because she couldn't really hear anything, she was only aware of James' return to consciousness when his arms were removed from around her and she felt the hood loosening and finally being removed. For a long time, they merely looked at each other and it wasn't until Caroline ran the tip of her tongue over her dry lips that James moved. Returning from the bathroom with a glass of water, he held it to her lips and watched as, gratefully, she drank. When she moved her head away, indicating that she had had enough, James put the glass on the bedside table, bent his head and kissed her. It was an almost exploratory kiss, as if they both wanted to taste each other. When the kiss ended, James' fingers lingeringly explored the contours of her face. Caroline felt a nudge of fear; it was as if he was imprinting every detail on his memory in order to recall them when he was far away.

'James . . .'

'Ssh,' he whispered and then started to untie her.

For Caroline, it was a most sensuous experience. He started with the ropes which secured her ankles, untying the knots and kissing the marks left by the ropes before proceeding further up her body. When he reached her slit, he paused long enough to slip his tongue inside, playing with her clitoris unmercifully before removing his tongue from her delicious opening and running it up and across her nether lips. He paused when he reached her bound wrists and looked at her.

'I wonder . . .' he said, pausing significantly.

'What do you wonder?' she whispered, enjoying the game.

'I wonder if I shouldn't keep your hands tied. You might feel compelled to try and run away.'

The tone was light, belying the serious nature of the comment.

'I don't want to run away from you, James,' she assured him with total sincerity.

Still he hesitated, his fingers lingering on the tightly tied knots.

'Is there anyone else that you want to run from, Caroline?'

This time there was no lightness of tone. The question was a serious one. Wordlessly, Caroline looked at him. What could she tell this man? More importantly, what should she tell him? Earlier today, she had told Clive that she loved him and she had meant it. That was before she had first seen James. The irony was not lost on her. Through his desire to win a business contract, Clive had sought to use her to gain what he wanted. Instead, by pushing her into this man's arms, he may have lost something that she believed he counted much more important. If she confessed her thoughts to this man, what would he think of her? Indeed, what did she think of herself? Caroline shrugged that thought aside. She had long since given up on analysing her own behaviour. Since the day when she had rung the bell of Francis and Lynne's house, she had irretrievably lost a good part of the person she had once felt herself to be. All three men who had made their way into her life had continued the process of change. In one way or another, she had loved them all; all these men who had dominated and enslaved her, for a while at least, had also enslaved her mind. Now, for the first time, she felt a sense of freedom. She knew without a doubt what it was that she wanted. Caroline thought about Liam. She owed him and she needed to ensure that Clive kept his promise and saved Liam's business reputation. The price of that was her loyalty to Clive. She would have to stay with him; at least until he'd kept his promise. Caroline's lips tightened as she thought of what she must do: Francis, Liam and Clive had all used her. Now, perhaps, it was time that she did some using of her own.

Suddenly, James released her and got off the bed.

'We need to shower,' he said, pulling her to her feet. 'Before we go into the shower, I will untie you, but I shall replace the ropes with these.'

He held up a pair of metal handcuffs. 'Hands in front of you, please.'

She stretched her arms out and felt the reassuring cold steel snap into place on her wrists. He pulled her to him.

James pulled her into the bathroom and pushed her

into the shower cubicle. Immediately, she was dowsed with water as he turned the shower full on.

'James! It's cold!'

'Shut up, woman, or I'll have to gag you again. The water will soon warm up,' James said, barring her exit route from the cubicle.

He was right and the water was soon pleasantly warm. Caroline soaped James carefully, paying particular attention to his cock and balls, until James caught the connecting chain between the handcuffs and pulled her to him. Urgently, he probed her mouth with his tongue, while his fingers slid into her slit as he soaped her body. She felt herself responding to him and it seemed only natural when he pushed her into a kneeling position on the floor and pushed his cock into her mouth, holding the chain between her wrists to prevent any ideas of escape. Eagerly, she sucked and licked him, running her tongue up and down the shaft and letting the tip of her tongue occasionally flick over his balls. As he approached his climax, James pulled on the chain, loving the knowledge that she was such a willing captive. He spunked into her mouth and pressed her against him as he rode the waves of pleasure. Then he, too, knelt on the floor and took her in his arms. The water washed away the sweat and semen but not their passion. It wasn't long before his cock was again erect and he lay back on the floor of the cubicle while she positioned herself so that he could easily penetrate her. As they both reached the pinnacle of their pleasure, he rejoiced to see her bobbing up and down as she rode his cock; her hands chained together, denoting her submissiveness – her total enslavement to his every desire.

'You're looking very solemn, my darling,' James said, when he had recovered.

'Oh, James. There's so much that I want to tell you.'

'We have all night, my darling.'

'James, I can't tell you yet. There are things that have to be dealt with first, before . . .'

'Before?'

Caroline hesitated as the natural submissiveness in her personality shied away from putting into words what it was that she really hoped for.

'Caroline, you can say anything to me. I won't take offence. I know we hardly know each other, but if there are such things as kindred spirits, I think that's what we are. Please talk to me,' James urged, building up her confidence as he spoke.

'Before we can be together,' Caroline continued, hardly daring to breathe. 'That is, if you want . . .'

She didn't finish the sentence. James showed her exactly what it was that he wanted as he crushed her in his arms, almost hurting her by the fervency with which he held her.

'My darling, take as long as you need. I'll be waiting for you, just as I've been doing for most of my life. I will leave you a note of how you can get a message to me wherever I am. To fill in the time, just think about where you would like to live. I have homes in New York, New England and California. If you want us to live in the UK . . .'

'No, James. Please let's leave England. I'd love to live anywhere in America with you – but not here.'

Not disturbed by her vehemence, James hugged her.

'There are one or two conditions, my love,' James said, trying to look serious.

Caroline felt a sense of dread. James, too? Everyone seemed to want something from her before she was allowed to be happy.

'What is it?' she asked, her voice barely above a whisper.

'Don't look so worried, my darling, it's nothing too onerous. I want to feel that beautiful mouth on my cock. If you're a very good girl, I might bring you off – or I might carry out my earlier threat and beat you.' He smiled at her. 'Then, to round the evening off, I would like to have you sleep beside me. You'll be tied up, of course.'

'Of course,' Caroline agreed, laughing in the immensity of her relief. In turn, she became serious as she looked at James. How she could love this man!

'I love you,' she whispered so softly James was unsure of her words.

'What did you say, my darling?' he asked, giving his attention to unlocking the cuffs on her wrists.

'I said I love you,' she said loudly and then felt a fear that it was too early in their relationship. Maybe she shouldn't have said it.

Caroline's words really penetrated into James' consciousness. He looked lovingly at her. She was really his; his own personal, loving slave.

'I love you, too, Caroline, more than I can say,' James said, pressing her back against the floor and kissing her with increasing passion.

Eleven

As arranged, James joined Clive for breakfast. Pleading tiredness, Caroline excused herself from making up one of the party. The truth was that she was too upset after her parting from James and, as yet, she didn't feel able to face Clive.

'I trust that the evening was to your satisfaction?' Clive asked, shaking out his napkin.

James found it quite difficult to smile at Clive. Whilst still respecting the other man's business acumen, he now felt an active dislike for his breakfast companion. Caroline had not revealed anything further to him, but he was in no doubt that the man sitting opposite to him was the reason for her reticence. Somehow, James felt, Clive had some kind of hold over Caroline. Fervently, he hoped that she would memorise the number he had given to her in case she ever lost the slip of paper she had so carefully hidden. Thinking only of Caroline, James pretended an enthusiasm he did not feel.

'Clive, I feel absolutely tremendous. Your girl certainly knows how to give a man a good time!'

'I am very pleased to hear it, James,' Clive responded carefully. 'However, she is my slave – not my girl.'

James looked up quickly at the implied warning in Clive's voice. 'Of course – your slave. She is very well-trained, my friend,' James said, narrowing his eyes as he used the word 'friend'.

In his turn, Clive interpreted the warning and when

he spoke again, his tone was lighter. 'She is that indeed! I couldn't think of a nicer present to offer.'

'Bribe, I think, is the better word,' James said.

Clive looked up from the toast that he was buttering. 'Bribe, James? I don't believe . . .'

'Clive, I have a great respect for your business value. I also have a similar respect for your honesty,' James said.

Clive's pause was only momentary. In James, he felt he had met his match and decided to continue the discussion for what it was; two men of equal intelligence, who both knew exactly what they wanted.

'OK, bribe if you prefer. Getting this contract is very important to me, James. I think we can both benefit from a business relationship.'

'Why limit it solely to business?' James asked as he poured coffee for them both.

'I have no objection at all to including a more social side,' Clive replied. 'After all, we do share certain other – hobbies.'

'Indeed we do, my dear Clive, but I was thinking of setting our – friendship on a formal basis as well,' James said.

Clive frowned, trying to assimilate what might lie behind those words. 'Formal basis? I don't think I understand.'

James finished his coffee and leaned back in his chair. 'I am more than happy to enter into a business arrangement with you, Clive. However, there are certain things that I would like included in what I presume are the usual standard terms and conditions before I agree to sign,' he said, his voice firm enough to deny any prospect of negotiation.

'What additions do you propose?' Clive asked warily.

'The additions that I require – not propose – are mandatory before I sign any contract with you. They are quite simple. You will allow me unrestricted access to your home at all times; such access will also include your – slave. I am to be allowed to visit your home on giving you 24 hours' notice of my arrival. I will be allowed the use of Caroline during my visit and I may do with her whatever I choose. If you have a problem with these terms, I thank you for a most exciting and entertaining evening and I will now take my leave. If, however, you agree, I will expect these conditions to be incorporated into the contract which I will sign before departing,' James finished, demonstrating the decisive flair which had taken him to the top in the business world and kept him there.

Clive looked at his guest. There would be no minimising of the terms. He had been presented with an ultimatum: accept the terms or lose the contract.

'James, I need time . . .'

'That, my friend, is something that I cannot give you. I have to catch a plane in precisely –' James broke off to check his watch, '– three hours. Prior to that, I have things to do. The bottom line, my dear Clive, is that you get on your PC and amend the contract or you tell me that it's no deal. I don't have time to debate the issue.'

James' tone was flat and final. For once in his life, Clive experienced the unwelcome chaos of flustered thoughts. The pragmatist surfaced and he rose from his chair.

'I am more than pleased that my slave performed so well,' Clive said and, leaving his guest to help himself to a second cup of coffee, went to do as he was told.

Clive closed the front door behind his departing guest. Thoughtfully, he tapped the folded pieces of paper against his chin. He had the contract upon which he had gambled so much, but might the gamble prove to be too expensive? Frowning, Clive climbed the stairs to the room where Caroline lay. He felt that she had much to answer for. He remembered her fears of the night before

137

that she might let him down. It seemed that she had succeeded far too well.

Entering the room without knocking, he stood looking at her. She was sleeping and he reflected on how very innocent she appeared to be when asleep. He walked to the head of the bed and dropped the signed contract on to her pillow. As though she had been awaiting this, her eyes flew open.

'Clive, what . . . ?'

'You were successful, my darling. I'd like you to tell me all about it.' Clive's tone was harder than he had intended. For the first time in his life, he was fighting an alien and unwelcome intruder: jealousy.

'There's not much to tell,' Caroline said, hesitantly.

'I find that hard to believe, my love. I have just spent the past half an hour inserting additions to the contract.'

'Additions? What sort of additions?' Caroline said, struggling with the vestiges of sleep as she pushed herself into a sitting position.

Without any change of expression, Clive leant forward and pushed her back down.

'Stay on your back, my darling. That is where you seem to do your best work.' Clive's tone of heavy sarcasm filled her with alarm.

'Clive, I don't understand. I did what you asked . . .'

'Didn't you just! You did everything and more, my love, and that is why I want to know everything that took place between you. Did you remain tied up all night?'

'Partly . . .'

'How partly?'

'We – we took a shower together. He untied me for that.' Caroline faltered. She was frightened. She had never seen such controlled anger before.

'Did he tie you afterwards?' Clive asked in the same unrelenting tone.

138

'Yes, he did. He wanted to sleep with me like that. You know what he likes . . .'

'Oh, I do indeed, my dear. I do indeed. I think you'd better get up and have a shower right now. I can smell him on you!' Clive's temper was rising and, with an effort, he controlled it.

'Clive . . .' Caroline begged.

'Get in the shower right now!' Clive yelled. 'You are my slave and you will do as you are told!'

Without further hesitation and with a sense of relief at being able to leave his presence, Caroline quickly got out of bed. Before she could get into the bathroom, Clive gripped her arms painfully.

'I don't know what went on between you two, my darling, but I am going to find out and you are going to be punished! Now get out of my sight!'

Thoroughly frightened and with an unsatisfied curiosity about the mysterious additions to the contract, Caroline scurried into the bathroom. As she stood beneath the warm water and soaped herself, she wondered what had happened at the breakfast meeting between the two men. She could not suppress a twinge of excitement as she considered the possible additions that had apparently been made to the contract at James' insistence – and, because of Clive's anger, she must be the cause. Despite the warmth of the water, she shivered as she reflected on the punishment that Clive had promised she would endure. She had never seen him so angry and she knew that, if she could, she would have to find a way to placate him.

'Carol, I need you,' Clive said as he caught sight of Mrs Davies in the corridor.

'Master Clive?' Mrs Davies said respectfully.

Clive reached down and, with a finger, tilted her chin towards him. 'Clive. Remember?' he said in a sensuously soft voice.

Immediately responding, Mrs Davies blushed. Clive could see the hardening nipples beneath the black material of her dress. With some resumption of good humour, he smiled at the housekeeper. 'I need your help with Miss Caroline. She has been very, very disobedient and has badly upset me. I don't like to be upset, Carol. The only thing that will give me some relief is to see the little slut suffer – as only you can make her suffer, Carol.'

Carol Davies felt an immediate wetness between her legs. 'You want me to discipline her – Clive?'

'Yes, I do. I want her to tell me something – truth-fully. I want you to – encourage her to do that.'

'With pleasure, Clive, and – can I do anything else for you?'

As Clive looked down at the upturned pleading face, an idea came to him. 'Perhaps there is something, Carol,' he said, smiling at her as the idea gathered momentum. 'Perhaps you can demonstrate to Miss Caroline just how I like to take my pleasure.'

After she had showered, Caroline looked around for something to wear and saw Clive's black satin robe. She slipped it on and then went to the door. To her surprise, it was locked. She walked to the bed and sat down, wondering why Clive had locked her in. She was still concerned about his reaction, but felt secure enough in his affections to know that she could somehow convince him that everything was all right. She couldn't help wondering what it was that had been inserted in the contract and how she was concerned. Sighing, she got up and walked to the window. It was a fairly grey, un-pleasant kind of morning. She thought about James and, in her mind, followed his progress to the airport. She wondered what his homes looked like and when she would see them. Her smile faded as she thought of Liam and Clive. In one way or another, she had loved them both; but this was different. She had never felt so keenly alive and so anxious to resolve matters so that she could leave.

Caroline turned at the sound of the key turning in the lock. The door swung open and Clive stood there.

'Well, Caroline, have you decided to be truthful with me?' he asked, standing aside so that Caroline could see Mrs Davies.

'There's nothing to tell, Clive. James used me as you knew he would and now he's gone. You have the signed contract. Isn't that what you wanted?' Caroline swallowed hard. She was desperately trying not to show that she was concerned at Mrs Davies' presence.

'Oh, yes, my dear, I do have the contract. What I didn't expect is to have to play host to dear James on such a regular basis.'

Caroline could not stop the light that sprang into her eyes and was quickly suppressed; Clive saw it and a pulse beat strongly in his throat.

'James is coming here?' Caroline asked, trying unsuccessfully to hide the note of hope in her voice.

Clive strolled towards her, the very slowness of his movements expressing menace. 'Yes, my darling, as if you didn't know.'

'Clive, I swear I knew nothing about it!' Caroline gasped, as Clive stood before her and gripped her arms.

'Didn't you, my dear? I rather think that the two of you cooked this up between you, didn't you?'

Caroline could only shake her head, but Clive was in no mood to listen.

'Mrs Davies!' he barked. 'Get over here!'

Too excited by the exchange that she had just witnessed to feel offence at the manner of Clive's address, Mrs Davies scurried over to join them.

'You see, Mrs Davies, Miss Caroline has become extremely disobedient. She is not telling me the truth. I think you should perhaps beat it out of her   in your own inimitable way, of course.'

'It'll be a pleasure, Master Clive,' Mrs Davies said, positively drooling with anticipation as she looked at Caroline.

'I rather thought it might,' Clive said, relaxing his grip on Caroline's arms. 'Now you, my dear, will pay attention to what it is that Mrs Davies tells you to do. If you tell me the truth, I will see to it that she doesn't hurt you too much.' He moved his hands to stroke the black satin that covered her breasts.

Despite herself, Caroline felt her nipples spring to erection beneath those stroking fingers.

'Oh, Caroline, you are such a slut,' Clive murmured as his arms went around her, holding her tightly so that she was effectively pinioned in his embrace. He bent his head and kissed her, gently at first and then with a passion that was so intense she could not help responding. As their tongues entwined, she felt him moving her arms behind her back and gripping her wrists. Raising his head, but keeping his eyes intently on hers, he called to Mrs Davies. 'Carol, there is some rope in my pocket. Please get it and tie Miss Caroline's wrists together.'

'Clive, please . . .' Caroline whispered.

'Please? Is that what you said to James, my dear? Please, James, make him let you come and see me often?'

'No, Clive. We didn't talk about anything like that . . .' Caroline broke off with a gasp as Mrs Davies tied the ropes about her wrists.

'That's right, Carol. Tie her nice and tightly. After all, we don't want her getting away from us, do we?' Clive said, kissing Caroline to silence her protests.

Caroline knew that she should feel fear. She *wanted* to feel fear as Clive pulled her gently towards the bed and pushed her down until she was lying beneath him. He stroked her face.

'Don't worry, my love, we have all day. You can tell me the truth whenever you want to,' Clive said, his voice soft and gentle.

'Carol, I think we'd better have her ankles tied, don't you?' Clive asked, again without removing his eyes from her face. She felt the odd fascination that he instilled within her. Desperately, she fought against it. She would not give in to him. She felt her ankles being skilfully tied together and winced at the tightness of the ropes.

'Not *too* tightly, Carol. We don't yet know how long she is to remain tied up. Could be all day, couldn't it, my love?'

'Clive, please ...' Caroline began, before Clive pressed a gentle hand over her mouth.

'Not now, my darling. I think we had better have you gagged. It will give you time to think   concentrate the mind, don't you think?'

Mrs Davies held out a handkerchief to Clive, who looked at it for a moment and then shook his head. Looking back at Caroline, he stroked her hair and smiled at her.

'No, Carol, the hood, I think. I want her to have peace and quiet to think about what she is going to tell me,' Clive said, in that sensuously insistent voice which fuelled Caroline's sexual arousal. 'We'll leave you alone for a little while, my darling. Think on what I have said and then we'll decide what to do with you.'

As he spoke, Clive touched a finger to her slit and massaged the swollen bud that had emerged from its hood, before obligingly slipping his hand beneath Caroline's head to enable Mrs Davies to place the hood over her face. Caroline was plunged into darkness and felt the lacings being secured behind her head, but this only served to amplify the sensations that were flooding through her as Clive's fingers continued their smooth and sensuous massage. When she was on the verge of her orgasm, Clive's fingers were removed. Desperately frustrated, she tried to cry out in protest, but even to her own ears the sound was muffled. She twisted and turned on the bed, knowing her struggles to be futile. They had left the robe on her, even though it was fully open in front. Clive had used the sash from the robe to tie her elbows together, forcing her breasts into prominence. After he had tied her, she felt a surge of hope as she felt fingers stroking her breasts and tweaking the nipples. If only he would let her orgasm before he left her; it would give strength to her determination not to say anything further about James. She could just lie here and await her punishment. For James, it would be worth it.

The stroking fingers paused and then ran down her thighs, teasingly flicking her clitoris. She tried to part her legs as much as her tightly bound ankles would allow and was briefly rewarded as she felt a tongue licking her bud, almost triggering her orgasm. Suddenly, all those wonderful sensations ceased. She felt a movement of the bed and made desperate muffled noises through the hood as she begged Clive to come back.

The person who had got off the bed stood in front of Caroline and looked down at her with lascivious eyes. How good the slut had tasted, Carol Davies thought. The housekeeper smiled and flexed her hands. Master Clive had told her that he wanted Miss Caroline to be thoroughly spanked and she was determined to do a good job. She looked around the room, mentally selecting the chair that she would use. Master Clive had also hinted that he wanted Mistress Caroline's sexual frustration to reach a fever pitch even as she struggled with the pain of the spanking. The housekeeper smiled as she looked at Caroline.

Mrs Davies was very good at her job!

Twelve

Trapped within the confines of the hood, Caroline wrestled with her sexual frustration. She knew that Clive regarded this as part of her punishment and would be revelling in the thoughts of her discomfort. In the darkness, Caroline saw the faces of her tormentors: Clive, Mrs Davies and, yes, James as well. Surely James would have realised the sort of pressure that Clive would put her under. Perhaps it was James' way of punishing her for her reticence with him, just the same as Clive. Caroline determined that, no matter what Clive and Mrs Davies might do to her, she would not reveal anything other than the sketchiest of details as to what had occurred when she had been with James. Thinking of Mrs Davies made Caroline wriggle uncomfortably within her bonds. She was not really afraid of Mrs Davies; she was, however, annoyed with herself at the way the housekeeper could so easily arouse her. Thinking back on the things that Mrs Davies had done to her, Caroline wanted to feel disgust; instead, she was aware that her thoughts were resulting in an increased sensitivity along her nerve endings. She expected pain from the proposed punishment, but surely there would be pleasure as well.

Because the wearing of the hood caused a considerable impairment to her hearing, Caroline was unaware that she was no longer alone until a pair of lips fastened around her left nipple and a finger slid inside her wetness. The fastenings on the hood were loosened and she looked forward to being able to see who it was whose fingers were giving her so much pleasure. However, the hope was not to be fulfilled. Immediately the hood was removed, her eyes were covered by a scarf. As this was tied in place, Caroline heard a low chuckle and knew it to be Clive.

'Sorry to disappoint you, my dear,' Clive said. 'You will be allowed to speak and hear, but your other senses will remain under my control.'

Clive finished tying the scarf and then stood in front of Caroline. 'Now, my dear, do you have anything that you wish to say to me?'

Mutely, Caroline shook her head.

'I'm not sorry about that, my dear. Carol and I had anticipated your stubbornness and we both welcome it,' Clive said, drawing Mrs Davies closer to him. He rubbed one hand over the housekeeper's breasts, smiling at the immediate response. 'Carol has so been looking forward to spanking you, Caroline. During your punishment, one or other – maybe both – of us may be inclined to give you some pleasure. You, of course, will not know if and when that may happen – or who is responsible. You are very much in our hands, my darling.'

Both the women shivered in anticipation as they listened to Clive. The smell of arousal was very evident in the air and Clive was as excited as his two listeners. He pushed Carol away from him and knelt on the bed with his knees on either side of Caroline's head. Caroline heard the sound of a zip and knew what to expect even before she felt the hardness of Clive's penis pushing at her lips. Deliberately, she kept her mouth closed in expectancy of a hand grabbing a handful of her hair and painfully twisting it until she relented. She was not prepared for the fingers that closed her nostrils and forced her to open her mouth. Only when what felt like the whole length of the penis was jammed into her mouth were the fingers released. Eagerly, she licked and sucked at the intruder, tasting Clive's excitement. She knew that Mrs Davies would be watching and she also knew that the housekeeper fancied herself in love with Clive. She sucked at the hardness within her mouth with an enjoyment that was fuelled by the jealousy she knew she was creating. Slowly, Clive became aware of what she was doing and suddenly withdrew from her mouth. Caroline was totally unprepared for the hard slap to her face. Then the hand tangled in her hair, but only to pull her head upwards until she could feel Clive's breath on her face.

'I will decide what games are to be played, my dear. It is not for you to choose,' Clive said. Before releasing her hair, he kissed her with a passion that denoted his enjoyment of the situation. Recovering from her shock at being slapped, Caroline responded with an enthusiasm that made Clive laugh softly as he relaxed his grip on her hair.

'Carol, I'd like you to remove your clothes, please,' Clive said, fingering Caroline's nipples. 'I would like you to pleasure me.'

Caroline could heard the sound of Mrs Davies undressing and she opened her mouth to protest that she could give Clive the pleasure he sought. A hand was pressed firmly over her mouth, sealing a piece of tape across her lips.

'No, my dear, I do not want any interruptions,' Clive said and slapped her again. 'Carol, I am going to lie beside Caroline and I want you to use your lips and tongue to give me pleasure. Caroline, I suggest that you lie quietly, otherwise Carol has my permission to discipline you in any way that she likes – without restriction.'

Caroline could do nothing other than lie still beside Clive, listening to the sounds of Mrs Davies bringing him to orgasm. Occasionally, Clive would reach for her and stroke her breasts or insert a questing finger into her vagina. Other than that, she had to lie perfectly still and listen to the sounds of two people enjoying each other sexually, leaving her to mentally struggle with her own frustration.

'Why settle for one when I can have two?' Clive asked and Caroline felt him move into position close to her head. Without warning, he tore the tape from her mouth. 'Suck me, slut!' Clive said, his voice ragged with barely controlled passion and temper.

Almost gratefully, Caroline took his cock into her mouth.

'Carol! Lick my arse!' Clive ordered and Caroline could imagine Carol Davies on her knees behind him, running her tongue between the cleft in his bottom. It almost seemed to have become a competition between Caroline and the housekeeper: which one could give Clive the greater pleasure?

'Ladies, I'm getting bored,' Clive said warningly.

Immediately, the two women redoubled their efforts. Mrs Davies cupped Clive's balls within her hands, squeezing them gently as her tongue slipped inside the entry to his rectum. Unable to use her hands, Caroline had to be as inventive as possible with her tongue. She could feel Clive's excitement increasing as he thrust in and out of her mouth. She felt a sense of triumph as the hot semen flooded over her tongue. She and not Mrs Davies had done this!

Clive collapsed on to her and lay still for a few minutes. Mrs Davies was sitting on the floor looking disdainfully at Caroline. Eventually, Clive moved and levered himself off the bed.

'Thank you, ladies,' Clive said. 'Unfortunately, I cannot be sure which of you gave me the greater pleasure, but I want to assure you that it was quite wonderful.'

Clive wiped himself and went to sit in the chair that Mrs Davies had earlier selected for Caroline's punishment. Seating himself, he looked over at the two women. 'Carol, take the slut's blindfold off, then come over here.'

Mrs Davies pushed Caroline's head to one side and untied the knot in the blindfold.

'Use the blindfold to gag her, Carol,' Clive said in a bored voice.

With alacrity, Mrs Davies forced the scarf between Caroline's lips and tied it tightly behind her head. She was feeling almost as frustrated as Caroline. Looking down at the prisoner, who was now looking at her with ill-concealed triumph, Mrs Davies slapped her face. Without a word, she got off the bed and walked over to Clive.

'Can I do anything for you, Master Clive?' she asked, as she stood in front of him.

'I think it's more a case of what I can do for you, Carol,' Clive said, looking her up and down. Carol Davies was not bad for her age, he concluded. In her favour, as far as he was concerned, was the fact that she obviously worshipped him and really would do anything for him. Clive looked across at Caroline. 'Are you comfortable, my dear?' he asked. 'On balance, I think that Carol probably pleased me a little more than you did yourself. I think that she deserves a reward for that, don't you?'

Caroline screamed her frustrated anger into her gag. Clive smiled pleasantly before turning his attention to Carol Davies. 'Come closer, Carol. That's it. Just a little bit more.'

Carol stood in front of Clive, who had sited the chair at just the right angle to allow Caroline a good view.

'Part your legs for me, Carol,' Clive said, running sensuous fingers up and down the backs of the housekeeper's thighs.

Carol Davies obediently parted her legs and Clive slipped a finger inside her slit. As he had known he would, he encountered a great deal of wetness.

'Would you like me to bring you off, Carol?' Clive asked. 'Shall we do it here, or would you like me to tie you to the bed?'

Wordlessly, Carol Davies could only stare at Clive.

'I'll take your silence as acquiescence, Carol. I tell you what I would like you to do,' Clive said, his voice softly sensuous but loud enough to carry to the helpless listener on the bed. 'I would like you to untie Caroline's arms and push her face-down on the bed. Use the sash from her arms to tie around her wrists – nice and tightly – leaving a long trailing piece. Can you do that for me, Carol?'

The question was purely rhetorical. Carol Davies would have done anything that Clive asked of her. Quickly she walked over to Caroline and pushed the helpless girl on to her stomach. Swiftly untying the sash from her arms, she retied it over the ropes that already secured Caroline's wrists, laughing with a surge of sexual excitement as her prisoner gasped with shock. She stood back to show Clive that she had complied with his wishes and awaited his arrival at the bed. Clive examined the tightly tied knots with approval before standing on the bed and pulling at the loose end of the sash. Caroline's arms were jerked upwards as Clive tied the sash through a ring in the ceiling. When he had finished, Caroline was on her knees, trying to ease the strain on her shoulders and wrists. With approval, Clive eyed his resultant handiwork. He looked back at Mrs Davies, who was standing watching him, her eyes bright with sexual excitement.

'Get on the bed and lie down so that you are facing Caroline,' Clive instructed her. Without hesitation, Mrs Davies complied.

'Stretch your legs wide, Carol,' Clive ordered.

Expectantly, Mrs Davies parted her legs. Caroline's head was now an inch or so away from her slit. Clive walked to the head of the bed.

'Let's have your arms at the corners, please, Carol,' Clive said.

As Mrs Davies followed his instructions, Clive secured each of her wrists to the bed, tying the ropes tightly around the legs of the bed. He repeated the procedure with her ankles and then stood back.

'Comfortable, ladies?' he asked. 'I think we'll have this off.'

Reaching behind Caroline's head, he untied the gag.

'This is how it's going to be, ladies. Caroline, you will lick and suck Carol for as long as it takes to bring her off. At the same time, Carol, you will perform this service for me. The object is for you and I, Carol, to receive a great deal of pleasure. You, Caroline, will reflect on the wisdom of your continuing silence on the matter you know I wish to discuss. At the same time, my darling, you should also consider the punishment which Carol is going to inflict upon you.'

Clive climbed on to the bed and knelt so that he was facing Caroline, with his knees on either side of Carol Davies' head.

'Now, I suggest that you get to it, ladies. If you fail to give satisfaction, Caroline, you should remember that you are in a very good position to be severely whipped.'

By moving her chin forward, Caroline discovered that she was in fact fairly easily able to lick at Mrs Davies' proffered bush. She was aware that Clive was watching her every move, but she didn't dare raise her eyes to his. Instead, she concentrated on giving her tormentress an orgasm that she would not quickly forget. Caroline wondered how Mrs Davies liked it now that she was the one tied down and helpless. However, as her tongue continued to lap at Mrs Davies' juices, she realised that the woman was indeed a very sexual creature; she liked sex in all its forms and was quickly able to adapt to circumstances and enjoy submission or domination with equal fervour. As if a light had been shut off, Caroline felt that Clive was no longer watching her. Surreptitiously snatching a glance at him, she saw that his eyes were closed and that his thrustings in and out of Mrs Davies' willing mouth had become more urgent. She couldn't still the little voice of jealousy within her as she saw the ease with which Mrs Davies was succeeding at her task. Caroline's tongue slid sensuously across Mrs Davies' engorged bud and she could not suppress a smile as she watched the housekeeper struggle to avoid coming before she had been completely successful with Clive.

'Come on, you bitch!' Caroline silently urged. 'Orgasm now! Leave your Master slightly less than satisfied.'

Caroline had her wish and Carol Davies bucked in the paroxysms of her orgasm, pulling against her fastenings as she moaned with pleasure. As Mrs Davies momentarily lost concentration on Clive, he opened his eyes and looked straight at Caroline with a look which told her that, again, he knew exactly what she had been doing. She tried to drop her gaze, but he wouldn't allow it. Again, she felt the all-pervading fascination that he held for her, the power of which constantly surprised her. Mrs Davies chose that moment to renew her efforts and, very slowly, his eyes closed as the housekeeper's tongue caressed the length of the shaft of his penis. Why was it, Caroline wondered, that even beneath the closed lids, she could feel his power? Would she ever be free of him?

Clive and Mrs Davies took their time in recovering, while Caroline remained in her uncomfortable position, the housekeeper's juices slowly drying on her lips. Clive got off the bed and, in a leisurely fashion, untied Mrs Davies before walking over to Caroline and stroking the cheeks of her exposed bottom.

'Uncomfortable, my darling?' he asked, smiling at

her. 'That's a pity, because I'd like to leave you like that for a little longer. It would be such a shame to waste the opportunity . . .' Clive let his voice trail off.

With a satisfied air, Mrs Davies came to stand beside Clive. 'I could cane her if you like, Clive,' she said, with the confidence of one who has just shared an intimate experience.

'Nice idea, Carol, but I have other plans for that delectable bottom before you punish it in the agreed fashion,' Clive said, his voice hardening to remind Mrs Davies not to abuse her new position.

'Of course, Clive, whatever you say,' Mrs Davies said.

'We'll leave her like that for the moment. I do need some time to – recover. Come and take a shower with me, Carol. I'd like to be very carefully washed,' Clive said, never taking his eyes off Caroline. He was reminding her that she was nothing but a slave and that he would decide what to do with her in his own good time. Caroline's arms were beginning to ache and she decided to risk asking Clive to let her lie down.

'Please, Clive, won't you at least tie me a little more comfortably while you are in the shower? My arms are really aching.'

Clive smiled and then bent to kiss her. Raising his head, he smiled at her so gently that she thought he would agree. He moved out of her line of vision and she waited for the expected release of her arms.

'Of course, my dear. We wouldn't want you to be too uncomfortable while we're in the shower, would we, Mrs Davies?'

'No, Clive, we certainly wouldn't,' Mrs Davies replied in a tone that should have warned Caroline.

She was attempting to turn her head to look gratefully at them when a hand came from behind her and a piece of tape was pressed firmly over her mouth. Clive's face appeared close to her own and he smiled as he smoothed the tape into position.

'There, that's better, isn't it?' he asked. 'Now you won't have to bother trying to scream. Much more comfortable, I'd say.'

By the time she was released, Caroline's arms were almost numb. Clive untied the sash and laid her gently on the bed, rubbing her arms to help restore the circulation. He bent down and kissed her gently, first on her taped mouth and then all the way down her body, pausing at her slit and teasingly pushing his tongue inside. The rope had also been removed from her wrists and she raised her hands to her face, intending to peel off the tape.

'I wouldn't if I were you,' Mrs Davies said, her voice a curt reminder of her presence.

Clive looked up and shook his head at Caroline. 'Such a naughty girl, Caroline. Time for your punishment, I think,' he said, pulling her off the bed. As her ankles were still tied, he picked her up in his arms and carried her over to the chair.

'Carol, would you like to sit here?' Clive asked.

Still naked, Mrs Davies moved to sit in the proffered chair. Clive laid Caroline over the housekeeper's lap.

'Hands behind you, darling, you know the drill,' Clive said, his voice rich with enjoyment.

Caroline put her hands behind her and Mrs Davies quickly tied them together with soft rope.

'That's better. She's obviously not going to be too helpful, Carol, so I think the gag can stay on,' Clive said, slipping fingers wet with his own saliva into Caroline's anus.

Mrs Davies reached beneath Caroline and painfully squeezed the girl's nipples as Clive ran his cock over the exposed buttocks.

'Tilt her a little, Carol. I didn't fuck her arse after our shower. I think this could be even more exciting.'

Mrs Davies obliged, drawing her knees up and tilting

Caroline so that her bottom was even more exposed and she felt the hardness of Clive's cock pressing against the tight little entry hole. Momentarily, she tensed and immediately Mrs Davies slapped her hard across her bottom, making her moan piteously. She felt so humiliated being fucked by Clive whilst laid across Mrs Davies' lap that she struggled a little and was immediately rewarded with another stinging slap.

'Her behaviour is deteriorating, Carol. Perhaps you had better punish her first,' Clive said, withdrawing his cock and kneeling in front of Caroline. He leant forward and kissed her.

'You'd better behave, my love. Mrs Davies is an expert at spanking wayward girls. She could keep going all night,' Clive said, his eyes piercing her with their intensity. He was obviously enjoying the situation. 'Proceed, Carol.'

'How many slaps, Clive?' Mrs Davies asked.

'Until I tell you to stop, Carol. That's fair, isn't it, my darling?' Clive fixed Caroline with innocuously enquiring eyes. He reached forward and caught her chin in his hand, forcing her head to move with a nodding motion. 'She agrees, Carol. Carry on.'

Mrs Davies' hand slapped down on to Caroline's bottom, making the girl jerk. There was to be no respite as the unyielding hand came down again and again, sending stingingly hot waves of pain through Caroline. Her eyes pleaded with Clive to no avail. He simply smiled at her and occasionally leant forward to kiss her tear-stained face. Caroline lost track of the number of slaps as the heat in her bottom inexorably increased. Suddenly, Clive tore the tape from her mouth and kissed her savagely while Mrs Davies continued to spank her. Incredibly, she felt her body responding, her own passion rising in response to his. Just as suddenly, Clive got to his feet and disappeared behind her. A firm hand on Mrs Davies' upraised wrist stopped the spanking. Clive grabbed Caroline's abused buttocks and pulled her back towards him as he plunged his cock into her anus. Mrs Davies grabbed Caroline's breasts and tweaked the nipples just sharply enough to trigger the girl's long-delayed orgasm. Clive continued to pound into her as she came, but it wasn't long before he tensed his muscles to cope with his own explosion. With the strength of his orgasm, Clive's grip on her buttocks increased and she cried out.

Mrs Davies clapped a hand firmly over Caroline's mouth, as she harshly whispered to the helpless girl, 'This is how it should be! Master Clive wants to keep you and I'll help him in any way that I can. You'll never be allowed to leave us, you slut! Never!'

Thirteen

Dressed in a figure-hugging black lycra catsuit, Lynne walked downstairs, idly speculating on the outcome of her proposed visit with Caroline. The front doorbell chimed and she shouted that she would answer it. Opening the door, she stood frozen with surprise, unable to find her voice.

'Well, Lynne, aren't you going to ask me in?'

Lynne managed to smile as she looked at the imposing figure standing on the doorstep. 'Liam . . . How . . ?'

Somehow she gathered her thoughts and stood aside for Liam to enter. The addition of a moustache since she had last seen him only added to his good looks. She floundered for something sensible to say. What did he know?

'Aren't you pleased to see me, Lynne?' Liam asked, with a slightly hurt expression.

'Oh, Liam, of course I am!' Lynne cried and threw her arms around him.

Liam's arms went round her and his hands followed the contours of her body as he appreciated the way she looked.

'I wonder if Francis knows how lucky he is?' Liam asked, just as the man in question came into view.

'Lucky about what?' Francis asked and, with a broad grin, returned Liam's fond embrace.

'Lucky enough to have such a beautiful wife that I am not sure you deserve,' Liam answered with mock severity. 'How are you, Francis? I reached my hotel in

Rotterdam to find the messages that had been received at various locations and forwarded on.'

'It's your own fault for failing to stay in any one place long enough to be contacted!' Francis returned, unable to hide the genuine affection he felt for this man. 'Why didn't you let me know that you would be globe-trotting on such a scale?'

Liam's smile faded. 'I wasn't aware of it myself when I originally set off,' he said.

'Look, this is no place to have a reunion. Why don't we go into the lounge and I'll get Alicia to make us some coffee. Have you had any breakfast?' Lynne asked, looking accusingly at Liam as if he had a tendency to skip the more important meals.

'I ate on the plane. Still a worrier, I see,' Liam teased, putting his arm around her.

They went into the lounge and Lynne rang the bell for Alicia.

'And how is the lovely Alicia?' Liam asked as he settled himself comfortably on the deeply padded beige leather couch.

'She's well and will be glad to see you,' Lynne answered.

As they spoke, Alicia knocked at the door and entered the lounge. Her face flushed with pleasure when she saw Liam.

'Coffee please, Alicia,' Lynne said and then smiled as she noticed the exchange of looks between Liam and the maid. 'Unless you would like something else, Liam?'

Thus addressed, Liam tore his eyes away from the sight of the pretty maid and turned to Lynne. 'Coffee will be fine, thank you ... at least for now,' he said, returning his gaze to Alicia and admiring the long, shining dark hair beneath her maid's cap and the long, luscious legs visible beneath the tiny skirt.

'Alicia, perhaps when you have made the coffee, you would like to join us?' Lynne said, her voice containing the hint of a question.

As Alicia curtsied, her eyes conveyed the answer to Lynne's unspoken question.

'What's been going on, Liam?' Francis asked as the door closed behind the maid.

'You knew that my businesses were in trouble?' Liam asked.

Francis nodded.

'When I visited the States, I realised that something major had been going on that I and my business advisors had been totally unaware of. Someone has been fraudulently transferring funds over quite a long period of time – hence the lack of detection. The businesses suffered in minor ways at first, but then the gradual build-up of the effect of loss of funds became noticeable. By the time it came to the notice of the accountants, the damage had been well and truly done. I've lost money and – more importantly – the confidence of the investors. I've been visiting as many of them as I could. They're sympathetic but suspicious. Without any hard evidence, I can do nothing to regain their confidence.' Liam spread his hands. 'I think I'm sunk, Francis. There's nowhere else to go.'

When Liam had finished speaking, there was a long silence while Lynne and Francis digested what they had just heard.

'I suppose I can't blame her for leaving . . .' Liam said slowly.

'Who?' Lynne asked sharply, although she knew.

'Caroline. I went home first, of course. She's gone – taken all her clothes. Didn't even leave a note. She knew I was in trouble and must have got wind of just how much.' Liam paused and then gave a low laugh, in which there was little humour. 'Even Mrs Davies has gone! That I'm not surprised about, but Caroline . . . I really thought . . .'

'Liam, you've got it all wrong!' Francis cut in. 'She didn't just leave you. She thought that she could help you . . .'

Now it was Liam's turn to interrupt. 'Where is she, Francis?' he asked, his voice taut with urgency. 'Have you seen her?'

'Yes, we both have,' Francis said. 'Don't explode, Liam, but she's with Clive . . .'

'Clive! That bastard! What . . . ?'

Lynne ran over to him and put her arms around him. 'Please be calm, darling. We'll tell you everything, but you must be calm. We have lots to tell you and plans to make, but not now. Look, Alicia is here now. Let's have some coffee and you can calm down.'

'All right, Lynne, but first tell me one thing. Caroline, is she OK?'

Lynne smiled and touched his face with a gentle hand. 'I promise you, Liam, she's fine. We're going to help you, darling. Francis and I will do everything we can. In the meantime, we want you to stay here with us, don't we, Francis?' She turned and looked appealingly at Francis, who immediately joined them.

'We insist upon it,' he said, putting his arm around Lynne.

Alicia set the tray down on the coffee table and poured the steaming liquid into four cups. Liam watched her as she moved, remembering the occasions when he had seen her in much scantier attire even than that which she was now wearing.

'How are you, Alicia?' he asked, deliberately brushing her hand as he took the cup from her.

'I'm well, Master Liam, and very glad to see you again.'

Liam smiled as his penis responded to the invitation. Francis and Lynne watched this exchange and Lynne then turned to Francis. 'I think, Francis, if you will excuse us, I will borrow Alicia and we will make up Liam's room.'

Francis smiled his acquiescence and looked meaningfully at Liam. 'Liam, I'm sure that you are very tired.

After Lynne and Alicia have made up your room, per-haps you would care for an early night?' Francis asked.

As it was still morning, Liam quickly caught on.

'Indeed, Francis. I am in dire need of some rest and relaxation,' he agreed.

Lynne moved to him and dropped a kiss on his fore-head. 'As soon as you're ready Francis will show you to your room. Alicia and I will ensure that everything is in readiness for you,' she said. She walked to the door with Alicia and the two women paused in the doorway.

'It will be a pleasure to serve you again, Master Liam,' Alicia said.

Lynne blew them a kiss and softly closed the door. Francis got up from his chair and retrieved two cups from the tray. Returning to Liam, he sat beside him on the couch.

'While we're waiting for your room to be made ready, Liam,' Francis said, 'I need to tell you a bit more about Caroline.'

'Yes?' Liam said and waited for Francis to continue.

'From what I can gather she is staying with Clive as part of some sort of bargain. Apparently, Clive knows something about your business problems and has prom-ised to help, if Caroline agrees to stay with him.'

'Is she all right?' Liam asked in a strained voice.

'She's well and she misses you, but . . .'

'But?'

'There's something about this Clive, something between them that I don't really understand. Originally, she agreed to stay with him in order to help you out, but now I get the impression that she is staying because she wants to.'

Francis was startled by Liam's laugh. 'That I can be-lieve. You never knew, did you, what led up to the break between myself and Clive?' Liam asked.

'No, I didn't know. It seemed to be quite sudden,' Francis said.

'When Caroline was living in my house, Clive exerted

his fascination over her. Between them, he and Mrs Davies made her look on Clive as the man she really loved.'

Reacting to Francis' puzzled expression, Liam waved his hand. 'You never knew Clive very well, Francis. When he wants to exert it, he has this strange power over people – men and women. He can make them say and do things that, under other circumstances, they wouldn't countenance. He wanted to mark Caroline really mark her. He was going to use a bull-whip on her before I stopped him. Francis, it was like she was in a trance. She didn't want to be hurt but she was going through with it because she knew that that was what he wanted.' Liam frowned at the memories. 'Oh, as soon as she knew what he was really like, she was horrified and very contrite, but there was still some residue of power left. I knew that, but I hoped that it would fade. We were so happy together then, even with Mrs Davies still around . . .'

'Mrs Davies!' Francis said with a scowl.

'Yes, Mrs Davies. Caroline felt sorry for her and begged me to let her stay,' Liam said.

'Dear Mrs Davies is very much in evidence at Clive's,' Francis said quietly. 'She seems to exert a great deal of influence in the household.'

Liam frowned, regretting that he hadn't followed his instincts and sent Mrs Davies packing with Clive. Well, it seemed that they'd got together anyway.

'Liam, please don't worry about it now. We have to try to find out what it is that Clive knows about your problems and then we can deal with him and get Caroline back.'

'She may not want to come,' Liam said. 'She once told me that she nearly asked Clive to take her with him when he was planning to leave.'

'Liam, there's three of us now – maybe four,' Francis said, looking at his friend.

'Four? Who else is involved?'

'Not yet, my friend, as Lynne said, we have plans to make, but first things first,' Francis said, pulling Liam to his feet. 'By your own admission, you are in need of rest and relaxation and, now that you have friends to help you, that is exactly what you are going to get!'

Somewhere between the lounge and the door of the bedroom to which Liam had been directed, Francis disappeared. Intrigued, Liam knocked on the door and was rewarded with a series of giggles and then a loud shushing sound.

'Come in,' Lynne called and Liam opened the door and went in.

Lynne was lying on the big double bed, naked except for a black leather G-string. Alicia was sitting demurely on a chair with her hands tied behind her.

'Well, ladies,' Liam said as he stood looking at them both.

Alicia was naked, her long dark hair flowing in loose waves across her shoulders.

'Francis thought that you might like some relaxation,' Lynne said, smiling at him.

'Francis?' Liam queried.

'Well, both of us. Francis has some work to do but he sees no reason for you to be kept waiting,' Lynne explained. 'Neither do I.'

Liam's cock stiffened at the obvious invitation. He had always liked Lynne and here she was available to him and with the consent of her husband.

'Alicia?' Liam asked, his eyes on Lynne.

'We thought that you might like to relieve some of the pressure by disciplining Alicia. She has been very naughty today, haven't you Alicia?' Lynne asked.

'Oh, yes, miss, I have,' Alicia confirmed.

Liam stood irresolute. The idea of chastising Alicia certainly held merit, but Lynne was also waiting.

'I can assist in the punishment, should you require,' Lynne said playfully.

'I think that would be just right,' Liam said, relieved at having the decision made for him. He started to remove his clothes.

'How would you like Alicia?' Lynne asked, getting off the bed and moving to the chair.

'I think she should be bent over the chair, her bottom appealingly presented for the cane,' Liam answered.

By the time he was completely naked, Alicia was bent over the chair in the desired position and Lynne was fastening a length of rope around the maid's slim waist.

'She is all yours, Master,' Lynne said as she finished securing the rope to the seat of the chair.

'Ours,' Liam corrected her.

He moved to the chair and stroked the white bottom so willingly presented.

'No marks,' he commented. 'You must have been a good girl, Alicia. When were you last caned?'

'A few weeks ago, Master,' Alicia said, trying to suppress sighs of pleasure at the gentleness of Liam's touch. 'My Master and Mistress have been very busy.'

Liam nodded as Lynne handed him the cane. He used this to stroke across the girl's arse and pushed the tip into the cleft between the cheeks of her bottom. Alicia struggled with pleasure, emitting little moans as she did so.

'The slave is quite noisy, Lynne,' Liam said.

'A gag, Master?' Lynne asked.

'I think so,' Liam answered as the tip of the cane slipped into Alicia's anus.

Lynne immediately tied a scarf over the girl's mouth. She tied the knot at the back of the dark head and then caressed the soft skin of Alicia's breasts.

'The slave is very wet,' Liam commented after he had inserted a finger into Alicia's slit. 'I think the caning had better be a severe one.'

Alicia wriggled in anticipation. Lynne moved to Liam

and put her arms around his neck. 'What should I do, Master?' she asked submissively.

Liam could no longer resist. He dropped the cane and gathered Lynne into his arms, pressing his mouth hungrily to hers. Lynne's mouth opened beneath his and their tongues entwined. Lynne felt her own arousal growing. She had always liked Liam and Francis had strongly supported her desire to comfort their friend. Only the muted sounds of protest from the prisoner brought them back to reality.

'First things first,' Liam said, laughing at Alicia's frustrated face.

Picking up the cane, Liam laid the first stroke across the white cheeks. There was a muffled scream from Alicia; born partly from pain but also from sexual pleasure. Lynne stood in front of her, letting her smell the mingled aromas of arousal and hot, moist leather.

'I have something better with which to gag her, Master,' Lynne said.

'An excellent idea, Lynne,' Liam said without pausing in his wielding of the cane.

Lynne pushed the G-string to one side, bent forward and pulled down the scarf which gagged the maid before pushing her shaven lips into Alicia's face. She moaned with pleasure as she felt the girl's tongue invading her slit, massaging her clitoris and nearly provoking an orgasm that had been steadily growing since she had tied Alicia's wrists together. Her eyes closed as she gave herself up to pleasure. Her climax was triggered in a most unexpected way, as Liam suddenly used the cane to lash her across the back of her thighs. She cried out with the pain, which fuelled her orgasm. From behind, Liam gripped her breasts and she felt the hardness of his cock pushing against the entry to her anus. Giving her consent, she pushed back against him and felt his cock slide into her.

'I always knew this was what you wanted, slut!' Liam shouted as he pounded into her.

'Liam . . .' she began, uncertain as to whether it would have been a protest or a cry of pleasure. She would never know, however, because Liam clapped a hand over her mouth and used his other arm to wrap tightly around her own arms, effectively imprisoning her.

'Slut!' Liam shouted again. 'Caroline! You slut!'

Lynne understood and struggled against Liam, more through her own reawakened arousal than through any form of protest. Alicia was still licking her as she came again, conscious of Liam's hot semen inside her rectum. Liam pulled her on to the floor and they lay still, wrapped together in sated exhaustion. Again, it was the sound of the groans of protest coming from the chair that aroused them. Smiling, Lynne attended to Alicia's needs, stroking the engorged clitoris only twice before the girl screamed out her pleasure.

Liam had risen from the floor and was seated on the bed after Lynne had untied Alicia and they had both joined him.

'Liam?' Lynne said gently.

Liam raised his head and looked at her. 'Lynne, I'm so sorry. For a moment I thought . . .'

'It doesn't matter, Liam. I know how you're feeling. Francis and I wanted you to be able to relax and shouting out her name like that was just what you needed. It really doesn't matter,' Lynne said, stroking the handsome features.

'I've said it before, Lynne, but Francis is a very lucky man,' Liam said.

'We're both lucky, Liam,' Lynne said. 'Now, I think that perhaps you and Alicia should spend some time together. I think Francis wants to give me some lessons.'

She stood up, settling her G-string into place.

'Lessons?' Liam queried.

'Yes. As you know, Francis has unlocked my submissive side to a certain extent. We're going to use that to good effect.'

166

Liam frowned in puzzlement. Lynne bent down and gently kissed the frown lines, before pulling back and smiling at him. 'You'll see her again, Liam,' she said. 'We're going to bring Caroline back.'

Fourteen

'Glad to have caught you in, Clive,' Francis said as he and Lynne were shown into the lounge by Mrs Davies. 'I've heard about a business opportunity that I think might be right up your street. As I had to bring Lynne over, I wondered if you might be free to accompany me.'

Not without suspicion at the suddenness of this 'business opportunity' but nevertheless reluctant to let anything which might be profitable slip by, Clive nodded his assent. 'Lynne will need to spend some time with Caroline, I presume?' he asked.

Lynne smiled. 'I would appreciate some "quality time" with the little slave,' she said.

'Then I think we had better leave you in peace, my dear,' Clive said. 'Francis, your kind offer is most gratefully accepted.'

'There is one thing, Clive,' Lynne said. 'I might need some assistance and would be grateful if Mrs Davies could remain with me.'

Clive smiled. 'An excellent idea, Lynne. Carol has proved herself to be invaluable in disciplining Caroline. I am sure that she will have no objection?' He raised his eyebrows questioningly in Mrs Davies' direction.

'I will be more than happy to be of service, Master Clive,' Mrs Davies responded formally.

'Then we'll see you two ladies later,' Clive said, ushering Francis to the door. 'I impose no restrictions on your treatment of Caroline, just be sure that you all enjoy it!' With this injunction, he smiled and closed the door.

After they had heard the sound of the front door closing, Lynne and Mrs Davies remained seated in the lounge. As the perfect housekeeper, Carol Davies awaited to be instructed to take Lynne to see Caroline. Being used to Lynne's rather forceful way of speaking, she was unprepared for the softness of the voice that eventually broke the silence.

'Mrs Davies – Carol – I'm glad that we are alone. Coming here to see Caroline was just a pretext. It's you that I really wanted to see.'

Astonished at the tone and content of Lynne's voice, Carol Davies widened her eyes as she looked at her visitor. 'Me, miss? Why me?' she asked incredulously.

'I know what you think of me, Carol. I know that I seem to be dominant and sure of myself, but I'm not. It wasn't until I met you and got to know you that I realised what I wanted . . .' Lynne let her voice trail off and dropped her eyes.

There was a silence, the length of which Lynne dared not break. She knew that she was gambling a lot on this woman's vanity and her desire for Lynne. At last, she dared to look up and then she knew that she had been right in her assumptions. Carol Davies was practically panting with lust as her eyes devoured Lynne. Submissively, Lynne looked away again. The sexual tension in the room was almost palpable.

'And what is it that you want?' Carol Davies' voice had lost its note of servility.

'I want . . . I want . . .' Lynne seemed unable to finish.

Carol Davies rose from her seat and went to sit beside Lynne. 'You can tell me, my girl. In fact, you had better tell me.' Mrs Davies' tone became forceful, although the fingers that stroked Lynne's hair were gentle.

Lynne turned to the housekeeper and clutched, apparently desperately, at Carol Davies' hands. 'Please, Carol . . .' She stopped as the housekeeper frowned at the familiar use of her name. 'I'm sorry . . . Mrs Davies,' she amended.

'Mistress will do,' Carol Davies said, gently pulling at Lynne's hair.

'Yes, of course, Mistress,' Lynne said, flushing prettily in a way that made Carol Davies' nipples harden.

'That's better. Now, my dear, tell me what your Mistress can do for you.'

With growing confidence, but also a real sense of fear, Lynne smiled at the woman she must now call 'Mistress'.

As the grip on her arm tightened, Lynne reminded herself that Francis knew where she was and that, in any event, Mrs Davies would not dare to go too far without Clive's permission. She had managed to convince the woman that she, Lynne, was serious in her desire to be dominated and treated as a slave by Mrs Davies. She had professed an admiration of the woman and her techniques, working on the woman's self-satisfaction and pride. Lynne had indeed succeeded and, as she was dragged down the stairs towards the cellar, she could only hope that she hadn't succeeded too well.

Lynne was pushed into a small room, whose only illumination came from a bare bulb suspended from the middle of the ceiling.

'Get undressed!' Mrs Davies ordered.

Not daring to hesitate, Lynne removed the soft leather dress that she wore, feeling just a twinge of resentment as the dress was torn from her hands and thrown across a rickety chair.

'On your knees, slave!' Mrs Davies ordered.

Now naked, Lynne obeyed, trying not to cringe openly as her knees encountered the rough wood of the boarded floor. There was silence as Mrs Davies walked around the shivering woman consideringly.

'Too cold for you, is it?' Mrs Davies snapped. 'Don't worry, my dear. I'll soon have you warmed up!'

The housekeeper stopped behind Lynne and used the toe of her shoe to push against Lynne's buttocks, indicating that she should spread her knees. Obediently, Lynne did so and was suddenly plunged into darkness as a scarf was tied across her eyes. She made a small cry of protest, only to be rewarded with a hand over her mouth.

'Keep quiet, my girl, or I'll have to gag you and I really don't want to do that yet,' Mrs Davies said, her tone betraying the level of her enjoyment.

Lynne felt the woman's breath against her face.

'No, my dear, I don't want you gagged just yet. There are a number of things that I want to know: for instance, why this sudden urge to be my slave?'

Lynne felt her arms being drawn behind her and soon felt rope securing her wrists together.

'You see, I'm sure that you thought you could fool me, didn't you? I don't know what you're after, but I want to be sure that you mean what you say,' Mrs Davies continued.

Lynne felt a surge of fear. Had she been hasty in her assumption of the woman's gullibility? If she were not to be believed, what might she expect from her captor? The idea was frightening and yet undeniably exciting. She felt her nipples harden as she became conscious of a wetness between her legs.

'Of course, Mistress,' Lynne said, turning her head towards the area that she imagined Mrs Davies to be occupying.

The world exploded into pain as a whip lashed across her thighs. Lynne crouched further down as she endeavoured to minimise the damage, knowing before Mrs Davies spoke what had been her error.

'I didn't give you permission to turn around, did I, slut?'

'No, Mistress. I deserve the pain and I thank you for inflicting it,' Lynne said, knowing the litany off by heart.

How often she had extracted such words from her own slaves!

'That's better. Do you know how I am going to prove your sincerity?' Mrs Davies asked, stroking the handle of the whip across Lynne's breasts.

Lynne had a fair idea, but pretended innocence. 'No, Mistress.'

She heard the sound of Mrs Davies kneeling in front of her.

'I am going to have to treat you as the commonest of all sluts and see how you react. If you are truly a submissive, you will enjoy this treatment. If, on the other hand, you are only pretending, you are in for the most humiliating and painful experience that you are ever likely to experience. I can be a very cruel Mistress, but I can also be very kind,' Mrs Davies said, gently pushing the whip handle between Lynne's legs. 'We can have a lot of fun together, but it is up to you. Convince me that you are genuine or be prepared to bear the pain which my anger, if justified, will force me to inflict upon you!'

Trying to ignore the burning sensation in her buttocks, Lynne adjusted her position to take the pressure off her knees. She was scrubbing at the wooden floor, trying to eradicate the stain which her own urine had left. Mrs Davies considered it good training for a slave to piss in public and to be made to clean up after herself. Lynne also tried to ignore the pulsating of her clitoris. So far she remained frustrated. She had to admit to a sneaking admiration for the woman who stood over her. The housekeeper certainly knew how to treat her slaves!

'That'll do!' came an imperious voice.

Lynne stopped scrubbing the floor and watched as Mrs Davies slowly walked around her.

'Next time, I might make you lick it up,' Mrs Davies said, stroking the whip handle across Lynne's face.

'It would be no more than I deserve, Mistress,' Lynne dutifully commented.

Her reward was a sharp tap across her back.

'You will speak only when spoken to!' Mrs Davies growled, relishing the reverse in their respective roles. There was a short silence, as though the housekeeper were carefully thinking.

'All right, slut! I am satisfied that your apparent conversion is a true one. No one of a truly dominant nature could have taken what you have. I will accept your service as my slave.'

Drawing a deeply reluctant breath, but knowing well what was expected of her, Lynne crouched down in front of Mrs Davies and touched her forehead to the floor.

'May I speak, Mistress?' she asked.

Mrs Davies stroked the whip down Lynne's back and smiled. 'You may, slut.'

'I live only to serve you, Mistress,' Lynne said submissively.

She became aware of the sound of Mrs Davies bending lower; felt the hot breath on her neck as she hoped that her meekness would result in the housekeeper allowing her some satisfaction.

'I think my little slave has earned some fun,' Mrs Davies crooned.

Lynne heard the housekeeper move away and then there was silence. After a while, she dared to raise her head and look around her. She saw Mrs Davies standing in front of a chair, as if assessing its suitability. Eventually, she turned towards Lynne and smiled.

'Come here, my dear girl,' the housekeeper invited.

Lynne felt she had come so far that a show of resistance was redundant. She got to her feet and walked towards Mrs Davies. When she reached the housekeeper, she was totally unprepared for being enfolded in a suffocating embrace. Mrs Davies' lips literally ravaged her own, but that in itself was sexually exciting. Lynne found herself responding and Mrs Davies tightened her grip. Carol Davies allowed her tongue to invade Lynne's soft mouth brutally. Lynne responded with as much energy as she dared, reminding herself that she was playing the submissive. At last, Mrs Davies pulled her mouth away and looked at Lynne. 'Sit in the chair, my darling,' she crooned and Lynne obeyed.

Lynne was not surprised to find her arms being drawn behind the chair. What did alarm her was the way that she was tied. Her wrists and elbows were drawn together and tied tight. More rope was securely tied around her waist and thighs and her knees and elbows were similarly pinioned. Lynne looked at Mrs Davies, unable to keep the concern from showing in her face. Mrs Davies stroked a gentle hand across her hair and face.

'There, there, my little girl. There's nothing to worry about. Mrs Davies is just going to make you feel good.'

Slightly, but not completely, reassured by these words, Lynne allowed herself to relax a little, until she saw Mrs Davies' next intention.

'No, Mistress, please . . .' Lynne began, but her protest was effectively silenced by the scarf which was tied over her mouth.

'You never say "no" to me, my girl!' Mrs Davies declared, standing in front of Lynne. 'I think you are forgetting yourself!'

Lynne was totally unprepared for the stinging slap across her face.

'There now, my dear,' Mrs Davies continued, again gently stroking Lynne's hair. 'You see what happens when you make me lose my temper.'

Mrs Davies gently stroked Lynne's body, going lower and lower until she reached her slit. Lynne felt herself responding, especially when Mrs Davies' tongue slipped between her nether lips. She forgot the discomfort of the restraining ropes and gave herself up to the sheer pleasure of the moment. She arched her body against the ropes as her pleasure grew. Mrs Davies seemed insatiable, letting her tongue lap at Lynne's clitoris and then her breasts. Occasionally, she stopped long enough to slap Lynne across her face, only exacerbating the woman's passion. Lynne felt her orgasm becoming unstoppable as she writhed against her bonds. She felt Mrs Davies' teeth grazing her flesh as the housekeeper nibbled at her breasts. Then, as the housekeeper's firm tongue once again invaded her slit, Lynne came swiftly and strongly.

Mrs Davies stood back and allowed Lynne to recover from the throes of her orgasm. 'There, my dear. Isn't that better? Mrs Davies knows what you need,' the housekeeper said. 'It's a pity that you're such a deceitful little girl.'

Lynne's eyes flew open. She looked at Mrs Davies, who returned the look with one of scorn, laced with pity. 'You didn't really think that you had fooled me, did you? I've seen you with that slut, Caroline. Always strong and enjoying your dominance. Your sort don't become submissive overnight. Perhaps you would like to tell me what you are really up to?'

Even though she was gagged, the question directed at Lynne was not a rhetorical one. Lynne tried to clear her thoughts. What could she say in her defence? Mrs Davies had seen right through her charade and further attempts at concealment were obviously useless; yet she certainly could not tell the woman the truth. It was important that neither Clive nor Mrs Davies knew of Liam's return. Raising her eyes, she shook her head. Mrs Davies walked over to her and slapped her across the face.

'Then I really think that Master Clive had better have a word with you, don't you, my little slave?'

'Ah, Carol. Is Lynne ready?' Clive asked. He was feeling very amenable. The project that Francis had introduced him to had definite possibilities as a real business proposition.

'I'm sorry, Master Clive, but madam left some time ago,' Mrs Davies answered, with the coolness of an accomplished liar.

'Are you sure, Mrs Davies?' Francis asked. 'The arrangement was that I was to take her home.'

'She asked me to apologise, sir. She said that she had something that she needed to do and would see you at home tonight.'

Mrs Davies looked meaningfully at Clive. With the barest hesitation, Clive put his arm around Francis.

'Typical woman!' Clive said jovially. 'Never can make up their minds. Thank you for letting me come with you today, Francis. I feel we can do some good business together.'

Francis shrugged and allowed himself to be propelled towards the door.

'I'll be in touch about that, Clive. Thanks for looking after Lynne, Mrs Davies.'

'It was my pleasure, sir,' Mrs Davies responded with sincerity. 'It's always a pleasure to look after madam.'

'All right, Carol. What's going on? Where is Lynne?' Clive asked as soon as the front door had closed behind Francis.

'Madam is safely locked up downstairs. I thought that you would want to talk to her before she went home,' Mrs Davies said, looking at Clive archly.

'And why should I want to do that?'

'She came here with a cock and bull story about wanting to be my submissive ...' Mrs Davies began, only to be interrupted by Clive's gasp of disbelief.

'Lynne? Your submissive? Carol, have you been drinking?'

Carol Davies looked thoroughly put out. 'Master Clive! You know I don't drink!'

Immediately contrite, Clive put his arms around her. 'I'm sorry, Carol, but this is all a bit of a surprise.'

Returning his embrace, Carol Davies relayed the day's events to Clive.

'You're sure that she is up to something?' Clive asked and then, seeing Mrs Davies' look of incredulity, nodded his head. 'Of course you're right. Such a conversion is far too sudden and unlikely to be genuine. Do you have any idea what she really wants?'

'No, I don't,' Mrs Davies replied. 'She really thought that she had me fooled for a while, but I've set her straight. I told her I would leave it to you to extract the truth from her and I've left her tied up nice and tight waiting for you.'

Clive bent his head and kissed the parted and waiting lips. 'Carol, you are indeed a treasure. You're a perfectly invaluable assistant.' Clive kissed her again. 'How is she tied?'

'I have her tied to a chair, Clive,' Mrs Davies answered, looking raptly up at him.

Clive nodded thoughtfully before looking intently at the housekeeper. 'Carol, I want you to do something else for me,' he said.

'Anything, Clive! You have only to ask!' Mrs Davies responded, her eyes clouded with obsessive passion.

'Take Lynne to my room and secure her to my bed.'

Concealing her disappointment as well as she could, Mrs Davies nodded. 'Yes, Clive, but isn't there anything else I can do for you?'

Clive looked into eyes that pleaded with him for a sign that Mrs Davies' passion was in some way reciprocated. 'Later, Carol,' he said, his eyes promising more than he was prepared to give. 'First, we have to deal with our guest!'

Lynne felt an unreasoning fear as she heard the key turn in the lock. She didn't dare to turn around as footsteps approached so she had no way of knowing who it was that tied the blindfold over her eyes. She could only be grateful as the unknown person released her from the chair. Her relief was so great to have the strain on her tightly bound arms removed, that she did not even mentally demur as her wrists were forcibly drawn behind her and a pair of metal handcuffs reaffirmed her captivity. If she had been able to speak, she would have asked if this was Clive or Mrs Davies and where Francis was. What had they told him and how long were they intending to keep her prisoner? In continued silence, she was pushed from the room. Cold wooden boards giving way to carpeting against her bare feet told her that she was being taken upstairs. The strong grip on her arm ensured that she concentrated on maintaining her footing, which left little room for further conjecture. She was aware of doors opening and closing and then she was pushed on to something soft. Her wrists were released from the handcuffs but she was allowed no opportunity for exploring her freedom before her wrists and ankles were drawn to the sides of the bed that she presumed she was lying on and there tied tight. In spite of the uncertainty of her situation, Lynne realised that she was sexually aroused. She strained her ears for some clue as to who it was that was so expertly tying her, but she was only able to pick up the sound of someone's breathing.

Suddenly, there was a deeper silence, which told her that she was alone. She struggled with her bonds, only to be confirmed in her guess that such struggling was pointless. At last, she lay still. She hadn't heard a door closing. Maybe the person who had brought her here was still in the room? Maybe she was being watched?

The voice that broke the silence was the more surprising because of the uninterrupted silence that had preceded it, giving no hint of the speaker's presence.

'Well, Lynne, I wonder what you're up to?' Clive said. 'Carol tells me that you appear to be unwilling to talk. I'm here to see if I can persuade you and you know just how persuasive I can be, don't you?'

Fifteen

Liam came out into the hallway as Francis unlocked the front door. Francis smiled, relieved to see that Liam was beginning to lose the haunted look that had seemed ever-present since he had learned about Caroline's defection to Clive.

'Hello, Francis. Successful day?' Liam asked.

'As it happens very. Is Lynne back?'

'Lynne?' Liam queried. 'No. I expected her to come back with you.'

Liam did not add that he had been hoping that there would also be a third member of the party.

'When Clive and I got back, Mrs Davies said that Lynne had already left. Apparently she had something to do.'

Liam knew Francis very well. As they went into the lounge and he poured drinks for them both, Liam shrewdly looked at his friend. 'You're not worried, are you?'

As he accepted the glass that Liam proffered, Francis shook his head. 'No, of course not. Lynne is a very independent woman. She's well able to take care of herself,' he said, although the frown remained on his face. 'I'm just a bit surprised, that's all.'

'Maybe she was upset that she didn't succeed,' Liam suggested. 'It was a little unlikely that Mrs Davies would fall for her suddenly submissive bit and follow her back here with Caroline in tow!'

Although he made light of it, Liam was disappointed.

Although, initially, he had expressed some derision at Lynne's plan, he had felt that anything was worth a try.

'Liam, Caroline cares about you. She proved it by going to live with Clive in return for his promise of help. She can't prefer Clive to you,' Francis said.

'Thanks, Francis, but you don't know Clive as well as I do. I saw the effect he had on Caroline before. She was ready to take an enormous amount of pain – because that was what he wanted. If he'd asked her, she would have gone with him. Clive is a user – but a very clever one. He has the ability to impose his will on people – and make them do whatever he wants.'

'That may be true, Liam, but not after all that Caroline now knows about him. She wouldn't . . .'

'Are you thinking of going into business with him?' Liam asked abruptly.

There was a silence while Francis thought back over the day's events. It was true that he had been impressed with Clive's business knowledge and the ease with which he had handled negotiations. Flushing a little, Francis looked at his friend. 'I have to admit that I am. Liam, the man is a business genius . . .'

'Believe me, I know,' Liam said, unable to keep the bitterness from his voice.

'Liam, I'm sorry. I don't mean to be insensitive, but . . .'

'Business is business,' Liam said and smiled. 'It's all right, Francis. I am well aware of Clive's talents and powers of persuasion. Once I've got my little problem sorted out, I might go into business with him myself.'

Francis stared at his friend.

'Why not?' Liam asked. 'He made me a lot of money before and I'm certainly not averse to letting him do so again.'

Francis remembered how Liam had bid for Caroline on the night he himself had lost her. Liam had not hesitated to keep Caroline, even though he had promised Francis that he would return her after only one night. Liam was not exactly a user, Francis reflected, but he knew what he wanted and would do whatever it took to achieve his aim. He hadn't let the long friendship between himself and Francis influence his decision on whether or not to keep what was once Francis' own treasured possession.

'What about Caroline?' Francis asked.

'Caroline? I am rapidly coming to the conclusion that I've lost her. I know Clive and I know that he wants her – just as I once did.'

'You had the money to pay for her, though, remember?' Francis said.

Liam finished his drink and smiled. 'I most certainly do remember. The money wasn't so important to me then. When I saw Caroline that night at your house, I wanted her. It was as simple as that. You could have named your price, Francis, and I would have paid it. When I took her away, I didn't expect to renege on the deal and not return her. There was something about her that made me know I had to have her, and she seemed to like me, you know,' Liam said, smiling at Francis as they both remembered. 'I thought we were happy together, even when there was that little episode with Clive.' Liam's face hardened as he remembered how he had stopped Clive from marking Caroline with a bullwhip. She had seemed to be besotted and it had taken a lot of persuading before she accepted the realities of Clive's personality. 'It wouldn't have taken much, you know,' Liam continued, looking at Francis. 'I know that originally she went to Clive from a desire to help me, but the bastard controls people; that's what he does best. I don't blame her.'

Seeing his friend's resignation, Francis sat beside him and put a comforting arm around his shoulders. 'We'll get her back, Liam. We don't yet know what success Lynne has had. Just don't give up on Caroline. Lynne's absence might well mean that she is working on a plan that we know nothing about. Let's just wait and see.'

Clive sat on the bed and began to run his fingers lightly over Lynne's helpless body. He had a fairly good idea of the thoughts that would be going through Lynne's mind as she lay in enforced inertness. She would of course be wondering as to his plans for her. She would be determined not to be unduly influenced or intimidated by him. Part of Clive was suspicious – certain that Caroline was at the root of her motive, whatever that might have been. There was, however, a far larger part of Clive's personality that responded with relish to this unexpected challenge. Lynne was a beautiful woman. She was also a dominatrix who had openly demonstrated her enjoyment of cruelty in his presence. Now the tables were well and truly turned. What delicious irony, Clive thought, that Lynne herself had instigated her present predicament. She had come willingly to his house and had expressed a desire to be a slave, albeit not his.

'Have you ever thought, my love, about the delightful vagaries of life? You came here today to be one person's slave and you have now been passed to me for my particular – attentions. How, I wonder, would Francis react if he knew where you really were?' Clive's tone was as soft and smooth as the most luxurious of ice-creams. 'Of course, when – and if – you are able to tell him, I wonder if he will be as entertained as I am?'

Clive stroked his fingers across her face, lingering at the blindfold and gag as if to emphasise his prisoner's helplessness. He had felt her muscles tighten when he had talked about her seeing Francis again. He had no intention of keeping her here, but he wouldn't tell her that just yet. He wanted her to mentally dwell upon the image of herself in prolonged bondage to him. He wanted her to imagine what her life would be like if she were to be kept in enforced slavery. Most of all he wanted to get the truth out of her, but he could wait – and in the meantime, he intended to have some fun.

'You see, my darling, if Francis comes back to me and reports that you have yet to come home, I will be the most concerned of persons. I will offer to help him in any way that I can during his search. I will invite him here so that we can plan out our search. How would you feel about that, my love? I would make sure that you were in the next room so that you could hear everything that was going on. Of course, you wouldn't be able to join in the discussion because you would be very securely tied and gagged. I would have Carol Davies look after and guard you. I'm sure that you'd like that, just as much as Caroline, wouldn't you, my love?'

Lynne struggled as much as she could against the restraining ropes, which had been expertly and very tightly tied by the housekeeper.

'Easy, my pet. Carol's ropes are not easy to loosen. In fact, struggling seems to make the knots even tighter,' Clive said, running his fingers over Lynne's bound wrists. 'You have such lovely skin, my dear, far too beautiful to mark unnecessarily.'

Lynne felt fear lodge in her throat: fear that she would never see Francis again; fear that she would become a slave to Clive and Carol Davies and a very real fear that she would lose control of her mind. She wanted to clear her mind and concentrate. She wanted to think of a way out of the mess she had got herself into. Overriding all of this, however, was her desire that Clive would not stop. His stroking fingers were evoking a sensuousness in her that would not respond to reason. She was glad that she couldn't see him: she was helpless and had been deprived of some of her senses, making her into a vessel of feeling that could do nothing other than respond in kind. Her nipples were hard and she wanted those stroking fingers to encircle them. She was wet and

183

her clitoris pulsed its need. She wanted to feel his lips sucking at the swollen bud. She wanted him to take the gag from her mouth and savagely kiss her. She knew that she wanted him to invade her mouth with his tongue. As Clive continued to stroke her body, Lynne reacted to each touch with exquisite sensitivity.

'There's something missing,' Clive said. 'Something is not quite right.'

She could feel him studying her. She wanted to scream at him to touch her again and she felt that he knew that and was inwardly laughing at her.

'Of course, I know what it is. Won't be a moment, darling,' Clive said and she felt him get off the bed.

There was no sound in the room. She strained her ears, trying to pick up the slightest noise, but there was nothing. She had never known frustration such as this. She made muffled pleading sounds through her gag as she twisted her head from side to side in a desperate attempt to dislodge the blindfold that obscured her vision. She could have had no idea that Clive was standing and watching her, smiling at her futile attempts. When he decided that she had had enough, he spoke softly close to her ear.

'I'm sorry that I've been so long, darling. I hope you haven't been too lonely.'

Lynne jumped inwardly at the sound of his voice. Where had he been? She hadn't heard him walk in or, for that matter, out of the room. She felt him sit on the bed beside her and then felt his fingers at her throat.

'Such a beautiful neck, darling, but so bare. Slaves should never have bare necks.'

As Clive spoke, he strapped a soft leather collar around her throat, buckling it at the back of her neck.

'There, that's much better, my love. Just another minute alteration,' Clive said, snapping a small padlock on to the buckle. 'I'm afraid that I don't have a key for that padlock, darling, but we won't want to take it off, will we?'

Before Lynne could react to his words, she felt his mouth close over her left nipple. As his tongue swirled around it, his teeth gently grazed the skin. Suddenly, she didn't care about the collar. She only cared about the feel of his lips on her skin and the knowledge that her own restrained position made it all that much more enjoyable. Clive kissed his way down her body, stopping at her vulva. He knew that her body was on fire with wanting, but he also knew that his own purpose would be better served if Lynne were to suffer further frustration and perhaps a little pain.

'Are you ready for some conversation, my darling?' Clive asked, moving back up the bed.

Lynne felt his fingers at the back of her head, untying the gag. As it came free, she felt his lips on hers and then his tongue pushing into her mouth. He drew his head back and she felt him looking at her.

'You are such a lovely woman, Lynne, but now you really have to tell me what your plan was when you came here today.'

Lynne didn't know what to say in response, but she knew what her body needed. 'Please, Clive. I'll tell you what you want to know, but first . . .'

'First?' Clive asked, with a note in his voice that should have warned her.

'Please let me come, please,' Lynne begged.

'Let you come? Why should I? You don't seem prepared to answer my needs,' Clive remonstrated.

'Please, I can't think when I feel this way,' Lynne said.

'I see. You need something to apply the mind, is that it?' Clive asked.

'Yes. If you'll let me come then I can think straight.'

Lynne thought that she had succeeded when she felt Clive move and then felt his tongue on her clitoris. She strained against the ropes as she felt her climax gaining in strength and momentum. Surely he wouldn't stop now? Clive did. He knew exactly when to stop to gain the maximum frustration.

'No, no, please . . .' Lynne began, before Clive's hand covered her mouth and stilled her protests.

'Carol! Get in here! I need you!' he yelled, before softening his tone. 'Perhaps we can both persuade you to cooperate.'

Hooded and bound with chains, Lynne was taken to the cellar room where she had spent some time with Caroline. She was made to stand against something solid and, from the feel of the rough wood, guessed that she was being chained to some kind of post. She could hear and see nothing. The all-enveloping leather hood was well padded and excluded all sound. She guessed that she was going to be beaten and was grateful for the fact that she could no longer hear Clive's seductive voice. She now realised what Caroline had been up against. She was still fighting her own frustration and almost looked forward to the expected pain of a whipping, which would surely stop her bodily craving for sexual satisfaction – at least from Clive's hands. Before the hood had been placed on her, she had had to undergo the humiliation of having her blindfold removed and seeing Carol Davies' eyes alight with the prospect of her pain and of Clive's obvious disfavour, into which the prisoner had fallen. Carol Davies had enjoyed putting the hood on her, strapping it behind her head. At least, Lynne then reflected, she didn't have to see and hear the woman.

After she had been chained to the post, Lynne was stroked and probed by fingers which were sometimes gentle and sometimes cruel. She could barely move at all and had to endure this delicious torment in enforced stillness. Whose fingers were doing what to her, she couldn't have said. All she knew was that she was continuously brought to the pinnacle of her climax before everything stopped. There was no touching and, to all intents and purposes, she might have been left alone: except she knew she had been brought here for a purpose and that purpose was her pain. It was agonising to have to wait in dark silence; not knowing if there was anyone near her and when the first stroke of the whip would land on her unprotected body. To her horror, she realised that she was wet with sexual excitement. She didn't want to be whipped and yet there was an undeniable excitement in the prospect. Perhaps there was more of the submissive in her than she had realised.

She became aware of a delicate touch, which gradually intensified. Something was stroking along the inside of one of her thighs. Was it the whip? She tried to imagine the pain. Who would be wielding the whip: Clive or Carol Davies? Her legs trembled as the tip of the lash was trailed up her back and across her shoulders. She was not aware that she was making moaning noises which elicited smiles from her tormentors. It seemed endless; the gentle stroking and sometimes the handle of the whip being inserted into her slit. She was back to where she had been, trembling on the verge of her climax and yet not enough to send her over the edge. Then even that was withdrawn and she was again left in silence. She decided that being in sensory deprivation was not something that she enjoyed. The uncertainty was bearable – even exciting. What was infinitely more difficult was the inability to see and hear; the not knowing whether she was alone or accompanied nor how long this was likely to continue. She became uncomfortably aware that her excitement and tension was having a very deleterious effect on her bladder. She had been chained with her legs slightly apart and so she did not even have the dubious comfort of squeezing her legs together. She realised that it would not be long before she had to undergo the humiliation of very publicly pissing. Knowing, however, that she had no choice, Lynne felt a huge relief as she gave way to her innate desire and let the warm liquid at first dribble and then cascade violently between her legs. The relief quickly gave way to a tense period of waiting. Surely she would be punished for her transgression? Gradually, Lynne became aware of the softness of a tongue licking its way up first one leg and then the other. It had to be Carol Davies. Surely it couldn't be Clive who was cleaning up her piss in such a very intimate manner. The tongue slowed each time it neared her clitoris. At each long, languorous stroke, she tensed as she felt the warmth of someone's breath against her skin. Surely this time she would receive gratification. Occasionally, the warm tongue touched her clitoris, making her knees buckle as much as they were able within the confines of the chains, but always the tongue then moved on, making her shiver with frustration. If only they would whip her. At least the pain would be something for her frustrated body to feed on. Was she always to be disappointed?

The licking stopped and she was again left alone. Now her frustration was growing untenable. She would go mad if something were not done to her. If only she didn't have the obstruction of the hood. She would scream and scream until someone helped her and relieved her aching need.

Suddenly, she had her wish. Fingers were busy behind her head at the lacings of the hood. She blinked as it came away and she had her senses restored to her. At first, she couldn't use them. The light was blinding her and there seemed to be a roaring in her ears. Before she realised that both problems had been caused by the sudden and unexpected restoration of her senses, she became aware of Clive's face, which seemed to fill her vision.

'Well, Lynne. We can keep this up all night. Can you?'

Sixteen

'Do you mean that you've kept my wife here all night against her will?'

Totally unflustered, Clive looked at Francis. 'Why don't you ask her that yourself?' he asked, looking in the direction of the lounge door.

Francis stood up and turned to see Lynne standing there. Her hair was loose and she wore a black satin robe. Her eyes looked tired and Francis ran over to her and folded her into his arms. 'My darling, I've been so worried. When Clive phoned and said that you were here but that you didn't want to return home until this morning, I thought . . .'

'Come now, Francis. We are friends and soon to be business partners. I never do that sort of thing to my colleagues,' Clive said, his tone as smooth and unruffled as a mill pond. 'As you know, Lynne came here of her own free will. It was only when her attempted deception was uncovered that I exercised my right to find out the truth.'

'Your right!' Francis yelled, turning to Clive and then advancing threateningly towards him. 'When does keeping someone prisoner come under the banner of a "right"?'

'Francis! It wasn't like that! Please listen!' Lynne pleaded with her husband.

Francis turned to her and saw that her eyes were full of tears.

'Are you all right?' he asked gently.

She nodded and Francis calmed somewhat.

'Please sit down, Francis. Lynne and I will explain everything over a drink. What will you have?' Clive simulated the perfect host with ease.

'Whisky, please,' Francis said. 'I think I need it.'

He resumed his seat on the couch and beckoned for Lynne to join him. Ever since he had received Clive's late-night call, he had been first concerned and then frustrated as he tried to puzzle out what might be happening. He had briefly spoken with Lynne over the telephone and she had reassured him that she was fine but that she and Clive had some things to discuss. Assuming that it concerned Lynne's plan to get Caroline back, he had discussed the matter with Liam. They had both decided that Lynne was probably better able to deal with the matter on her own and that, unsatisfactory as it appeared, they would just have to wait. Francis had arranged to pick up Lynne the following morning and had declined Liam's offer to join him.

'I think not, Liam. Clive is still unaware of your return and I think we should keep it that way until we hear what Lynne has to say,' Francis had said, with far more calm than he was actually feeling.

Now that he had been reunited with his wife and had seen for himself that she was indeed OK, he felt a return of his intense curiosity. Clive mixed their drinks and handed one to Francis. Lynne declined his original offer but, in any event, Clive pressed her to accept a glass of whisky. Having completed the formalities, Clive sat in a chair opposite them and sipped from his own drink.

'Well, is anyone going to enlighten me?' Francis enquired, looking from one to another of his companions.

Clive laughed apologetically. 'I'm sorry, Francis. I'm not sure where to begin.'

'You know why I came here, Francis,' Lynne suddenly said, taking the initiative. 'Clive knows that I came here to get Caroline back.'

Francis looked at her, trying to work out from the expression in her eyes exactly how much she had told Clive and whether there was any subtext to be deduced from her words. Deciding that a non-committal approach would be the best option, Francis sat back with an expression that told of his desire to listen.

'As you know, my intention was to persuade Mrs Davies that it was her who I was interested in so that she would come to live with us and I could persuade her to bring Caroline along with her,' Lynne said, her words tumbling out as if she wanted to say them as quickly as possible and have done with it.

'Yes, I know all that,' Francis said carefully, conscious of Clive's expectant gaze.

'Well, I didn't consider Mrs Davies' devotion to Clive. She played along with me for a while in order to find out what I was really up to,' Lynne continued.

Francis reached for her hand and squeezed it comfortingly. He felt her discomfort and just wanted to let her know that he understood.

'I wouldn't tell her what she wanted to know and so she . . .'

'Told me,' Clive finished for her. 'I must say, Francis, that I'm disappointed in you,' he said, returning his piercing gaze to Lynne's companion. 'I thought that we had begun to reach an understanding, you and I.'

'Clive, there are things of which you are probably unaware . . .' Francis began.

'Do you mean your original possession of Caroline?' Clive queried pleasantly. Rising, he went to the drinks table and poured himself another whisky. Turning back to them, he smiled at Lynne. 'I must say, my dear, that it was very remiss of you not to mention the full extent of your previous relationship with our darling Caroline. I had no idea – and as to your introducing your husband to me as if he had never seen Caroline before . . .' Clive shrugged his shoulders as though he could still not believe this fact.

Francis looked at Lynne. He still did not know exact-ly what Lynne had told Clive, but decided that it was time to take some of the initiative himself. 'OK, Clive. Cards on the table. Sure, Lynne and I had Caroline as our slave at one time and then we lost her to that bas-tard who called himself our friend for which, by the way, I will never forgive him. Then, by the strangest fluke, we get the chance to be reunited with her. Surely you can understand that it was too good an opportunity to pass up?'

Reflectively, Clive sipped his drink. As an expert gam-bler and a true master of the art of bluff, he could not avoid looking for the angles and deceptions in someone else's 'truth'. 'Who is this "friend"?' he asked.

Desperately, Lynne squeezed Francis' fingers. She hadn't mentioned Liam. Surely Francis was not going to.

'You know him very well, Clive,' Francis said coolly. 'You used to live in his house and you were once busi-ness partners.'

Lynne sucked in her breath. Well, he had done it now! She opened her mouth to speak, to try and repair the damage, but was disarmed by Francis' smile as he brought their entwined hands up to his lips and kissed her fingers. 'It's all right, darling. Clive might as well know the truth,' he said, warningly narrowing his eyes as he looked at her.

'Yes, of course you're right,' Lynne said and smiled at him to show that she understood.

It took Clive a few minutes to digest the latest infor-mation that he had received from Francis. Eventually, he raised his head and looked at him. 'Caroline has told Lynne why she is here?' he asked.

Francis nodded.

'And how do you feel about that?' Clive asked.

'A man who would treat my one-time friend as you did is someone with whom I would very much like to do business,' Francis said, looking at Clive with as much sincerity as he could muster.

For another few minutes, Clive kept his eyes fixed on Francis. It was almost as if he was trying to probe into the recesses of his companion's mind in order to elicit the truth. Finally, Clive stood up and walked over to Francis. He held out his hand and smiled. 'It will be a pleasure to do business with you, my friend.'

After a delicious lunch, served by an almost triumphant Mrs Davies, Lynne and Francis relaxed on the couch. Clive was not in the room, having excused himself in order to make some important calls. Unsure of the proximity of the treacherous housekeeper, Lynne and Francis kept their conversation light and general. Francis was aching to find out exactly what had transpired here last night and Lynne was equally desperate to know what plan Francis had for dealing with this new situation. Eventually, Clive returned to the lounge and sat in his usual chair facing them.

'Well, it's all sorted,' he said, smiling at Francis. 'We are in business!'

Francis and Lynne showed their pleasure at this news. Clive's eyes raked Lynne's now sexily-clad body. He felt a stirring of sexual desire as his eyes unashamedly travelled the slim length of her shapely body in all its PVC-covered glory. Francis didn't mind this open admiration of his wife. In fact, it made him feel proud of his proprietorship.

'There is one small problem, though, which you might be able to help me with,' Clive said, regretfully forcing his mind back to business matters.

'Anything, Clive, name it,' Francis said expansively.

'In order to get this business deal started, I will need to be away for two or three days. I would be grateful if you and Lynne could take care of Caroline for me – at your house.'

Lynne and Francis looked at each other, surprised beyond measure. Here was an unexpected and large bonus. Clive was asking them if they would mind doing exactly what they had been plotting and scheming for. They both looked back at Clive, unable to hide their delighted surprise.

'You know what Lynne intended and yet you are prepared to accede to what we want?' Francis asked.

'Not without a guarantee, Francis. I am a businessman used to risk-taking but always preferring the safe investment,' Clive answered. 'I intend to allow you to take Caroline with you this afternoon, provided that you also take Carol Davies.'

Francis' frown showed his lack of understanding of Clive's motives. Before he could ask any questions, the door behind him opened and a confident voice spoke to him.

'I will consider it a pleasure to join yourself and madam, Mister Francis,' Mrs Davies said.

Francis and Lynne both rose and turned to the door. Caroline was standing there, dressed in a figure-hugging black lycra bodysuit and a pair of black PVC boots. A chain was attached to the collar around her neck and Carol Davies had a very firm grip on the leash. The housekeeper was dressed in her usual black dress and she smiled in a slightly superior way at her intended hosts.

'Come in, Carol,' Clive said. 'You see, Francis, Carol is my insurance. You already have ample evidence of her devotion to me. She cannot be bought and I rely on her to give me regular and truthful reports. For instance, if you or Lynne were to attempt to take Caroline out of the country, Carol has immediate recourse to myself or – in an emergency – one of my associates. She will not allow you to do anything of which I would not approve.'

Francis looked at both Clive and Mrs Davies, before spreading his hands in an acknowledgement of defeat.

'As ever, Clive, I bow to your superior game-play. I believe that I speak for Lynne when I say that we will be delighted to look after Caroline pending your return.'

Clive bowed his head slightly and smiled at Lynne and Francis. 'One more favour, please. I would like to take my leave of my slave in private. Perhaps you would both like to go with Carol who will – look after you.'

Francis indicated to Mrs Davies that he and Lynne would follow her and the three of them left the room. Mrs Davies led them to Clive's study and offered to make them drinks. While she busied herself preparing these in one corner of the room, Lynne and Francis spoke in whispers.

'What are we going to do?' Lynne asked. 'When Mrs Davies sees Liam, she'll go straight to Clive.'

'Leave it to me, my love,' Francis reassured her, as he spoke keeping an eye on Mrs Davies. 'In the meantime, be very careful what you say. With Carol Davies "looking after us" Caroline may not be the only one under her watchful eye!'

Closing the door behind his guests, Clive turned to Caroline. She was standing in the same position as she had been when Mrs Davies had gripped the leash of her lead. Clive went up to her and, without warning, slapped her hard across the face, sending her sprawling to the floor.

'On your knees!' he yelled at her.

Sobbing as much from the shock of the slap as from any pain, Caroline did as she was told. Clive grabbed the lead that trailed from her collar and walked behind her.

'Hands behind your back!'

Again, Caroline obeyed. She was confused and frightened by Clive's attitude, but knew better than to question him. She felt the soft leather of the lead being wrapped around her wrists before being knotted into

195

place. Clive remained where he was and stroked the silkiness of her long hair. Slowly, he walked around to stand in front of her, but she kept her eyes lowered. Clive had several strands of her hair wound around one of his hands and he spent some moments looking at them.

'You are a very good slave, Caroline. I am very pleased with you,' he said.

Startled by the softness in his voice, Caroline looked up at him. Her reward was another stinging slap across her face. This time, his hold on her hair prevented her from falling. She gasped in pain as the hand in her hair became a cruelly twisting fist. He bent down and put his face close to hers.

'That was just a reminder, my love – not that you need one, of course – to be on your best behaviour. I need you out of the house for a few days. James is coming and he expects to see you. Because of my new business commitment with Francis, I shall explain to him that I had to make several unexpected trips away from home. I shall also explain that Mrs Davies had already asked me for permission to visit her daughter in the country. Being a very kind employer, I had of course acceded to that request. So, in all the circumstances, what else could I do but let my good friends Francis and Lynne take you to their place for a few days? I will inform Francis that on no account is he to let you see James. I will leave it to him to come up with a suitable excuse. A clever man, Francis. I'm sure that he won't let me down.'

Caroline could not have spoken, even if her fear of Clive had not already put an embargo on such speech. Her thoughts were too full of James and of how she was to be prevented from seeing him. Clive watched the play of emotions across her face and reinforced his grip on her hair.

'He's really got to you, hasn't he, my love?' Clive

asked, shaken by the depth of his feelings. He wasn't used to being challenged in this way and it made him angry at the person responsible. 'That's a pity because, as I think I've already told you, I don't like to lose. Having got you at last, I do not intend to let you go! So think on that, my love. Carol will remind you of it, if she sees that you are in danger of forgetting. She has my permission to chastise you as she thinks necessary. I have also told her to ensure that your sojourn away from me is such that you are longing to be returned to me. I can trust Carol; she will not let me down. Do you understand, my pet?'

Using the tight grip that he had on her hair, Clive brought her face closer until his eyes filled her vision. Gasping with the pain, both from his hold on her and the knowledge that she would not be able to see James, Caroline nodded.

'Good girl. Now, how about a farewell present for your Master, h'mm?'

As Clive spoke, he unzipped his fly and allowed his penis to protrude. It was already erect with a tear of fluid escaping from its knob. Knowing what was expected, Caroline opened her lips and took the stiffness into her mouth. At first, Clive was not gentle, thrusting hard into her until she almost choked. He was excited by the whole situation: the pretty submissive bound and kneeling at his feet taking her Master's cock into her mouth; the knowledge that, even when she was not with him, he had total control over her and the thought that other powerful men wanted her but could not challenge his ownership. As his passion took over, leaving no room for anger, Clive became gentler. Confident in the certainty of his mastery over her, he could afford to be magnanimous. He released his grip on her hair and stroked his hands down across her breasts, to be rewarded by the hardness of her nipples.

'You are such a little slut, Caroline. Your body

197

dictates your behaviour, doesn't it? No matter what you may think you want, your beautiful body can be played like an instrument. You were scared of me earlier, weren't you, little one? Not now, though. Now, you want me as much as I want you. Your body craves it and you can't get enough. What a perfect little sex slave you are!'

Caroline heard the words and knew that they were true. When Clive's hands were on her body, he could make her do whatever he wanted. She would do anything in the hope of a reward. Caroline's mind rebelled even as her body continued its slow climb to full sexual arousal. She wasn't like that! She wasn't that fickle! She started to shake her head to confirm her thoughts but, as though he could read her mind, Clive resumed his tight grip on her hair.

'No, my little darling. Don't let me down now. Come on, slut, suck me! Make me come!'

With his other hand, he again slapped her face. Instead of causing her pain, she was only aware of the increased pulsating in her clitoris that such treatment produced. As Clive became more excited, she pulled against her bonds, wanting to feel the inescapable tightness of the bindings. She licked and sucked hard on Clive's penis. She wanted to make him come. Surely, as her reward, she could expect reciprocal relief. Clive was pulling harder on her hair, but she didn't mind. It was further evidence of his excitement and the proximity of his climax. With his free hand, he sharply squeezed each nipple.

'That's right, my little darling! Oh, you're good! You're very good!'

Clive was almost yelling as he approached his climax. The grip on her hair was forcing tears to Caroline's eyes, but that only excited her. As she tasted the first drops of Clive's semen in her mouth, she renewed her fervent hopes that she would be allowed some relief herself. She greedily drank the warm fluid that flooded her mouth and was aware of Clive's urgent fingers rubbing against her swollen clitoris through the thin fabric of her suit. She opened her mouth and let Clive's penis slide from her lips as she cried out her pleasure. Clive pushed her to the floor as her orgasm overwhelmed her, making her hips buck against him as he lay on top of her. He waited until she had quieted and then gently kissed away the semen from her mouth.

'Remember, my love. There will be plenty more of this – if you please me. If you don't, well, we know what happens to errant little slaves, don't we?'

Caroline opened her eyes and looked at Clive. He was smiling, but, belying the softness of his smile, there was a coldness in the eyes that stared at her which left her in no doubt as to the sincerity of his words.

Seventeen

The journey home to Lynne and Francis' house was an awkward one. Caroline and Mrs Davies sat in the back seat. Lynne and Francis had noted the fact that Caroline's left wrist was handcuffed to Mrs Davies' right. Clive had obviously meant what he said and was not about to take any chances. Lynne and Francis sat in the front seats and, with Francis driving, could do no more than exchange troubled glances. Both were thinking the same thing. Liam was at home awaiting their return. He would certainly not expect to see them accompanied by Caroline and Mrs Davies and it was important that Mrs Davies was not yet made aware of Liam's return. As they neared their home, Francis pressed a number on his car phone which retrieved the stored number of their house. As Francis had hoped, Liam answered.

'Hello, Alicia,' Francis said. 'Thought I'd better ring to let you know in advance that we will shortly be home and that we are bringing two guests. Please ensure that the spare rooms are made ready. See you soon.'

Francis hung up and glanced at Lynne. He could only hope that Liam would realise that Francis had made a deliberate mistake and that it would be better if he were not around to greet them on their return.

As the car turned into the familiar driveway, Caroline swallowed hard. In a way, it was like coming home, but so much had happened since she had last been here and so much now was unresolved. She didn't know what to expect, but she knew one thing with absolute certainty.

Somehow she had to make contact with James, and she had to do it soon.

Francis removed the key from the front door lock and called out loudly that they were home. Lynne followed him inside as did Caroline and Mrs Davies, the latter being the only one not to have been in the house before. She looked around with curiosity.

'Well, Mrs Davies,' Francis said, relieved to find that his call had obviously done the trick, 'welcome to our home. I hope that you and Caroline will both be very comfortable here.'

'I am sure *I* shall, Mister Francis,' Mrs Davies said. 'As for the slave, well, her comfort should not be of concern to you.'

Caroline looked desperately uncomfortable with Mrs Davies' response to Francis' politeness. She remembered how she had stood in this very hallway, dressed in a sheer plastic cape, as she waited to be taken away by Liam. She wondered where he now was and hoped that he was OK. Clive still maintained that he would keep his promise and save Liam's businesses and reputation and she believed that, through James, she could enforce the keeping of that promise – if only she could make contact with James. As she thought of this, she looked at Mrs Davies, the seeds of an idea beginning to germinate in her mind.

'Lynne, perhaps you would go and see Alicia to make sure that she has prepared the guest rooms,' Francis said, hoping that his wife's usual quick uptake was still in good working order. Turning to Mrs Davies, he ignored her earlier abuse of his good manners and tried again. 'Mrs Davies ... or may I call you Carol?'

'Mrs Davies will do, sir. I am here for one purpose only and that is to look after Master Clive's property. I suggest, therefore, that we observe the usual formalities.'

Suitably chastened and also fairly annoyed, Francis changed his tone. 'Then may I offer you some refreshment – if not for yourself then perhaps for your prisoner?'

Realising that she and Caroline were likely to be here for several days, Mrs Davies moderated her attitude somewhat. 'Certainly, sir. That would be much appreciated.'

Francis showed them into the lounge and poured a whisky for himself, a mineral water for Mrs Davies and an orange juice for Caroline. As he pressed the drink into Caroline's hand, he took a few seconds to gently massage her fingers before sitting on a chair opposite to the couch on which the two women sat.

'Now that we're safely inside, Mrs Davies, would it not be sensible in terms of comfort for you both to remove the handcuffs?' Francis asked conversationally.

Mrs Davies bridled. 'She is in my charge, Mister Francis, not yours. I will take the necessary action when and if I deem it to be appropriate.'

Well, well, thought Francis. It certainly is a truism that a little power can go straight to some people's heads!

'I appreciate that, Mrs Davies, but . . .'

'There are no buts, Mister Francis!' Mrs Davies retorted. 'As I said, *I* will make the decisions regarding the slave . . .'

Francis had had enough. He banged his glass down on to the coffee table and stood up. As he advanced angrily towards her, Mrs Davies shrank back into the couch.

'Kindly remember, Mrs Davies, that you are in my house. Whilst that situation continues, *I* will make the decisions as to the comfort of my guests, not you! I suggest that you remove those handcuffs right now!'

Mrs Davies scowled at him, but complied. As the cuff was taken from her wrist, Caroline looked gratefully at

Francis who, ignoring Mrs Davies' outraged glare, bent down and kissed her gently on the lips. Straightening, he looked challengingly at Mrs Davies. 'Caroline and I are old friends, Mrs Davies, and perhaps it would be as well for you to remember that – especially as you are under my roof.'

He had the satisfaction of seeing Mrs Davies drop her eyes and look distinctly uncomfortable. Having established some ground rules, Francis resumed his seat feeling a lot happier about the new arrangement.

Lynne found Liam in his bedroom. He was lying on his bed and did not look up as she entered. She sat on the bed and took one of his hands in both her own. He looked so tired and drawn that she felt an aching sadness in empathy with his state.

'She's here, Liam,' Lynne said softly.

'I know. I was watching from the window.'

There was a silence. At last, Liam turned to face her. 'I also saw Mrs Davies. What's she doing here?'

'Liam, we've got Caroline back – with conditions,' Lynne said.

'What conditions?' Liam asked.

'Clive had to go away for a few days on business so it suited him to let us bring Caroline back, provided that Mrs Davies came, too.'

'As a sort of wardress?' Liam asked, his voice heavy with sarcasm.

'Liam, at least she's here. We must find a way to let Mrs Davies know that you're back. If she can be persuaded not to tell Clive . . .'

'Persuaded!' Liam shouted, swinging his legs over the side of the bed. 'I have to persuade my former housekeeper not to tell my former business partner that I'm back?'

Lynne put a placatory hand on his shoulder. Liam shook it off and then turned to her, his face distorted with rage. 'No, Lynne, I'm sorry! I'm not going to play dead! I'm going to see Mrs Davies right now! She can do what she likes!'

He jumped to his feet and stormed from the room. Lynne ran after him, fearful of the consequences of his action.

'Where is she?' Liam demanded as he reached the bottom of the staircase. 'In the lounge?'

Without waiting for an answer he wrenched open the lounge door and stood on the threshold, his anger momentarily stilled as he saw Caroline. Everyone in the room seemed to be frozen as in some kind of tableau. For a few seconds, no one spoke. Almost on tip-toe, Lynne slipped past Liam and joined her husband on the couch.

Caroline slowly rose to her feet, her eyes wide with surprise. Liam started towards her and then stopped as Mrs Davies also rose and gripped Caroline's arms meaningfully.

'Things have changed, Mister Liam,' Mrs Davies said. 'This slave belongs to Master Clive now and I am here to make sure that that situation remains unchanged.'

Liam scowled at Mrs Davies and pushed her away from Caroline. 'I don't give a fuck why you're here, Mrs Davies. I want to talk to Caroline in private and neither you nor anyone else is going to stop me!'

Mrs Davies opened her mouth to protest, but Liam knocked her back on to the couch.

'Caroline, I believe there are things that we need to discuss!' Liam said, grabbing the startled girl by the hand and almost frog-marching her from the room.

'Liam, please listen . . .' Caroline pleaded, attempting to rise from the chair into which Liam had angrily pushed her.

'Shut up!' Liam yelled, pushing her back down. He had dragged her to his bedroom and seemed in no mood to listen to her pleas.

'Liam, I know that you're angry, but ...' Caroline tried again as she rose from her seat, but Liam turned on her furiously.

'Yes, I'm angry ... You can't know how angry I am!'

'Please listen to me,' Caroline begged, but Liam was not in a listening mood.

'Sit down, you filthy little slut!' he yelled at her.

Shocked at his treatment of her, Caroline merely stood and stared at him, infuriating him further. Pushing her forcibly back into the chair, he looked around and saw a bathrobe hanging on the back of the bedroom door. Grabbing the belt, he pushed Caroline to the floor and used the belt to tightly tie her wrists together behind her back. Grabbing her ankles, he forced her into a bow shape by tying them to her bound wrists.

'Liam, please! You're hurting me!'

'Not half as much as you've hurt me, slut!' Liam growled.

'I only tried to help you,' Caroline said, choking back tears.

'By going to your old boyfriend and begging his assistance! Oh, yes, my love, I've heard all about it! You just couldn't wait, could you? Was it very difficult for you having to live with me whilst you plotted with your boyfriend behind my back?'

'Liam, Clive isn't my boyfriend! I didn't know and didn't care where he was until Mrs Davies said that he could help you!'

Liam administered a stinging slap across her face. 'You are a lying little slut! You might have been able to fool Lynne and Francis, but did you really think that you could try that on with me?'

'Liam, please listen to me! I'm telling you the truth!'

Liam saw the thick leather belt that she wore around her slim waist. Swiftly unbuckling it, he pulled it from her. Caroline screamed at him as she realised his intention. 'No, Liam! Don't ...!'

The rest of her protest was muffled as the belt was wrapped tightly over her mouth and then buckled at the nape of her neck. Liam then stood in front of her as she struggled helplessly. Coldly, he stripped off his clothes before kneeling almost casually in front of her and putting his hands in the neck of her suit. Ignoring the pleading in her eyes, he balled his hands into fists and ripped the flimsy fabric all the way to her crotch. Having done that, he got to his feet and stood over her. She saw that he was fully erect and, in spite of the circumstances, the sight excited her. Liam watched her nipples hardening and spat out his words. 'You slut! That's all you want isn't it? When I wasn't here to supply it, you went out and found another source! Was he good, slut? Did he make you feel good?'

Desperately, she shook her head. Liam turned to his discarded jeans and pulled the belt from them. He wrapped the supple leather around his hand, watching her as he did it. Even in his anger, he was careful to position the silver buckle in the palm of his hand so that it would not strike her flesh. Reaching down, he pushed two fingers into her slit, which was revealed between the torn shreds of her suit. Bringing them out, he sniffed them, smiling coldly at her.

'Ready for it as always, slut! It excites you, doesn't it, being tied and being beaten?' Liam asked, unfurling a length of the belt. 'Best quality hide,' he said, studying the leather. 'Only the best for you, my love. You deserve it!'

As he said this, he tore the rest of the suit away from her body and then contemplated her nakedness. He had almost forgotten how beautiful she was and the thought made him even angrier. An image which he couldn't dismiss filled his mind: the image of Clive fucking her. To shut that image out of his mind, he started to hit her with the belt. His strokes were methodical, sometimes on her bottom and sometimes on the front of her thighs. Her muffled cries pleased him. She wouldn't be thinking of Clive now! As the beating continued, both of them became more and more sexually aroused. As Liam threw the belt away from him and lay on top of her, he wondered if she hadn't been gagged whose name would she be shouting – his or Clive's? He thrust into her, biting her nipples as his excitement neared its peak. He knew that Caroline was very near to an orgasm and he was strangely pleased. He found himself in a mental competition of his own making. He would make her feel better than Clive had ever done and he would get her to admit it. Somehow, he would make sure that Clive knew it, too – knew who was best. He screamed out Caroline's name as he climaxed and felt her complementary shudders beneath him. On this occasion at least, he had won.

Passion and anger spent, Liam released Caroline. She buried her head in his shoulder, sobbing out her sorrow. 'Liam, I'm so sorry. I shouldn't have gone to Clive, I know that now, but I wanted to help you.'

She raised her head and looked at him. 'You're wrong about me wanting to go with Clive just because you weren't here. I honestly hadn't seen him since you ordered him out of the house six months ago! I swear it!'

Tenderly, Liam brushed her tears away with gentle fingers. 'I believe you, Caroline. It was just seeing you again and knowing where you'd been. I'm the one who's sorry, darling, but it really doesn't matter now, does it?'

Alarmed, she looked at him. 'What do you mean it doesn't matter?' Caroline asked.

'Mrs Davies was right when she said things are different, Caroline. It's not your fault or mine. It's just circumstances.'

Caroline looked at his familiar face, wanting to feel the stirrings of old feelings. She stroked his face, knowing that, for whatever reason, those feelings had gone. What they had just experienced was a mutual lust engendered by their separation. She couldn't expect Liam to forget about the time she had spent with Clive and, even though he knew nothing about James, he sensed that she was different. Not for the first time, Caroline wondered about her apparent lack of faithfulness. At one time, she had really loved this man. She still cared for him – but not in the same way. How could her feelings have undergone such a tremendous change?

Liam looked at the intentness of her gaze and smiled. He stroked her cheek with his finger. 'You are looking particularly fierce, my love,' he chided gently.

'Introspection always does that to me. I look inside and don't always like what I see.'

Liam folded her into his arms, knowing that he still cared deeply for her but also realising that something very precious had gone from their relationship. As he held her, he almost felt that he was saying goodbye to her. He felt sad, but not as devastated as he might have expected. Perhaps, because he had been mentally preparing himself for this, the ending was not so abrupt as he might have feared.

'What now, Liam?' Caroline asked.

'We are still friends, Caroline – good friends. I always look after my friends. If you want to go back to Clive, I won't try to stop you,' Liam said. 'Clive and I have a lot of things to discuss. I understand that, as his hold over you, he promised that he could help me. I want to find out just how he thinks he can do that.'

Caroline shivered at the mention of Clive's name. With some concern, Liam looked at her. 'What is it, Caroline? Are you afraid of Clive?'

'I'm not sure. I'm afraid that he won't let me go,' Caroline said. She couldn't tell Liam about James. That would hurt him too much and she had already done enough of that.

'You have nothing to fear from Clive,' Liam said, holding her close. 'You're not alone now, Caroline. You're among friends who will help you.'

Caroline looked at Liam, desperately wishing that she still felt the same about him, but knowing that that was impossible. Liam did not know that Clive was a much more powerful man than when he had known him and he also didn't know how strong Clive's powers of persuasion really were. She looked at Liam with love and gratitude in her eyes. He had been through so much. Now was not the time to tell him of her fears. She needed to contact James and Mrs Davies was her only hope.

'Liam, until we know how Clive can help you, I think we should keep Mrs Davies sweet.'

Liam looked at her in surprise. 'Mrs Davies? Why?'

'She is supposed to report to Clive regularly. If she doesn't he'll know that there's a problem. If you apologise to her . . .'

'Apologise to Carol Davies? You're mad!' Liam said, looking incredulously at her.

'Liam, be sensible! Until you know what information Clive has that can help you, you need to pretend that there is no question of my not being returned to Clive.'

Liam thought about this for a while before turning to her. 'And is there?'

'What?'

'No question of your not being returned to Clive?' Liam asked with a seriousness that made her long to be totally honest with him.

'I don't know. I don't know what I want. Clive can be – irresistible when he wants to be.'

'I know. Remember that I've seen him at work,' Liam said.

Caroline turned to him knowing that he was referring to the time when he had interrupted Clive just as he had been about to savagely mark her – with her consent. She returned to him and put her arms round him.

'Both of us will never forget that,' Caroline admitted. 'I have to be able to make a decision about whether or not I go back to him free of any pressure from him or anyone.'

Liam smiled and kissed the tip of her nose. 'All right, my sweet. It shall be as you desire. I'll make peace with the old dragon and let her make her reports – on one condition.'

Caroline frowned. 'What condition?'

Liam laughed and put his hand down to cover her vagina.

'For old times' sake?'

Liam walked into the lounge with Caroline following behind. Her head was bowed in a suitably submissive posture. Mrs Davies cringed back in her seat as Liam walked towards her. She was not more amazed than Lynne and Francis when Liam held out his hand to her.

'Carol, I owe you an apology.' He had difficulty in refraining from laughing as he watched conflicting emotions chase across the housekeeper's face.

'An – an apology, Mister Liam?' she eventually managed to say.

'Yes. Caroline has told me the whole situation. I'm sorry that I jumped to conclusions. Of course you have the care of Clive's slave and you were quite right to be angry with me. When I came back and realised that Caroline wanted to be with Clive and not with me, I guess I just lost it. I'd be grateful if we could forget all about it.'

Cautiously, yet not wanting to appear truculent, Mrs Davies put her hand in Liam's.

'Thank you, Mrs Davies. I will return Caroline to your very capable care,' Liam said, standing to one side and gesturing Caroline forward.

Caroline stood in front of the housekeeper, carefully keeping her eyes lowered. There was a silence, during which time she felt Carol Davies' eyes raking her from head to toe. Deciding that now was the time to begin her campaign, Caroline respectfully looked at her wardress. Her authority fully restored, Mrs Davies looked unflinchingly at her prisoner until Caroline turned her back and put her hands behind her. Smiling with satisfaction, Carol reached forward and snapped the handcuffs on to her wrists.

'I think you are due for some punishment, don't you?' Mrs Davies said, gripping Caroline firmly around her arms.

Raising her head slightly, Caroline flashed a look of gratitude at Liam before again bowing her head and nodding her assent.

'Perhaps someone could show us to our rooms?' Mrs Davies enquired.

Always quick on the uptake, Lynne rose from her seat and went up to Mrs Davies. 'I can do better than that, Mrs Davies. Perhaps you would like to take your little slave to our dungeon? You will find all that you need for whatever punishment you have in mind.'

Mrs Davies inclined her head. 'That would be very kind, Miss Lynne,' she said, prepared to be magnanimous now that she was getting her way.

'Not at all, Mrs Davies. Perhaps you need some assistance?' Lynne offered.

Caroline held her breath. She needed to be alone with Mrs Davies.

'Thank you, Miss Lynne. Maybe later. Right now, I need to have a formal one-to-one chat with the slave,' Mrs Davies said, tightening her grip on Caroline in order to leave her in no doubt that the conversation would be a painful one.

Eighteen

Lynne led the way down the stone steps. Caroline was glad to feel that there was no decrease in the warm air. When she shivered, it was with the knowledge of what she had to do.

'Here we are,' Lynne said. 'I think that you will find everything you need.'

Mrs Davies looked around. 'This will be perfect. Thank you, madam,' the housekeeper said, keeping a firm grip on Caroline.

Remembering Liam's face when she had seen him in his room, Lynne could not help feeling that Caroline was going to get her just deserts. Smiling, she walked over to a rack along one wall which displayed an array of whips and selected a thin riding crop.

'As your hostess, I hope you will allow me to show you one of our best implements,' Lynne said, as she returned to stand beside Mrs Davies. 'I have found that the use of this crop achieves the desired result. Please feel free to use it and any other item that you may find here.'

Mrs Davies took the crop and appreciatively ran her hand across the smooth surface. 'Thank you, madam. This will be fine.'

'If she gives you any trouble, Mrs Davies, don't hesitate to call on me,' Lynne said, allowing herself a vindictive glance at Caroline before ascending the steps and leaving prisoner and captor alone together.

Caroline felt tears sting her eyes as she realised that,

once again, Lynne was blaming her for the situation with Liam. She found that this knowledge merely strengthened her resolve. Mrs Davies was indeed the only person she could turn to in order to get in touch with James. Taking a deep breath, she turned to the housekeeper, who was still admiring her surroundings.

'Mrs Davies ... Mistress?' Caroline began.

With some annoyance, Carol Davies looked towards Caroline. 'What is it, slave?'

'Can – can we talk ... Please?'

Mrs Davies was intrigued at the pleading tone in Caroline's voice and at her strange request. She was also very excited to be in a real honest-to-goodness dungeon, albeit one without the expected cold stone walls, dripping with water. The walls were indeed of stone, but central heating had very obviously been installed. By twentieth century standards, despite the iron-barred cell and, arrayed around the walls, various instruments capable of restraining and inflicting pain upon transgressors, this dungeon was really a surprisingly comfortable place to be – especially when one was in control!

'If you are going to plead with me for leniency, it would be as well for you to save your breath. Master Clive has put you in my care and he would expect nothing less than the administration of severe discipline,' Mrs Davies said, tapping the crop against the heel of one hand as she spoke.

Caroline fell to her knees before the unyielding form of her captor. 'Please, Mistress. I have been longing to talk to you for some time. I need you to know that I –' Caroline swallowed. She was finding this harder than she had expected but, if she were to see James, she had to continue. Mrs Davies was looking at her expectantly. '– I love you,' Caroline finished. It was not hard to accompany her words with a look of wide-eyed sincerity. She desperately needed to succeed.

Mrs Davies looked incredulously at her. Liam had dressed her in one of Lynne's short rubber dresses before he brought her back downstairs. Mrs Davies had to admit that it was a very pretty sight indeed to have such a beautiful penitent, her hands cuffed behind her, kneeling at her feet.

'You love me? I don't believe it!' Mrs Davies said, although her voice clearly indicated that she would like to.

'Please, Mistress! Give me a chance to show how much I adore you,' Caroline pleaded.

'In what way could I do that?' Mrs Davies asked, although her mind was already supplying the answer.

'Humble me! Beat me! Humiliate me! Whatever you want, Mistress. Only let me love you – please.'

Mrs Davies used the tip of the riding crop to lift Caroline's chin. 'Why should I believe you? What's brought on this sudden display of devotion? What is it that you want?'

'Nothing, Mistress, except to serve you. All the time that I've been the slave of a man – Francis, Clive, Liam – they've all used me and then discarded me. Except you. You've never discarded me. You've always been there for me. I haven't always been a good slave to you, I know that, but things will be different. If you'll let me serve you, I'll show you how different things can be!'

Mrs Davies looked at Caroline. She wanted to believe her, like she had wanted to believe Lynne when she had also professed such a desire. That one had proved to be a scheming little liar. Why not this one? 'I want to believe you, but . . .' she said, before Caroline resumed her pleading.

'Punish me for all the times that I've ignored or offended you. Maybe that will make it all right,' Caroline begged, feeling an unexpected sexual arousal at such a prospect.

The idea also showed its merits to Mrs Davies, who

leant forward and kissed Caroline gently on the lips, then pulled away and looked at her. Seeing the same look of pleading sincerity in the slave's eyes, she dropped the riding crop and fell to her knees in front of Caroline. Putting her arms around the helpless girl, she kissed her savagely, brutally pushing her tongue into the girl's mouth and delighting in her response. Both women were excited when she pulled away and looked at Caroline.

'I'm going to punish you for all the wrongs that you have done to me. You know that, don't you?' the housekeeper asked, her mouth salivating at the prospect.

'I would welcome it, Mistress,' Caroline said with more than a little meaning behind her words.

Mrs Davies looked around until she caught sight of two heavy iron rings suspended from the ceiling. In her excitement she quickly got to her feet, dragging Caroline with her. Pulling the girl toward the rings, she grabbed some rope from one of the shelves close by and feverishly unlocked the handcuffs. With a fierce grip, she held Caroline's wrists in front of her while she positioned the girl beneath the rings. Looping the rope through them, she forced Caroline to rise on to the toes of her bare feet as she tightly tied each wrist to the corresponding ring. She knotted the ropes so tightly that she made Caroline gasp with surprise, but merely smiled at her slave. 'If you want to serve me, my girl, you won't always be comfortable! You'd better get used to that!' the housekeeper said, her voice thick with sexual passion and excitement.

'I am here to serve you, Mistress,' Caroline whispered submissively.

Mrs Davies finished tying the ropes and then invaded Caroline's mouth with her tongue, squeezing the girl's nipples as she did so. Impossibly aroused, Caroline responded. Flushed with excitement, Carol Davies tangled a hand in Caroline's hair, pulling the girl's face close to her own.

'I'm going to test you out and you'd better not be lying to me, you little slut!' Mrs Davies warned Caroline and then released her grip on Caroline's hair before retrieving the riding crop. She walked behind Caroline. Nothing happened for a few moments as Mrs Davies pulled up the short skirt of the rubber dress and then studied the marks left by Liam's belt on the white flesh.

'I am glad to see that Master Liam has not lost his touch,' Mrs Davies commented. 'It gives me something to try and improve upon, doesn't it?'

The question was obviously rhetorical and Caroline did not attempt to reply. She stood in silent anticipation of the first stroke. Instead, she felt the riding crop being gently stroked over her buttocks. In spite of the discomfort from her tied wrists and the fact of the enforced teetering on her toes, Caroline felt her muscles relaxing. The stroking was extremely sensuous. Not for the first time, she wondered at Mrs Davies' amazing ability to stimulate and excite her. She drew in a startled breath as she felt the intrusion between her legs, but automatically parted them a little wider to allow the riding crop greater access to her slit. The crop brushed her sensitive clitoris and she gasped with pleasure. From behind her, Mrs Davies reached forward and stroked her left nipple. Within her bonds, Caroline swayed with the exquisite feelings flooding through her.

'Oh, Mistress, that feels so good,' Caroline whispered.

'Pleasure before the pain, my darling,' Mrs Davies said.

Caroline could not tense her muscles. The intoxicating power of her sexual arousal would not allow for it. Abruptly, the crop was pulled from her, but the expected stroke was not delivered. Instead, Mrs Davies appeared before her half-closed eyes. The housekeeper was smiling as she thrust the crop between Caroline's teeth.

'Something for you to bite on, my darling,' Mrs

Davies said. 'I think you deserve to be whipped, don't you?'

With the crop jammed between her lips, Caroline could not make a verbal reply, but she could tell that a response was expected. Slowly, she nodded her head and Mrs Davies leant forward to kiss her.

'That's a good girl. I know what Miss Lynne said, but I think there is nothing to equal the pain of the whip, don't you agree?'

Again, Caroline nodded. Mrs Davies appeared to be satisfied and lowered her head to suckle Caroline's nipples, making the girl want to spit out the crop and beg for Mrs Davies to bring her off. As if she had read her prisoner's thoughts, Mrs Davies raised her head and looked warningly at Caroline. 'I would advise you not to attempt to remove your gag, my dear. If you do, I will only replace it with something which is a lot more uncomfortable.'

For the first time, Caroline noticed the whip that Carol Davies held in her hand. It had a very thick leather handle and she certainly had no desire to have it thrust between her lips. Mrs Davies smiled as she perceived that her message had properly registered. She didn't, however, walk away from Caroline but started stroking the whip across the girl's breasts. Caroline swallowed. She could taste her own juices on the leather of the crop between her teeth and that, coupled with the strands of leather brushing sensuously across her breasts, caused an increase in the juices between her thighs. Mrs Davies was obviously conscious of this, too. She chuckled as she looked at Caroline, before drawing the whip strands down Caroline's body until they slithered over her naked pubis. 'You are such a naughty girl, aren't you?' Mrs Davies asked.

Caroline nodded as the housekeeper's face pressed closer to her own.

'Naughty girls such as you need to be punished, don't they?'

Again, Caroline nodded. This was a game and she knew that she had to play her part well if she was going to achieve her object. Besides, she knew that she wanted Mrs Davies to beat her. Such was her arousal that she believed that it would only take one or two strokes of the whip to bring her to the orgasm she really needed.

'Then I'd better see to it, hadn't I?' Mrs Davies said and disappeared behind Caroline.

The first stroke was such a shock to her system that, even though she had been expecting it, she opened her mouth wide as she yelled. She felt the crop dislodge from her mouth and heard the clatter as it dropped to the floor. She was too busy dealing with the waves of stinging pain that pervaded her buttocks to be concerned about her failure to retain the crop in her mouth. She was returned to full reality when an abusively large rubber ball-gag was forced between her lips and strapped tightly behind her head.

'Disobedience will not be tolerated, my girl!' Mrs Davies shouted at her, although the smile of enjoyment on her face belied the anger of her words. 'Now you will really have to be punished!'

The next stroke of the whip caught her between her thighs, making her clamp her legs together in order to try and ride the pain but also to prevent a recurrence. Mrs Davies would not let her get away with that, however, and forced a wooden leg-spreader between her legs and strapped the ankle-cuffs attached to each end of the implement tightly around each ankle. She then stood in front of Caroline. 'You will find, my girl, that I will not tolerate disobedience or the placing of obstacles in my path. Any such actions from you will result in very severe punishment. Do you understand?'

Caroline could only nod helplessly. Now she knew that Mrs Davies would make a point of whipping her on that most sensitive area between her thighs. She tried to twist her wrists within their bindings, but only succeeded in being reminded of just how tightly she was tied. She was correct in her assumption as she discovered when Mrs Davies resumed the punishment. The next four strokes were rhythmically delivered to the insides of her thighs in meticulous rotation. Caroline's yells were effectively muffled by the large rubber ball strapped into her mouth. She found, however, that the fourth stroke was not as painful as the others because she was learning how to ride the pain and turn it into sexual pleasure. Mrs Davies saw the change in the writhings of Caroline's body and guessed the reason. She increased the severity of the lashes; first across Caroline's buttocks and then across the backs of her thighs. Breathless with excitement, Mrs Davies dropped the whip and ran to stand in front of Caroline as the girl twisted against her bonds with the strength of her orgasm. Mrs Davies dropped to her knees and greedily suckled the juices seeping from Caroline's sex. The feel of those avaricious lips on her clitoris made Caroline orgasm again and again until she felt that she could no longer stand it. When Carol Davies removed her mouth from its delicious watering place, she sat back and licked her lips. Caroline sagged within her bonds, until the pain in her arms reminded her to straighten up. Mrs Davies got to her feet and walked around Caroline, smiling with pleasure at the marks which she had inflicted. She resumed her position in front of the girl.

'I want you to do something else for me now, my darling girl. Let's just untie your poor wrists from these rings. I'm sure that you'd like a rest, wouldn't you?'

Relieved and exhausted, Caroline nodded.

'Then I think that you'd better lie down, my darling, and I know just the place,' Mrs Davies said as she removed the leg spreader and untied the ropes securing Caroline's wrists to the rings. She caught the girl as she fell, her legs unable to support her satiated frame.

'I hope that you're not too tired, my darling girl,' Mrs

Davies said solicitously. 'We haven't finished yet, you know. Not by a long way!'

Only half-aware of what was going on, Caroline was helped across the floor of the dungeon by Mrs Davies. She was urged to lie backwards on to some form of wooden support. It was only when Mrs Davies was spreading her arms outwards and at an angle from her body that she realised what was happening. She remembered the existence of the bondage cross from a previous visit she had made to the dungeon when she had been living in this house and being used as a slave by Francis and Lynne. She knew she was right when Mrs Davies strapped her wrists tightly to the wood, using the leather cuffs that Caroline had seen before. Moving further down, Mrs Davies made her spread her legs so that her ankles could be strapped to the bondage cross. Finally, Mrs Davies drew a thick leather strap across Caroline's waist to secure her even more firmly. When she had finished, Mrs Davies used the winch to raise the cross to an almost vertical position. The bondage cross consisted of pieces of wood shaped into an X, to which a prisoner could be strapped, as Caroline was, or with the head inverted. It could also be rotated. Caroline looked down at Mrs Davies and saw that the woman was smiling, apparently well pleased.

'You look very pretty, my dear. There is something that I want you to do for me, but I can see that you need your rest and I do so want you to be refreshed for what I have in mind. I'm going to leave you for a little while then, my dear, to let you get some sleep. In any event, although this dungeon is very well equipped, there is something which I need that doesn't appear to be here. I'll see you soon, my love,' Mrs Davies said and blew her a kiss.

Caroline tried to speak, but the ball-gag only allowed the feeblest of whimpers to issue from her mouth.

'No, no, my love. Don't strain yourself. Just get some rest and I'll be back soon,' Mrs Davies said, before turning and climbing up the stone steps.

Caroline's weariness deserted her. She spent a few minutes struggling against the straps that bound her to the cross, but it was a wasted effort. The straps had all been very securely buckled and there was no way that she could escape from her restraints. She sighed as she remembered that, in any event, she didn't want to escape. She needed Mrs Davies to believe that she truly desired to be her slave. Caroline swallowed to try to ease the dryness in her throat. She wished that she had not lost her hold on the riding crop. The ball-gag was stretching her mouth in such a way that it made her jaws ache. Caroline wondered what it was that Mrs Davies had in store for her. At least the aching need between her thighs had been satisfied but, even as Caroline thought this and pondered on what else she might be able to expect, she became aware of further stirrings in her clitoris and knew that it would not take much to fully arouse her again.

She did not have long to wait. She heard footsteps descending the stone steps and twisted her head as Mrs Davies came into view. She went immediately to the winch and returned the cross to a horizontal position. As she was winched lower, Caroline saw that there were chains looped over the housekeeper's shoulder. Caroline looked at them with interest because they were quite delicately wrought, but she soon discovered that the delicacy of the links hid a solid strength. Mrs Davies apologised for her absence as she unwound the chains and proceeded to tie them across and around Caroline's breasts.

'There, they do look as nice on you as I thought they would,' Mrs Davies said, moving further down with another length of chain. 'Are you quite comfortable, my dear?' She asked and then looked up. 'Oh, silly me. Of course you can't speak. Never mind, it's for the best, my dear. You won't be tempted to say something silly, will you?'

Caroline moaned her frustration into her gag. Surely Mrs Davies wouldn't keep her gagged all the time? She needed to be able to speak to the housekeeper.

'Now, I think you'll look very pretty with some chain around your waist and in your cunt, don't you?'

Caroline watched as Mrs Davies wound some of the chain over the waist-belt and then down between her legs where it was pulled tight before it was brought back up behind and secured to the waist-belt. Mrs Davies adjusted the chain between her legs so that it was pressing against her clitoris. She looked at Caroline almost conspiratorially.

'We don't want that slipping out, do we?' she asked and then inserted two fingers into Caroline's slit. 'Yes, very pretty and plenty of room for you to perform for me.'

Surprisingly, Mrs Davies unbuckled the straps that secured Caroline's wrists. She smiled at the girl's evident confusion. 'It's all right, my dear, I haven't gone quite mad. You can't possibly reach the straps at the back of your waist-belt and, with that still in place, you cannot reach down to unstrap your ankles. Besides which, the chains are very strong and are padlocked, of course.'

Mrs Davies moved closer to Caroline's head and kissed her gently on the mouth. At the same time, she pushed something into Caroline's hands. Drawing back a little, she smiled almost sympathetically at Caroline as she wound a further length of chain over the girl's mouth, firmly imprisoning the ball-gag in place. Caroline heard the snap behind her head as a padlock was locked into place. The message was clear: her hands might be free but it was Mrs Davies who would decide when and if the gag were to be removed.

'Now it's time for your little entertainment, my dear. I want you to bring yourself off while I watch.'

She moved away and operated the winch, again bringing the cross to an upright position. Caroline looked down at her hands and saw that it was the riding crop which had been thrust into them. Helplessly, Caroline watched Mrs Davies, who had dragged a chair in front of the cross and was obviously waiting for her to begin. Caroline felt herself blushing with embarrassment. In spite of all that she had been through, she found the idea of bringing herself off in front of this woman to be a totally humiliating one.

'Begin, my dear. I think I'd like to see you play with yourself first,' Mrs Davies said, in a tone of voice that clearly indicated she would not be denied. 'You are my slave, my dear, and you said that you would do anything for me,' she continued, angry at Caroline's continued hesitation. 'Now begin! I think I'd like to see you play with your nipples. Do it now!'

Hesitantly, Caroline tucked the crop into the belt at her waist and then touched her hands to her nipples, almost jumping at their extreme sensitivity. Her face burning, she stroked the burgeoning hardness, conscious of the intensity of Mrs Davies' eyes upon her and of her own sexual arousal.

'Now push the chain to one side so that you can stroke your clitoris, my dear,' Mrs Davies said. Caroline could see that the woman's eyes were glittering.

Caroline did as she was told, pulling the chain so that it moved slightly, enough for her stroking middle finger to arouse her further. Mrs Davies leant forward in her chair, almost as if that would urge the girl to greater efforts.

'Keep stroking your clit like a good little girl,' instructed Mrs Davies. 'Use your other hand to take out the crop.'

Caroline extracted the riding crop from the waist-belt and opened her eyes.

'I want you to fuck yourself with the riding crop,' Mrs

223

Davies ordered and, as Caroline looked into those implacable eyes, she knew that she had to obey.

Caroline felt an excitement overcoming her embarrassment at the idea of fucking herself in front of this woman. Slowly and sensuously, making a real performance for her audience, she began to push the riding crop into her vagina. Now the fingers that were busy at her clitoris increased their speed. She could no longer hold the housekeeper's gaze and closed her eyes as the delicious sensations of her approaching orgasm overwhelmed her. She was only vaguely aware of Mrs Davies urging her on in a tone of rising excitement. She was conscious of her own needs alone as the rhythm of her stroking fingers matched that of the crop as she manipulated it inside herself. Had she been able to think clearly, she might have known that Mrs Davies was masturbating to her own climax. She might even have taken a pride in the fact that it was the skill of her own performance which was responsible. All she knew, however, was that she was being carried on a huge wave of orgasmic feeling which came crashing down with bewildering force.

Caroline realised that someone's hands were releasing her from the restraints which had held her so tightly. When the gag was removed, she sucked in a deeply cleansing breath of air. She felt drained, but pleasantly so. As she opened her eyes, she managed a smile at Mrs Davies, which was not returned. The housekeeper's eyes were glittering with sexual excitement. She ran her hands over Caroline's body, which was now soaked with the sweat of her passion.

'Your dress is sticking to you, my darling,' Mrs Davies said. 'It makes you look even sexier and much more delicious. You have performed well for me and I am pleased with you. There is only one more test that you need to undergo and, if you are successful, then I will be satisfied.'

Now fully alert, Caroline struggled to sit up. She realised that she had not even been aware of Mrs Davies returning the bondage cross to its horizontal position.

'Mistress, I will gladly do anything that you may ask of me,' she said.

Mrs Davies leant forward and kissed her. 'You have received a lot of pleasure, my darling?' she asked.

Caroline nodded. 'Oh yes, Mistress, more than I deserve,' she responded fervently.

'Good. Then I feel that it is my turn, yes?'

Caroline knew that this might have been expected and, yes, it *was* fair enough. She was feeling warmly satisfied and it would certainly not hurt her to give Mrs Davies some pleasure in return.

'Yes, Mistress. It will be an honour,' Caroline said, reaching forward with the intention of undoing the buttons of Mrs Davies' dress.

'No, no, no, my love. Don't be so impatient. There is plenty of time and I want to tell you what I would like you to do for me,' Mrs Davies said, rising from where she had been sitting perched on one corner of the bondage cross.

'Of course, Mistress. Please forgive my impatience,' Caroline said and lowered her eyes.

Mrs Davies reached down and helped Caroline to stand. 'Now, my darling, Mrs Davies will tell you what she has in mind,' the housekeeper said, stroking Caroline's hair. 'Sit down on the chair and I will tell you what it is that you are to do for me.'

Immediately, Caroline sat on the chair so recently vacated by Mrs Davies when she was watching her slave's performance. Mrs Davies came up behind her and continued stroking the long, blonde hair.

'You have such beautiful hair, my darling. It is a pleasure to own a slave such as you. Now, I'm just going to tie your hands and blindfold you.'

Obediently, Caroline put her hands together behind

her back and soon felt the rope that was being used to secure her wrists being tied tightly. A dark cloth of some kind was used to cover her eyes as she sat quietly waiting to be told what it was that was expected of her. She heard Carol Davies walk around to stand in front of her. She heard the sound of clothes being removed and dropped to the floor. She felt the warmth of a body close to hers and then felt something soft being rubbed against her lips. Realising that it was one of Mrs Davies' nipples, she opened her mouth and sucked on the increasing hardness which was obligingly pushed between her lips. She did not pause in her sucking as Mrs Davies outlined to her what she wanted.

'I have a great need, my love, to feel those delicious lips of yours sucking at my clit and bringing me off. I also have another very pressing need which you can also attend to. I need to relieve myself and I want to do that over your pretty little face.'

Caroline stopped what she was doing before she inadvertently bit on the nipple in her mouth. She heard a quickly indrawn breath and knew that she had made a mistake.

'You never have liked that, have you, my darling slave? I had thought that perhaps you would now have such a desire to please me . . .'

Caroline, horrified at the coldness in Mrs Davies' voice and at how close she had come to completely wrecking her own carefully laid plans, slid off the chair and knelt at the housekeeper's feet.

'Please, Mistress, I'm so sorry. I was just . . .'

The cold voice interrupted her. 'What were you just, my little slave?'

'I was just so thrilled to be able to serve you in this way, Mistress. The honour took me by surprise.'

Caroline held her breath as she waited for Mrs Davies' response. Had she gone too far? Perhaps even Carol Davies would not be taken in by such an obvious attempt to appeal to her gullibility. She felt the stroking hand again in her hair, but couldn't relax until she heard the resumption of warmth in Mrs Davies' voice.

'You are indeed a very good little slave. You have passed the final test.'

Mrs Davies was urging her to rise and Caroline did so.

'Mistress, do you not want me to serve you in this way?' Caroline asked.

'There is no need, my dear. By your willingness, you have proved your loyalty.'

Caroline hesitated, but only fractionally. Mrs Davies was offering her an out but she knew that it couldn't be taken. Because of the enormity of what she intended to ask of Mrs Davies, she had to prove herself beyond doubt.

'There is a need, my Mistress. I want to make you feel good and I would consider it an honour to be allowed to serve you in this way.'

The stroking stopped and then Caroline felt the touch of lips on her forehead.

'My darling child, you really have changed. You are prepared to do this for me, even though I've told you that there is no need.'

Mrs Davies' voice was so full of gratitude   humility almost   that Caroline felt a twinge of guilt. She was deceiving this woman in the worst possible way.

'Mistress, I really want to do this for you.' Caroline said and was surprised to find that she really meant it. In view of her plans, it was the least that she could do.

'Sit on the chair then, my love. There is no need for you to be uncomfortable.'

Mrs Davies gently helped Caroline to sit on the chair and then stood before the willing girl. 'Thank you, my darling. No one has ever been so good to me,' she said, so softly that Caroline had to strain to catch the words.

Caroline leant forward and used her tongue to find

the fleshy slit and the pleasure bud within. She reminded herself that this was all in a good cause – albeit a very selfish one – and applied her tongue and lips in the best way she knew to elicit maximum pleasure. As she licked and sucked, she was on her guard for the first sign of the stream that she knew was to come. Initially, it was disguised within the increased juices that Mrs Davies was manufacturing, but soon there could be no doubt as to the identity of the liquid that filled her mouth. Caroline used every ounce of her willpower to stop herself from gagging and pulling away. She had to pretend that she liked and wanted this and, worse, she had to drink it. She was grateful for the blindfold; grateful for the ropes that bound her wrists and grateful for the hand that tangled in her hair and forced her head to remain in position. She tried to think of James; tried to picture his face and remember the feel of his hands on her skin: but there was only the reality of the pungent liquid filling her mouth and spilling over her chin to run in warm rivulets down over her rubber-clad breasts. The stream ended at last and she felt the hand in her hair tighten and the muscles of the woman's pubis contract as she climaxed, screaming out her pleasure. Caroline was glad that she had done this for the woman who had made her feel so good and whom she was so cruelly about to deceive.

Nineteen

'Hello, my name is James Ogilby. I believe that a friend of mine is staying here and I'd like to see her, please.'

Lynne stared at the stranger. He was handsome with a cultured American voice. He was dressed in a well-cut business suit and conveyed an impression of friendly good manners with an underlying strength.

'The name of your friend?' Lynne asked.

'Her name is Caroline and I believe that she may not be a totally willing guest,' James answered with engaging frankness which may have had a lot to do with the fact that Lynne was a very beautiful and, dressed as she was in her usually sexual way, desirable woman.

Painfully conscious of the fact that her nipples were erect and very obviously so as they pressed against the thin latex of her black dress, Lynne found herself momentarily flustered. 'I'm not sure . . .'

'However I am,' James interrupted, fixing her with a piercing gaze that did nothing to hide his admiration – and determination.

Not trusting herself to say any more, Lynne stood aside to allow James to walk into the hallway.

'You have a lovely house,' James said, looking appreciatively around him.

'Th – thank you,' Lynne murmured, wishing desperately that Francis were here. 'Would you like a coffee, or something stronger?'

'Coffee would be very nice, thank you. Do I take it that my information is correct?' James asked pleasantly.

'Information?'

'Yes, I had a telephone call from Mrs Davies. You know her?' James was enjoying himself. Now that he knew Caroline was here, he could afford to relax a little and play whatever game this lovely woman had in mind.

'Mrs Davies. Yes – yes, I know her. She's here too. I'm afraid that my husband is away . . .'

James moved quickly towards her and folded her into his arms, kissing her firmly on the lips.

'Was that really necessary?' he asked as he released her.

Almost breathless with surprise at the stranger's audacity and not a little perturbed by the feelings he had aroused within her, Lynne straightened her dress. 'What?'

'The information that your husband was not at home. If that was an invitation, I enjoyed it. If not, then I apologise for my mistake.' James smiled as he regarded her discomfiture. He was not unused to having this effect on women.

Lynne flushed and decided that the best course would be to avoid answering. Mrs Davies' appearance at the top of the stairs gave her the excuse that she needed.

'Ah, Mrs Davies. This gentleman is looking for Caroline,' Lynne said, trying to recover her poise.

'Mr Ogilby?' Mrs Davies asked as she descended the stairs.

'Yes, Mrs Davies,' he replied. 'I believe that I have you to thank for identifying Caroline's whereabouts. I am most grateful.'

Mrs Davies was wearing one of her uniform black dresses. She studied James Ogilby from the bottom step of the stairway. She could see why Caroline had so wanted her to contact this man on her behalf.

'I would like to speak with you in private – if that is possible?' Mrs Davies asked, looking to Lynne for confirmation.

Highly intrigued, Lynne had no hesitation in granting the request. 'Certainly, Mrs Davies. You can use the lounge and I will ensure that you are not disturbed. I am not expecting Liam or Francis to return before lunch.'

'Thank you,' Mrs Davies said, rather enjoying the speculative curiosity that she could see in Lynne's eyes. 'Would you like to follow me, Mr Ogilby.'

'James, please,' James amended, observing that Mrs Davies was far from immune to flattery.

Mrs Davies led the way into the lounge.

'Oh, Mrs Davies, shall I call Caroline?' Lynne asked.

Mrs Davies turned in the doorway and smiled at Lynne. 'Miss Caroline has had rather a – busy time of late, Miss Lynne. She is asleep now and I think we should leave her to rest until after lunch.'

Comprehending the meaning behind Mrs Davies' words, Lynne nodded. 'Perhaps Mr Ogilby would like to join us for lunch?' she asked.

James smiled his thanks. 'I will look forward to it.'

Mrs Davies ushered him into the lounge and shut the door behind them. As Lynne turned to mount the stairs to her room, she reflected on James Ogilby and his presence in the house. What could it mean? Shrugging her shoulders, she continued on her way, making a mental note to instruct Alicia on the new luncheon arrangements. If James Ogilby was looking forward to it, he was certainly not the only one.

'Thank you for coming so quickly,' Carol Davies began as they sat in chairs facing each other. She had offered him a drink, but he had declined.

'I've been searching for Caroline for a number of days. You knew that I had told Clive that I was coming back to the UK and wanted to see her?'

Mrs Davies shook her head. So that was the reason for the sudden removal to this house.

'I was quite surprised to hear from Clive that the

231

house was temporarily closed up and that I wouldn't be able to see Caroline. Not getting a satisfactory response from Clive, I decided to come back anyway and try to find her. I had little success until I received your call. Tell me, what's your angle?' James asked, looking intently at Mrs Davies.

'Angle?'

'Mrs Davies, I am a very successful businessman. My success has, amongst other things, come from my certain knowledge that everyone has an angle. Knowing that, I look for a competitor's angle of self-interest and exploit it. So, I repeat the question, what's yours?'

Respecting his directness, Mrs Davies decided to reciprocate. 'To find a secure place to live and a situation in which I can be happy,' she said.

'I can respect that,' James said. 'How does Caroline come into that?'

'Miss Caroline is not above practising a little deception to get what she wants. I live with her and Clive now – at least, I did. I thought that she was going to be happy with Master Clive and he certainly seemed so with her. After your visit to his house, things changed. Miss Caroline seemed to be very restless and Master Clive became much firmer with her.'

'Firmer? In what way?' James asked with a sense of alarm.

'He put me in charge of her. Oh, I'd always looked after her when Master Clive was out, but this was different. He didn't want her to have any kind of freedom. He instructed me that, under no circumstances, was she to be allowed to write a letter or make any telephone calls. I presume that was to prevent contact between the two of you. Then, when he learned that you wanted to come back, he made sure that Caroline was not available to you. I was sent here with her to – look after her,' Mrs Davies said, flushing under the directness of this man's gaze, but also feeling a stirring of sexual arousal in his presence.

232

'She was your prisoner?' James asked.

'Yes. I am not – unused to having the charge of female . . .' Mrs Davies appeared to be searching for an appropriate word.

'Prisoners,' James supplied. 'Mrs Davies, I would prefer it if we could speak freely and honestly. I have a reasonable idea as to what has been going on and I am not likely to tell anyone else.'

'Thank you. Yes, I have handled Master Liam's prisoners – I prefer to call them slaves – and I was pleased to continue this service for Master Clive. I was especially pleased to look after Caroline. I was drawn to her from the first day that I saw her. She reminds me of – someone.' Mrs Davies looked away. She did not like to think of the lesbian lover who had left her a long time ago and whom she still badly missed.

'What was it that led you to contact me?' James asked, speaking gently as he sensed her distress.

'Miss Caroline was so desperate to see you that she pretended to – care more about me than she really did. I was taken in for a little while and, when she told me the truth, I decided that anyone who could do what she did in order to persuade me to help her deserved that consideration. She gave me your number and asked me to call you.'

'That can't have been easy for you,' James said, demonstrating another of the qualities that Caroline had sensed in him and to which Mrs Davies now responded.

'It wasn't, but I can see now why she went to so much trouble,' Mrs Davies said, smiling for the first time with genuine warmth.

'Thank you,' James said. 'What about you, though? I intend to take Caroline with me to America. Where will you go?'

Mrs Davies shrugged her shoulders. 'I would like to stay with Master Clive. I – respect him a great deal. Once Caroline has gone, he will need me more than ever.'

Carol Davies couldn't bring herself to tell this man just how much she cared about Clive. She acknowledged her own vanity but even she could not fool herself into believing that Clive cared anything for her, other than that she was sometimes useful to him. Carol Davies had long ago accepted the fact that she was a person who people used. She had allowed herself to be deluded by Clive, Lynne and Caroline because she had wanted to be. She told herself that she had no complaints. She had received much sexual enjoyment from her treatment of the slaves under her care and she had great hopes that, once Master Clive had recovered from Caroline's desertion, he would realise the benefits of keeping her on. She was well aware that he could use her in any way that he chose and that that would be all right with her. She jumped as she felt a gentle hand on hers. In her reverie, she had closed her eyes, forgetting that she was not alone. Now James was standing in front of her, a gentle and concerned expression on his face.

'He will want you more than ever, Mrs Davies. I promise you that. Will you trust me?' James asked, looking almost with affection at this woman who had been responsible for bringing him to Caroline.

Carol Davies blinked away some unshed tears and smiled. 'Yes, James, I will. Caroline is a very lucky girl. She loves you very much, you know.'

James smiled and nodded. 'Yes, I know that and I love her, too. I will look after her for you, Mrs Davies. You will be welcome to come and see us. We will insist upon it.'

Lunch was an informal and very pleasant meal. James had been introduced to Francis and Liam and the three men had hit it off immediately.

'What are we going to do about Clive?' Francis asked as they settled back with coffee after the delicious lunch.

Lynne sat on the couch between James and Liam. As she did so, all three men eyed her appreciatively.

'I have great plans for Clive,' James said expansively. 'And for you, too, Liam.'

'Me?' Liam asked in some surprise.

'Yes. I've been looking into Clive's business dealings. He is a very clever man and will be very useful to me – as long as I can have someone who I trust to look after him while I am in the States,' James said, looking meaningfully at Liam.

'You're not suggesting what I think you are ...?' Liam said, building up to an immediate rejection of any such plan.

'Indeed I am, Liam. Having met and talked with you, I think I am a good enough judge of character to place my trust in you.'

'Surely you know that my businesses are on the point of collapse?' Liam asked.

'Engineered by Clive. Yes, I'm aware of that,' James said.

'Engineered by ...?' Liam exclaimed.

'Clive,' James finished for him. 'Liam, as I told you, I've been looking into Clive's business activities. I did this when I was last here because we had talked about doing some business together. What I found was very interesting. I had some idea of what Clive had been up to, but not in such detail as I am now informed of. For some months, Clive has been working behind the scenes to bring you down. He was almost successful, but I can stop him – for a price.'

'What sort of price?' Liam asked suspiciously.

'The price of your silence and of your service to me. You see, Liam, the way in which Clive has operated to destroy you has been rather clever. He has gone about it with a single-mindedness that is really quite admirable, were it not for the fact that it was done as a means of revenge. I have the means to stop his plans and I intend to use them. I can do that quite simply. All I need is your assurance that he will never know that you

235

know, thereby allowing for you to join with us in a very profitable business enterprise.'

'Profitable for whom?' Liam asked.

'There is room for all of us,' James said, his glance taking in Lynne and Francis as well as Liam. 'I need someone or some people who I can rely on to keep a very careful eye on Clive so there will be no danger of him doing to me what he tried to do to you. Liam, if you agree, I can get a contract drawn up very quickly. If I'm right about this project, it will make us all extremely rich.'

'And if you're wrong?' Liam asked.

'I rarely am, Liam, and that is not false modesty. I can show you the plans in great detail. Francis, I think that you and Lynne might be interested. At the very least, I'd like all of you to go over the details,' James said and then turned to Liam. 'If I'm wrong, Liam, well, there are always risks and I think that you are one of those people who are prepared to take a chance. Your companies, however, will be quite safe. With all of you keeping an eye on Clive, I think we can cut the risks to a minimum.'

Liam smiled. He really liked James and felt that he could trust him. He held out his hand. 'James, you've got yourself a deal.'

They shook hands. Liam raised his glass in a toast. 'James, I would back you against Clive any day. It will be a pleasure to have him think that we've buried the hatchet and that I trust him enough to work with him again. He won't like losing Caroline, though,' he said.

'He'll have to get used to the idea. I am more powerful and wield a lot more influence than he can even imagine. I love Caroline, Liam. She will be quite safe with me.'

'I can see that you do, James, but I warn you that you'd better look after her. If you don't, whatever your power, I'll come after you,' Liam said with a sincerity that no one could doubt.

'You need have no fear on that score, Liam. Caroline is very lucky in the men she has known – well, most of them anyway,' James said, raising his own glass in a toast to Liam and Francis.

'Caroline is a very lovely woman –' Liam said '– if a sometimes rather fickle one!' He laughed as he realised the truth of his own comment.

Twenty

Caroline heard the laughter as she peered over the banister above the stairs. There seemed to be people in the lounge. Francis and Lynne must be entertaining. Having tried unsuccessfully to shake off her lethargy, she relinquished the effort and returned to her room. Stripping off the satin robe she had earlier pulled on, she fell on to the bed and, with relief, closed her eyes. Mrs Davies had really been getting her 'pound of flesh', using Caroline in whatever way she pleased in return for the favour that the girl had begged from her. As Caroline shifted about in the bed, trying to find a more comfortable position for her well-striped bottom, she reflected that it would all be worth it – if Mrs Davies were successful in her attempt to contact James. Exhausted by her recent experiences, Caroline gave up the battle and let sleep reclaim her.

She was dreaming but, as with most bad dreams, was unable to force herself into wakefulness and thus effect an escape. She was in a house, of which all she could see were the endless lengths of corridors. There were many doors lining her route and she tried them all, but was unable to open any of them. She was growing increasingly frantic, because of the footsteps of which she had become aware. They followed her; stopping when she stopped and speeding up or slowing down in conjunction with her own. She heard herself calling, 'Oh, please, leave me alone! Go away!' She tried to scream, but each time she opened her mouth to form the word 'Help' her throat closed and she couldn't utter a sound. The footsteps were coming closer and she found herself clawing at the handles of the doors, but nothing helped and the footsteps were coming closer. He – she was sure it was a man – must be right behind her. She tried to turn and face her persecutor, but she suddenly found that she couldn't move. She felt the hands grab her from behind. One hand gripped her left arm; the other clamped hard across her mouth. She tried to struggle so ferociously that she woke herself up to find that it was all happening. This was no dream. The hands that held her were only too real. Feverishly, her mind grappled with what was happening. Who was it? It must be an intruder who had come into the house and, realising that everyone was fully occupied, had decided to explore the upper rooms for anything worth stealing. Her imaginings were confirmed by a gruff voice.

'What a stroke of luck! I thought that I might find something precious in the bedrooms and I was so right!'

Having had her worst fears confirmed, Caroline renewed her struggles. If only she could attract attention from one of the people downstairs. Desperately, she bit at the fingers that covered her mouth.

'Oh, no you don't!' the voice warned her and suddenly she couldn't breathe as a thumb and finger covered her nose. 'Be very still, girlie, and I'll let you breathe! Your choice!'

With a huge effort, Caroline nodded, flaring her nostrils to get as much air as she could when the obstruction was removed.

'That's better. Now listen to me, I don't want to hurt you, but I will if you give me any trouble. Those people downstairs sound to me like they're having a very good time. They won't help you. So it's just you and me, baby. As I say, you can make this difficult or easy. I think we could have a really good time or it could be a really bad time for you – so which is it to be? Are you going to give me trouble?'

Caroline shook her head. Whoever this man was, he could be dangerous. She would have to play along with him until someone came looking for her. 'That's a good girl. I knew you would be cooperative if I set it all out for you.'

Caroline felt a slight movement, as if the man were reaching into his pocket for something.

'Now listen to me, darling, I'm going to take my hand away from your mouth. if you attempt to scream, I promise you that you'll be very sorry. Do you understand?'

Caroline nodded. She wished that she could see the man; use her eyes to plead with him to leave her alone. Then she caught her breath as she heard the unmistakable sound of sticking plaster being peeled from a roll. Before she could usefully think of something to say to prevent it, her lips were sealed shut.

'Close your eyes, darling,' the voice said.

Caroline knew what he intended and moaned desperately behind the tape.

'I said close your eyes!'

There was no mistaking the firmness of purpose in the voice and Caroline closed her eyes. She felt another strip of tape being sealed across her closed lids.

'That's a good girl. After all, I wouldn't want you picking me out in a police line-up, now would I?'

It was the satisfaction in the voice that made Caroline turn on the bed and try to scratch and claw at the stranger. Laughing, he imprisoned her hands and forced them behind her back.

'I was going to have to tie you up anyway,' the stranger said as he tied her wrists tightly together. 'Better have the ankles tied as well. Don't want you wandering off now, do I?'

Caroline tried to place the stranger's accent. She

would need to be able to give the police as good a description as possible. She kept changing her mind; sometimes she thought that he might be Irish and then at others thought that she could detect some West Country in the voice. All such thoughts left her as she was pushed on to her side. She felt the stranger's gloved hands running gently down her back. She would not let him arouse her, she thought desperately. Surely, given the circumstances, she was too afraid to feel sexually aroused? She couldn't deny, though, that the shivers running up and down her spine could not be totally blamed on the fear that she was feeling. There was something very sensuous about those hands – stranger's hands – encased in the softest of leather. They stopped at her buttocks. She could almost feel the stranger's enquiring eyes on her marked flesh. He ran his fingers lightly across the raised weals, making a tutting sound.

'Oh, dear, we have been a bad little girl, haven't we? Bad enough for someone to whip you, I think. That's an interesting idea. When I saw you lying naked on the bed, I only had in mind that it would be kind of nice to fuck you, but perhaps there are other things that you might prefer. What do you think, darling. Shall I whip you before I fuck you?'

Caroline fought with her bonds, but most of all with herself. She could not now deny that she was incredibly turned on. Her fear was only exacerbating her arousal. Somehow, she felt that this man would not really hurt her. After all, she was in a house where there were other people around; the man had bound her eyes with tape so she was not a threat to him for future identification. He would probably leave her like this to be discovered by someone who could help her. Just fractionally, Caroline relaxed. The stranger must have noticed this, for she felt a stinging slap across her face.

'Feeling better now, are we? Are you so sure that I won't hurt you? Didn't anyone ever tell you never to assume anything?'

241

Caroline struggled as she felt the man push her on to her back and then lie on top of her. He was heavy and, tied as she was, such struggles were fairly futile.

'That's better, girlie! I like my women to have a bit of life in them!'

She tried to twist about in an effort to dislodge him, but felt him fumbling with his trousers and knew that he was freeing his penis. She imagined that it would be big, because she felt that the stranger was a fairly big man. Inconsequentially, she wondered how she would explain to the police that she could probably identify the man's penis. It wasn't exactly the sort of thing that would be expected on an identification parade otherwise there would never be a shortage of volunteers! She even inwardly smiled at this thought, but was rudely returned to reality by another hard slap on her face.

'Don't go to sleep on me, girlie! That would be very insulting and I would have to punish you for that!'

Immediately, Caroline moaned behind the tape to let him know that she was indeed awake. She felt the hardness poking against her slit and automatically tensed herself, to be rewarded with another slap.

'You like it rough, do you? OK, baby, I know just what you need!'

Caroline was pushed on to her side and she felt the man lie behind her. She had no time to tense her muscles before the hardness of his cock pushed against the entry to her anus.

'Relax, darling, or I'll hurt you! Push down and let me in or I'll force it and you won't like that! Make it easier on yourself, baby!'

Caroline did as she was told and felt the intruder slide into her anus. At the same time, she felt arms close around her and leather-clad fingers stroking her breasts. The stranger certainly knew how to pleasure a woman, she thought. It would be so easy to let herself enjoy what was happening to her. She felt his thrusts become

242

more urgent and felt herself responding. Her erect nipples were being squeezed between his gloved fingers and she began emitting little moans of pleasure behind her gag. They rode together to a mutual climax which, for Caroline, was suffused with guilt at her enjoyment of what should have been a terrifying ordeal.

For a while, there was silence in the bedroom. It was Caroline who moved first, causing the man's newly limp penis to slip from her rectum. Hazily, she wondered what she could now expect. Would the man be satisfied? Would he want more? He had threatened to whip her. She hoped that he wouldn't remember that. Her buttocks were still very sore from Mrs Davies' attentions and had caused her no little discomfort as the stranger had ridden her so roughly – and yet there had also been a strange tenderness. Caroline shook her head and felt tears welling in her eyes, but unable to escape because of the tape. Thank goodness James could not see her now. Thinking of James only increased the anguish that she felt at their separation. Yes, she was glad that he could not see her now but, conversely, she wished that he was here with her so that he could take her in his arms and tell her that everything would be all right. She was unaware that her body was shaking with silent sobs until she felt strong but gentle hands cradling her.

'Hush, baby, it's all right. I won't leave you again, I promise.'

Strange how the voice had lost its gruffness. It was warm and gentle, reassuring and – very American!

'It's all right, darling. I'm sorry, I shouldn't have done it. It was only a game. Please forgive me.'

James! It was James! She made some urgent pleading noises into her gag.

'Oh, my poor darling! I'd forgotten! Hold still!'

Very, very gently, James unpeeled the sticking plaster from her lips and then she felt his mouth close over hers.

243

As his tongue entered her mouth in a very welcome intrusion, she responded with all the pent-up longing that she had lived with since he had left her.

'James, is it really you?' she asked when the kiss ended.

'Yes, my darling. Hold perfectly still,' the unmistakable voice that she had been longing to hear told her.

Very gently and carefully, James peeled the sticking plaster from her eyes and she was able to see that it really was him. She looked at him with such intensity that he laughed and kissed her again.

'After such an inspection, I hope that I measure up,' James said.

'Measure up?' Caroline asked, but she was not really listening. She was still trying to convince herself that it was true – that James was really there with her.

'To the ideal you may have built up in my absence. You looked as if you were trying to assure yourself that I really was as you'd remembered me.'

'James, would you please stop talking rubbish and untie me. I want to hold you,' Caroline said.

James pushed her on to her side and started to untie the ropes at her wrists, but then stopped.

'Just a moment,' he said and rolled her on to her back. 'That sounded like an order to me. I think we need to establish a few ground rules before I take you off to America.'

'America? James, are you really going to take me back with you?'

'Once we've established who's in charge here,' James said with mock severity.

'Oh, darling, I'm sorry. What I meant to say was please, Master, would you be so kind as to untie me and then I can show you how very much I love you?' Caroline said, very submissively,

'I might – but then I might not,' James said teasingly, pretending to consider the matter seriously.

'James, please, someone might come in.'

'We're among friends here, my darling. I think you will find that neither Francis, Liam, Lynne or Mrs Davies will be interested in untying you if I express a preference to the contrary,' James said and kissed her on the lips.

'James,' Caroline said, her voice serious. 'What about Clive? Is everything all right?'

James leant down and kissed her. 'Everything is fine, my love. Don't worry about Clive. I'll make sure that he doesn't trouble you again,' James promised.

'James! You wouldn't . . .!'

He laughed and kissed her again. 'No, my darling, I wouldn't. Clive and I are business partners and that is fine with me because it means that Liam and I can keep an eye on him.'

'Liam? You've met Liam?' Caroline asked anxiously.

James laughed at the concern in her voice before he relented and told her everything that had been agreed.

'So you see, my love,' he finished, 'everything has been sorted out. As well as looking after my business interests, Liam is also going to ensure that Mrs Davies has a good home with Clive. Clive well knows that to incur my anger is really not a very good idea.'

James lowered his head and took Caroline's left nipple into his mouth. Biting her gently, he raised his head and smiled. 'Now are you satisfied?' he enquired.

She returned his smile and nodded.

'Then there is only one problem remaining,' James said, frowning slightly.

'What is it, James?' she asked anxiously.

'If I decide not to untie you, how do I explain to the air stewardesses why it is that my most beloved companion is accompanying me with her wrists and ankles so tightly bound?'

He appeared to be considering this question seriously and, for a moment, Caroline studied him anxiously.

Suddenly, his face creased into a smile as he gathered her into his arms. She found herself laughing with him.

'Oh, darling James, I love you! I love you!' she said, smothering his face with kisses.

'I love you, too, my darling, very, very much!' he said, the sincerity in his voice matched by that in his eyes.

'Then please will you untie me! I'm asking very, very nicely,' Caroline pleaded.

'Yes of course I will, my darling,' James responded. 'Just as soon as –' He broke off, apparently considering his next words.

'As?' Caroline asked.

'As soon as I've spanked you for being so bloody impatient!' James said, smiling but raising his hand to confirm the seriousness of his intentions.

NEW BOOKS

Coming up from Nexus, Sapphire and Black Lace

Nexus

In For a Penny by Penny Birch
November 1999   £5.99   ISBN: 0 352 33449 5

Penny Birch is back, as naughty as ever. *In for a Penny* continues the story of her outrageous sex life and also the equally rude behaviour of her friends. From stories of old-fashioned spankings, through strip-wrestling in baked beans, to a girl with six breasts, it's all there. Each scene is described in loving detail, with no holding back and a level of realism that comes from a great deal of practical experience.

Maiden by Aishling Morgan
November 1999   £5.99   ISBN: 0 352 33466 5

When Elethrine, Princess Talithea and their maid, Aisla, threaten to spank the sorceress Ea, they are punished by being transported to a distant part of their world. *Maiden* charts their journey home through a series of erotic indignities and humiliations, throughout all of which Elethrine is determined to retain her virginity. What she doesn't realise is that this will involve far more humiliating encounters for her than for her companions.

Bound to Submit by Amanda Ware
November 1999   £5.99   ISBN: 0 352 33451 7

The beautiful and submissive Caroline is married to her new master and the love of her life, James, at a bizarre fetishistic ceremony in the USA. He is keen to turn his new wife into a star of explicit movies and Caroline is auditioned without delay for a film of bondage and domination. Little do they know that the project is being financed by James' business rival and Caroline's former master, the cruel Clive. Clive intends to fulfil a long-held desire – to permanently mark Caroline as his property. Can her husband save her from his mesmeric influence? A Nexus Classic.

Sandra's New School by Yolanda Celbridge
December 1999   £5.99   ISBN: 0 352 33454 1
Nude sunbathing and spanking with a lesbian, submissive girlfriend lead hedonistic Sandra Shanks to the rigours of Quirke's school, where adult schoolgirls are taught old-fashioned submission, in the stern modesty of too-tight uniforms. In a school without males, the dormitory fun of 'all girls together' is as deliciously naughty as Sandra imagined – until she learns sadistic Miss Quirke's own guilty secret.

Tiger, Tiger by Aishling Morgan
December 1999   £5.99   ISBN: 0 352 33455 X
Aishling Morgan's third novel is a study in gothic eroticism. Her world is populated by strange half-human creatures, like Tian-Sha, the tigranthrope, a beautiful blend of girl and tiger. In this bizarre fantasy world a complex plot of erotic intrigue is played out against a background of arcane ritual and nightmare symmetry.

Sisterhood of the Institute by Maria del Rey
December 1999   £5.99   ISBN: 0 352 33456 8
The strict Mistress Shirer has always kept the residents of the Institute on a tight rein. Her charges are girls whose behaviour is apt to get out of hand and who need special discipline. Now they've opened a male dormitory and all manner of strange goings-on have come to her attention. Determined to restore order, Mistress Shirer sends Jaki, her cross-dressing slave, into the dormitories to find out exactly what is going on. A Nexus Classic.

NEXUS BACKLIST

All books are priced £5.99 unless another price is given. If a date is supplied, the book in question will not be available until that month in 1999.

CONTEMPORARY EROTICA

THE ACADEMY	Arabella Knight	
AMANDA IN THE PRIVATE HOUSE	Esme Ombreux	
BAD PENNY	Penny Birch	
THE BLACK MASQUE	Lisette Ashton	
THE BLACK WIDOW	Lisette Ashton	
BOUND TO OBEY	Amanda Ware	
BRAT	Penny Birch	
DANCE OF SUBMISSION	Lisette Ashton	Nov
DARK DELIGHTS	Maria del Rey	
DARK DESIRES	Maria del Rey	
DARLINE DOMINANT	Tania d'Alanis	
DISCIPLES OF SHAME	Stephanie Calvin	
THE DISCIPLINE OF NURSE RIDING	Yolanda Celbridge	
DISPLAYS OF INNOCENTS	Lucy Golden	
EMMA'S SECRET DOMINATION	Hilary James	
EXPOSING LOUISA	Jean Aveline	
FAIRGROUND ATTRACTIONS	Lisette Ashton	
GISELLE	Jean Aveline	Oct
HEART OF DESIRE	Maria del Rey	
HOUSE RULES	G.C. Scott	Oct
IN FOR A PENNY	Penny Birch	Nov
JULIE AT THE REFORMATORY	Angela Elgar	
LINGERING LESSONS	Sarah Veitch	

THE GOVERNESS AT ST AGATHA'S	Yolanda Celbridge	
THE MASTER OF CASTLELEIGH	Jacqueline Bellevois	Aug
PRIVATE MEMOIRS OF A KENTISH HEADMISTRESS	Yolanda Celbridge £4.99	
THE RAKE	Aishling Morgan	Sep
THE TRAINING OF AN ENGLISH GENTLEMAN	Yolanda Celbridge	

SAMPLERS & COLLECTIONS

EROTICON 4	Various	
THE FIESTA LETTERS	ed. Chris Lloyd £4.99	
NEW EROTICA 3		
NEW EROTICA 4	Various	
A DOZEN STROKES	Various	Aug

NEXUS CLASSICS
A new imprint dedicated to putting the finest works of erotic fiction back in print

THE IMAGE	Jean de Berg	
CHOOSING LOVERS FOR JUSTINE	Aran Ashe	
THE INSTITUTE	Maria del Rey	
AGONY AUNT	G. C. Scott	
THE HANDMAIDENS	Aran Ashe	
OBSESSION	Maria del Rey	
HIS MASTER'S VOICE	G.C. Scott	Aug
CITADEL OF SERVITUDE	Aran Ashe	Sep
BOUND TO SERVE	Amanda Ware	Oct
BOUND TO SUBMIT	Amanda Ware	Nov
SISTERHOOD OF THE INSTITUTE	Maria del Rey	Dec

Please send me the books I have ticked above.

Name ....

Address ....

....

....

.... Post code.........................

Send to: **Cash Sales, Nexus Books, Thames Wharf Studios, Rainville Road, London W6 9HT**

US customers: for prices and details of how to order books for delivery by mail, call 1-800-805-1083.

Please enclose a cheque or postal order, made payable to **Nexus Books**, to the value of the books you have ordered plus postage and packing costs as follows:

UK and BFPO – £1.00 for the first book, 50p for the second book and 30p for each subsequent book to a maximum of £3.00;

Overseas (including Republic of Ireland) – £2.00 for the first book, £1.00 for the second book and 50p for each subsequent book.

We accept all major credit cards, including VISA, ACCESS/MASTERCARD, AMEX, DINERS CLUB, SWITCH, SOLO, and DELTA. Please write your card number and expiry date here:

....

Please allow up to 28 days for delivery.

Signature ....